LONG TIME COMING

ALLIE MCDERMID

Copyright © 2022 by Allie McDermid

All rights reserved.

The right of Allie McDermid to be identified as the author of this work has been asserted by her in accordance with the Copyright, Designs and Patents Act 1988.

No part of this book may be reproduced in any form or by any electronic or mechanical means, including information storage and retrieval systems, without written permission from the author, except for the use of brief quotations in a book review.

All characters and events in the publication are fictitious and any resemblance to real persons, living or dead, is purely coincidental.

ALSO BY ALLIE MCDERMID

Love Charade

Love Detour

Love Magnet

1

Dani Hamilton gripped the small sink with both hands. She shouldn't have downed that beer. It sat heavy in her stomach, sloshing with every movement, threatening to make a reappearance.

She blew out unsteadily, her eyes locked with her own gaze until her attention was stolen by murmuring outside: a chorus of 'Hey! There's a queue.' Followed by a familiar voice telling them to shut up.

She smiled, temporarily forgetting she was close to having a whitey.

'Dani, you good?' her sister Kirsty called through the door. When she didn't answer the question, a sharp rap against the wooden frame followed. 'Dani?'

'Yeah, yeah. I'm fine,' she lied. 'Won't be long.'

She wanted to curl up and lie on the cold tiles. This was the only downstairs bathroom, though. She wouldn't get away with it for long.

But it wasn't just the booze making her feel like shit. Lying down could only solve so much.

Another deep breath and she was braced for the party

outside. The atmosphere was heavier than the alcohol sitting in her. Something was decidedly off, but she couldn't quite put her finger on it.

Any event with Ashley and Hazel was always tough – as was expected when the love of your life shacks up with someone else – but today was different. It was like walking through a familiar corridor in the pitch black. It should be safe. It probably was safe. But her head was screaming *run, get out!* Instead of legging it, she was self-medicating with booze.

Why cha—

'Dani!' Kirsty snapped.

'Alright, alright.'

She ran a hand through her long brown hair before making a final adjustment of her backwards cap, repositioning it. *Okay.* Presentable.

She yanked the door open to be met with a sigh of relief from the next in the queue. The guy barged right past her without a word.

Kirsty guided her to the side, her eyes searching her sister's face for clues on her current mood. 'What's up with you today?' she hissed, attempting to keep her voice below the listening volume of the ever-growing line for the loo.

Dani shrugged. 'Nothing.'

No comeback: just a glare.

Dani knew better than to argue. 'Look, it's fine. I just feel off today. It'll pass – let's enjoy ourselves.'

Kirsty chewed on her cheek, unconvinced.

'Dani, there you are,' Ashley's sister, Leanne said, rounding the corner from the kitchen. Was this some kind of sibling inquisition?

Dani surveyed her options. She was trapped at the end of the hall, unless she wanted to dart into the dining room and launch herself out the window. She was no match for two older sisters; no point in trying to escape.

Kirsty's sour face softened as Leanne came level with her, but a pump of her sister's eyebrows told Dani the issue wasn't dropped.

'What's up?' Dani asked, hoping for something trivial.

'Mum's got something to say. She needs you in the garden, now.'

Dani's stomach just about hit her feet, the alcohol only adding to its swift descent. Something was definitely up.

'Just me?' Dani asked, stabbing a finger at her chest.

'No, no. Everyone. Mainly you two, though.'

'Me?' Kirsty and Dani exchanged a quick glance. She and Ashley were close, but only through association. This was Dani's second family. If Kirsty was also involved, this was major.

'Yep, now come on. I need to find Uncle Jeff. He's gone AWOL again.' With a blasé wiggle of her head, Leanne was off, ushering the remaining people in the toilet queue to head out as she passed.

'This doesn't feel right,' Dani said, rooted to the spot.

They ignored the weird look the toilet guy gave them when he exited. It was a free country, they could block the corridor outside the loo if they wanted to.

'It doesn't, does it?' Kirsty looked over her shoulder, as if the answer might have sneaked up on them. 'Have you spoken to Ashley much?'

The truth was, Dani had been actively avoiding her. The longer Ashley and Hazel were together the more insufferably coupley they became, and these days it felt like they were joined at the hip. Seeing Ashley with someone else was hellish.

It was her own fault: Dani had had her chance and blew

it. Nearly twenty years of chances, to be exact. She'd never been ready before now. Never been good enough. She'd made changes though, and pulled her socks up.

Which, of course, was exactly when Hazel had come on the scene. Talk about crummy timing.

'She's been busy,' Dani said, avoiding Kirsty's curious eyes.

There was no fooling her. 'Busy. Yeah. Well, Rhona and I thought she was a bit weird, to be honest.'

Dani's muscles stiffened. 'Weird? How?'

'Dunno – she just seemed a bit jumpy.'

The queue for the toilet fizzled out, as did the chatter surrounding them, most people choosing to go outside rather than face the wrath of Leanne.

'Jumpy?'

'Are you just repeating what I'm saying?'

'Are you just repeating what I'm saying?' Dani whined, screwing her face up.

Kirsty playfully grabbed at her ribs. 'Right, look. We need to go outside.'

'Or' —Dani countered, raising a finger in the air— 'I go home and you tell me what's going on later.' She made to pass Kirsty, only to be pulled back into place.

'I know that was a joke, but it wasn't funny.'

'When did I say it was a joke?'

Leanne's face appeared from the kitchen. 'Dani. Now.'

If Kirsty was bossy, Leanne was something else. Dani marched outside in silence, Kirsty hot on her heels.

The small garden of the Dumbreck villa was rammed with people. The air was electric with excited talk. Dani led them up the back and into the space carved out by their friends.

'You okay?' Sarah, or Trip to her pals, asked, concern clear.

'Yeah, just drank that beer too fast.'

'I told you not to neck it.' She bumped into Dani's shoulder with a smile, holding up a fresh bottle of booze. 'Got you another, though.'

Trip: an angel in disguise. She always knew what Dani needed.

Dani had only managed a sip when Ashley's dad, Brian, called for silence. The garden fell quiet, the static in the air growing tenfold.

He cleared his throat. 'Hello friends, family, and possibly a few gatecrashers!' Polite laughter peppered the crowd. 'Thank you for joining us to celebrate my birthday...'

Dani tuned out. She'd heard this speech a thousand times. Brian's birthday bash was as fixed in the calendar as Christmas Day. He and Mary would exchange well-practised banter, summing up the last year and wishing well for the next. They'd all have a clap and return to socialising.

So, why did it feel like the air was getting heavier? Like this was secretly building to something much bigger?

Dani studied her friends' faces as they watched Ashley's parents. Kirsty was perched on the arm of Rhona's chair, an arm around her shoulder as her girlfriend scooped her close. They'd been together nearly a year now. It wasn't long, but Rhona felt more like a sister with every passing day.

They didn't seem bothered by the changing atmosphere.

Next, she darted her eyes to Kim and Trip. Opposite in height and personality, but they'd do anything for each other. That's what made their group work: they looked out for one another. No matter what.

No concern from them either.

It was only Izzy who met her gaze with the glint of suspicion in her eye. The tall blonde sidled closer to Dani, ducking level with her ear and keeping her voice low. 'Something's going on.'

Dani had to contain the exclamation that nearly popped out of her like a gunshot. She gritted her teeth, trying to keep a smile on her face. 'I know, right?'

'You think someone's ill?'

Dani looked between Brian and Mary; they seemed healthy enough. And Ashley would have told her if anything was going on with her.

'Nah. Something else.'

Izzy stepped back, her glass of wine resting against her bottom lip as she thought.

So, Dani wasn't imagining it. Something was brewing.

Brian's eyes turned wistful as he came to the end of his speech. He held up a hand to delay any applause. 'Before you return to your bevvies, Ashley and Hazel would like to have a quick word.'

Dani's heart skipped a beat before working double time.

She held her breath, scared to miss a single word.

'Hi, everyone,' Ashley said, nerves clear in her voice. She'd never liked public speaking. She took Hazel's hand in her own, and they shared one of the looks that turned Dani's stomach. She looked beautiful. Her blonde hair was usually styled in a ponytail but today it was fashioned into an elegant updo. Her normal jumper-and-shirt combo had been switched for a gorgeous floral dress, cinched at the waist with a bow. It was all adding up. She'd made an effort for this. Dani gulped. 'I'll keep this short and sweet. Dad's rambled on long enough and I know you want to get back to your drinks.' Brian protested and another ripple of laughter played through the crowd. Dani swallowed hard as a smile pulled at Ashley's lips, so strong it was stopping her from talking. Finally, after another look at Hazel, she spoke: 'I'm thrilled to announce that Hazel and I are engaged.'

The sound of Dani's beer bottle smashing off the slabs as it slipped from her fingers echoed in her ears.

2

Negotiating guests as she crossed the garden was harder than the assault course Hazel had made her compete in this summer. To make it worse, there was only one person Ashley Davidson really wanted to see, and she was nowhere in sight.

After a thousand hugs, cheek kisses, and well wishes from relatives, she was finally with her friends.

'Congratulations,' Trip beamed, pulling her in for a hug.

Soon she was in the middle of the huddle, an outpouring of adulation surrounding her as much as Trip's arms. Something about it sounded flat though, like they were saying it because it was expected. Or maybe she'd just heard too much in a short space of time. They were happy for her, surely?

She stepped back from the embrace, scanning the faces around her.

'Where's Dani?' Ashley asked, hoping the question sounded off the cuff.

'She needed the loo,' Kirsty said, her eyes betraying the fact she was lying.

'I'll go find her,' she replied, stepping back from the throng, only to be hooked by Rhona's hand on her arm.

'Give her a min,' Rhona suggested. The way her eyes locked with Ashley's hinted a minute probably wouldn't be enough though.

The words *Is she mad?* sat on her tongue, like a vice on further conversation. Asking would be admitting there was a problem, though. It was a no-brainer that today would be tough. She'd dreaded it since Hazel proposed.

Why couldn't Dani just be happy for her?

She'd made it abundantly clear there were no romantic feelings on her side: fair enough, so why act like Ashley was her property? She could be such an insufferable brat at times. Would it really kill her to grow up and be pleased Ashley had finally found someone who valued her?

'How did Hazel propose?' Izzy asked, pulling Ashley from her internal rant. 'I'm guessing she was the one who did it, or did you ask? Ohh, spill all.'

Ashley swallowed down her bad mood. This was a day for being happy, not focusing on Dani's shortcomings. She'd wasted enough days on her as it was.

'Hazel asked me,' she replied, smiling at the memory. 'She took me to the Hermitage, remember the place near Dunkeld with the waterfall and stuff?' There were nods of understanding but Ashley felt the need to elaborate further. 'It's a woodland walk; it's lovely. It's where we first said *I love you*.'

'Awww,' Izzy gushed.

'She went down on one knee on the bridge. It's like something from a fairy tale, all rustic, mossy, and old. I'll put the photos on Facebook later.'

Izzy was doe-eyed at the recount. Polite smiles plastered the faces of everyone else.

She had no reason to think her closest friends had a problem with Hazel. That was Dani's personal grudge to bear. And yet, there was always something a little sour about their interactions. Trip especially. She was the master of masking emotion, but the hushed conversations, sideways glances, and change in tone when Hazel was involved didn't go amiss. There was nothing malicious in her friend's actions, quite the opposite, but Ashley was finely tuned to see it. And once you see it, you can't stop spotting the signs.

'You must be so happy,' Kirsty said, and sounded like she meant it.

'Yeah, super happy. I can't still can't really believe it, if I'm honest.'

'Let's see the rock, then,' Kim chirped, pulling Ashley's left hand into the centre of the circle.

Another chorus of *ooh*s and *ahh*s erupted.

'That's pretty,' Izzy said, fawning.

Ashley admired the platinum ring: an oval diamond sat in its centre with a blue sapphire either side. It was gorgeous. She'd always loved sapphire stones.

'You'll be next,' Kim joked to Kirsty and Rhona.

'Slow and steady wins the race,' Kirsty quickly retorted, and Rhona suppressed a mischievous smile.

'I'm going to the loo,' Trip said, putting her empty beer bottle on the nearest table. 'Back in a mo.'

'I'll join you,' Ashley blurted, taking off before any could protest. Aside from Dani, Trip was Ashley's closest friend. She might be the master at deflecting how she really felt about Hazel but she could be counted on for her honesty with everything else.

She walked double quick, trying to keep up with Trip and avoid the guests desperate to talk to her. It was like being on a bad fairground attraction, people pawing and grabbing as she passed, smiles plastered on their faces. It was great they were happy, but all this attention was already too much.

'Trip, yo, hold up.'

Finally, at the steps to the kitchen's bifold doors, Trip slowed her pace. 'Sorry, just dying for a pee.'

'Is Dani okay?' There was no point beating about the bush.

Trip's features contorted as she thought. 'Yeah, totally. Why?' She stepped between Ashley's Uncle Tam and Uncle Robert and into the kitchen. What a stupid place to have a conversation; why were they standing in the door?

Ashley huffed. Thankfully, it was lost to the pop of Mum opening champagne. 'Ashley, darling! Great timing. Help me with these, please?'

'One minute.' They were in the hall before she could be cajoled into abandoning her mission with Trip. The queue to the toilet was long. 'Use my mum and dad's en suite; it'll be quicker.' Also, easier to talk without a hallway full of friends and family.

'You okay?' Trip asked over her shoulder as they ascended the stairs.

'Of course, why?'

'You're following me to the toilet,' she replied with a chuckle.

'No I'm not.'

Trip stopped on the landing, so abruptly that Ashley nearly toppled into her. 'Spill.'

Ashley fiddled with the tie on her dress as heat crept across her cheeks. 'Is Dani mad?'

Trip's face thawed to one of understanding. 'I think "shocked" is the appropriate word.'

Ashley nodded slowly while worrying her bottom lip with her teeth. 'Where is she now?'

'To be honest, I was hoping to find her on the way to the loo. She just kind of ran off.'

'Shit.'

'Yeah. Kirsty said to give her space.'

Her tongue was out of action again, words firmly clogged in her throat. The last thing she wanted to do was hurt Dani.

Trip offered a half-smile of reassurance. 'She'll be grand. Just give her time.'

'It's what she does now that worries me. No idea where she went?'

Trip shook her head. 'Look, I might actually pee while I'm here. The queue's massive downstairs.' She nipped into Mum and Dad's room.

Ashley leaned against the top bannister and looked to the floor below. The occasional guest wandered by, the tops of their heads the only clue to their identity. Where would Dani go?

She'd moved out long ago and Ashley's bedroom was now a glorified office, but it still had a sofa bed in the corner. It was as good a bet as any.

She hovered her knuckles over the door, her other hand on the handle, poised to enter. This was her room: why knock? Still, it felt wrong to barge in. Ashley opened the door slowly.

Sure enough, Dani was slumped on the sofa, an open bottle of wine in her hand. She jumped into action at the sight of Ashley, pawing at her eyes as if she'd be crying.

'You okay?' Ashley asked, uncertainty lacing her words.

Dani avoided eye contact, choosing to focus on the bottle instead. 'Me? Yeah, golden. Why?'

'Just wondering.' Ashley sat on the springy sofa. She'd never liked it. Far too soft.

She chanced a look at Dani. She'd definitely been crying.

'Congratulations, oh my God, sorry, that should have been the first thing I said to you,' Dani rambled, her bottom lip wobbling slightly as she spoke. In a flash, the bottle was on the ground and Ashley was held in a bearlike hug.

'How come you're up here?' Ashley asked, still holding onto Dani like they were lost at sea.

She felt Dani swallow against her shoulder.

'It was really busy downstairs. Just needed a moment by myself.' She sniffed and held Ashley a little tighter.

Dani wasn't a crier. With the exception of her father passing, it just wasn't in Dani's repertoire. She was a closed book. Even after all these years, Ashley still struggled to read her.

'These are happy tears,' Dani said with a forced chuckle.

Closed book or not, Ashley saw through that one like glass.

It was better to play along though. 'I know. Can you believe it?' Ashley released her grip, hoping Dani would too so she could look her in the eye.

Eventually, she leaned back, revealing tear-stained cheeks. She instantly pawed at them, getting rid of the evidence. 'I'm proper chuffed for you, Ash.'

Ashley snagged her gaze and held it as tightly as they'd hugged. 'I should have told you before I announced it like that. Sorry.'

Dani nodded, her attention back on the wine bottle she was turning between her hands. 'A heads-up would have been nice.' She paused, turning something over, as if debating to add the thought or not. 'I'll miss you.'

Ashley cut short the snort of laughter that escaped. 'Where am I going?'

Dani took a long, ragged breath. 'Marriage is massive. You know what I mean.'

She did. And the thought of it hurt like hell, but she'd come to terms with her unrequited feelings, shaping them into something new and moving on. A few years ago, the thought of not seeing Dani would have near killed her. Now, it only stung a little: they would change and adapt. Getting married and starting a family didn't mean you ditched your friends completely.

Dani look a long slug of wine, gulping the booze down as she winced.

'Since when did you drink wine?' Ashley asked with a smile, hoping to lighten the mood an ounce.

'A lot's changed recently. Maybe you were too busy to notice.'

'What's that supposed to mean?'

'That came out wrong.'

'It sure did.'

Dani held the bottle in the space between them like a peace offering. 'It's stinking, but you're welcome to have some.'

'Excuse me.' Ashley chuckled. 'That's one of Mum's classic reserves. It's not the wine's fault your taste is awful.'

Dani grabbed at Ashley's waist with her free hand, making her break out in giggles. 'No, no, stop!'

That only made her go harder.

Ashley was soon breathless, huddled over as Dani tickled her senseless.

'Ash?'

Hazel's distant voice made them both freeze. With a gentle cough, Ashley straightened herself. Her heart pounded. Not just from the tickles, but also from the sinking feeling she'd been caught doing something bad.

'In here,' she called, smoothing her dress out. Dani took another gulp of wine, her face stoic.

It wasn't long before Hazel poked her head round the door. Her warm smile melted Ashley's heart. 'There you are. Your mum wants to do a champagne toast.'

3

Dani reached across Kirsty to grab the soya milk, intent on finishing off the latte she was making.

The best thing about working in the family café was that there were no social expectations. She always brought her A game when it came to customer service but there was no forced conversation, no polite chit-chat with co-workers. Kirsty knew when to give her space and it was never awkward.

Nearly a week had passed since Ashley's announcement, and so far the only thing to shave off a slither of pain was her therapy session yesterday.

She'd started seeing Jenny not long after The Kiss (as she'd now come to refer to it in sessions). She was sceptical at first, but it was slowly changing her life for the better. A year on, she felt like a new woman. It was as if she'd carried around an impossibly heavy backpack since Dad died and every week Jenny removed an item. Sometimes it was small. Sometimes it was huge. Whatever the breakthrough, they all added up.

Drunkenly kissing Ashley in Ibiza had been the wake-up call she needed. She'd been thirty-three. It felt like a lifetime ago now. They were just seventeen the first time around. Now that really was a lifetime. Sixteen years between kisses and Ashley still did things to her insides that should be illegal. She either sorted her life out or it was game over. Ashley deserved her to be the best version of herself. Dani couldn't be that with the tricks her brain was playing on her.

'You good?' Kirsty asked, her eyes on Dani's coffee. 'You've been doing that fern for ages. You'll have more foam than coffee soon.'

She was right. *Shit.* 'Just thinking.'

Kirsty didn't push it. 'Do you want to pick up table nine's order, or will I?'

'What is it?' Kirsty didn't usually ask. They just cracked on with it.

'Four lattes, a mocha, one double espresso, a cap, and a flat white.'

Now it made sense: that was a lot. 'Business meeting?'

'Think so. Will we split it? You do the lattes and the espresso? I'll do the rest.'

'Deal.'

Dani had worked in Café Odyssey since leaving school and it was as much her home as the flat she and Kirsty owned together. With Mum in charge and nearly every other staff member family, it was a finely tuned machine, perfected over generations. There'd been a moment when it looked like Kirsty would go to university and do her own thing, but after Dad passed away she'd joined the ranks. Dani thanked her lucky stars for that every day. There was no one else she could imagine working with. Never mind living with.

Which reminded her: 'Is Rhona home tonight?' It was Dani's turn to make tea.

'Nah, she's in Brussels until tomorrow, remember?'

Dani nodded slowly, pushing the espresso button on the machine. She'd not been the best at retaining info this week. 'Aw, yeah. Sorry.'

Kirsty offered a small smile, silently telling her not to worry about it. 'I'll be glad when wedding season is over. It's been weird having her away so much.'

'Do you think she'll—' The words caught in Dani's throat. She coughed quietly, hoping that looked like the reason for her pause, not the fact the end of this sentence made her want to rip her own skin off. 'Do you think she'll do Ashley's wedding?'

Rhona was a high-end wedding photographer. Her prices might be a little out of Ashley's budget, but mates rates were a thing, yeah?

Kirsty wiggled her head, internal debate clear. 'Hazel already asked her at the party. Rhona said yes.'

Why did Kirsty's tone suggest that was some sort of betrayal? It was Rhona's choice who she had as clients; Dani didn't hold it against her. Maybe they needed to have a chat. Now wasn't the time or the place, though.

'That's amazing. I'm glad she could do it.' A realisation hit Dani square between the eyes. 'So, they have a date already?'

Kirsty put her finished flat white on the serving tray. 'Roughly, or at least that's what Hazel told Rhona. They want to aim for next August. Anniversaries and stuff. I guess it makes sense.'

That felt like no time. A measly year. Three hundred and sixty-five days. Although, maybe it would be better if it was even sooner. Rip the band-aid off in a swift motion, get it done with.

Kirsty's hand stilled over her uncompleted cappuccino before she placed the milk jug back on the counter. She took a deep breath. 'I'm only going to say this once, because I know you'll play it off, but listen to me, yeah?' She waited for Dani to nod. 'If any of this ever feels too much or whatever. Just say. I get it. We don't need to say a word. No questions. No discussion. You don't need to go to this wedding.' She picked up the jug and carried on with the cappuccino like she'd not said a word.

'Thank you,' Dani mumbled, finishing her first latte. It was appreciated, but Kirsty was right: she was more likely to play this whole thing off. Push it under the carpet. Only Kirsty, Rhona, and Trip had an inkling of how much this was killing her. They didn't know the half of it, though. Something told Dani that Jenny would be seeing a heck lot more of her in the coming months.

The bell over the café door jingled and a familiar voice filled the bar area. Trip.

'Ladies, how are we today?'

Kirsty's face creased with amusement. 'Since when do you call in at this time of day?'

Trip was an English teacher at the local secondary school. Seeing her during the week was as rare as a dairy-free mocha. It just didn't happen.

'Emergency dentist appointment. Crown fell off,' Trip informed her, pointing at her jaw. 'No point going back for thirty minutes.'

'Can you drink after something like that?' Dani asked.

'What? Booze?'

Dani chuckled. 'Always a one-track mind with you. No, doofus. You're here. I'm guessing you want a coffee?'

Trip's eyes brightened as she clicked, a lopsided smile pulling at her lips. 'Ah, gotcha. No, not really. Well, maybe. But I'd probably dribble. I actually wanted to see you.'

'Me?' Dani asked, pointing to her chest and looking at Kirsty.

'You, yeah.'

Ominous. 'What have I done?'

Trip laughed quietly and leaned on the counter, eying up the scones under a glass dome. 'They look good. Raspberry and white choc – can I get one? I'll pay, obviously.'

Dani put her hands on her hips. 'Trip.'

'Yeah?'

'Why you here?' Her tone left no room for confusion; she didn't have time for dallying.

Trip sucked her lips in, pulling a face like she'd been scolded by a parent. 'Sorry. It's about Ashley.'

Dani groaned, unable to stop her eyes from rolling.

'Now, now,' Trip continued. 'She's desperate to talk to you but doesn't know how.'

'Huh?' She had been strangely quiet on the text front this week, but Dani figured she was just giving her space or busy with wedding stuff.

Trip shrugged. 'Just reach out to her, yeah? Something's bothering her.' Ashley worked in the office of Trip's school; it shouldn't have been a surprise she was getting her to do ground work.

A wave of ice travelled down Dani's spine. Ashley wasn't going to warn her off the wedding, was she? Given their history, it would make sense. What else could be bothering her?

∼

'Have you texted her yet?' Kirsty asked, slumping into the armchair with a beer. They'd been to the pub a lot recently. They'd agreed to stay in tonight, only to cave and pick up beers on the way home. At least they'd saved some dosh. Plus, this way they got to enjoy them in joggers without the prying judgement of Kim and Travis, working the bar.

'Not yet. I don't know what to say. Why hasn't she just texted me?'

'Same problem, probably. She doesn't know how to start it.'

'It would be so much easier if Trip had said we could mention her.'

'But she didn't. So, buck up and get on with it.'

Dani sighed. The reason for Ashley's sudden need to see her was weighing on her mind. More so because a new solution had popped into her head this afternoon, and given the chance to run with it, her brain wasn't for dropping it any time soon.

It was ridiculous.

Even thinking it made her feel odd.

But it was there, a beacon in her mind, calling her closer, wishing her to believe it could be true.

Perhaps Ashley was finally going to declare her feelings, give Hazel the heave-ho.

She just needed to chat to Dani first, make sure they were on the same page. They'd been through so much together: was Ashley really ready to commit to someone other than Dani?

'You've still not sent it, have you?' Kirsty asked, peering over the gap between the chair and sofa.

Dani scrunched her face up. 'What would you say?'

'I thought you guys texted every day? Just throw an "everything alright with you?" into the convo.'

'We used to,' Dani replied, with a defeated sigh. 'Not so much these days.' Conversation had endured a slow decline since Hazel had appeared, but the first day Dani didn't hear from Ashley at all had stung like a motherfucker. Like everything, she got used to it over time. Didn't stop her heart skipping when Ashley's name flashed up on her lock screen.

God, this was worse than starting a conversation on Tinder. She'd only used that for casual hook-ups; words were easy when you could get straight to the point. Even then, she'd deleted that app more than a year ago. Talk about being out of practice.

Dani typed *Had a good day?* into the message box.

Nope.

She shook her head, backspacing the words away. *You okay?*

Nah.

Was there anything funny she could share? No images sprung to mind. Even their shared jokes were few and far between. She could feel Kirsty's glare boring through her, so she stabbed *How's the wedding planning going?* into the box and hit send.

'Talk about indecisive,' Kirsty teased with a breathy chuckle.

Dani didn't have the heart to rise to the bait. She chucked her phone on the couch and grabbed her beer off the table.

Chet the cat eyed her with malice for moving too much. He'd grown loads since Dani got him. She'd never intended him to be a replacement for Ashley, but the handsome grey tabby was now her best friend. Not that she would utter something so embarrassingly sad out loud.

Her phone buzzed and Chet stretched his legs out with a shake before getting comfy again.

Ashley. *Not really started, haha. Free for a drink tomorrow?*

Time to find out what this was all about. Dani's stomach flipped.

4

Ashley fiddled with the menu in the centre of the table, repositioning it for the thousandth time. Dani was late. Not by much, but enough to heighten Ashley's nerves. She'd already rearranged the sauces twice.

They'd agreed to meet in The Stables, a quiet, unassuming pub in the middle of Shawlands. It seemed as neutral a ground as anywhere, well, without leaving their Glasgow suburb and heading west or to the city centre. If she'd suggested that, Dani would have definitely known this was more than just a social gathering.

Ashley took in her surroundings, intent on not touching the sauce for a third time. The barbecue bottle was suspiciously sticky.

In her haste to meet Dani she'd clean forgotten that Lovefest, the suburb's annual love festival, was on, so the pub was busier than usual. Packed, in fact. It was a Saturday, yeah, but it was standing room only now. She'd been lucky to get a table. She felt bad for nursing the same glass of wine for the last thirty minutes.

There was no way she could have just met Dani at their

agreed time and launched into things, though. She needed time to adjust, time to let her nerves settle.

Her eyes traced the toy train track circling the room, suspended a few feet below the ceiling, running the length of the mahogany bar and passing over the patrons' tables. Years ago the toy train would chug around non-stop, but it was now parked at the station above the large flat-screen TV. Forever marooned until someone deemed it important enough to fix. Rumour had it that the train had taken a bend a little too fast, launching itself into some unsuspecting bloke's vindaloo, taking his pint out and breaking a wheel in the process. Now that would have been a sight to see.

She sipped her wine. It was like drinking milk straight after orange juice. Every drop sat heavy in her stomach.

Jesus, Ash. This was hardly the craziest thing in the world. In fact, this was a good thing. Why was she worrying Dani was going to freak out, get mad, and take offence?

She played with the stem of her glass, twiddling it between finger and thumb.

Hands on her shoulders made her jump.

'Shit, did I scare you?' Dani asked as she took a seat opposite her in the wooden booth. A devilish grin hinted she was anything but sorry.

'Just in my own wee world,' Ashley replied, hoping her heart returned to normal soon. She went to pick up her glass, only to find a slight shake to her hand. She played with the stem again instead. 'No hat today?'

Red flushed Dani's cheeks. She could hardly expect to be without her trademark snapback and not have it mentioned. Instead, her wavy brown locks were styled to one side, pushed out of her face. Ashley had seen Dani sans hat easily less than a dozen times. Most of them being formal events like weddings and funerals. Today was anything but special. She played it cool, not wanting to make Dani feel self-conscious.

She'd forgone her usual hoodie-and-jogger combo too and was sporting her nice denim jacket with a T-shirt. Something was definitely up.

Ashley's mouth went dry, anxiety now in full control.

'Just fancied a change,' Dani replied, already half-standing. 'Do you want another drink?'

She eyed her nearly empty glass. Was another one wise? The way her hand was still shaking said it was needed. 'Just a small one.'

Dani was off. Ashley fixed her gaze on the cars outside, parked at the traffic lights, waiting for them to go green. She eyed each driver and passenger with rueful jealousy. They looked like they were having a good day, not willing their hearts not to break through their ribs.

A full glass of wine appeared on the table, followed by a pint for Dani. She shimmied her jacket off as she sat down.

Her brown eyes met Ashley's and she smiled. 'So, what's been happening?'

Ashley swallowed hard. 'Not much, really. Mum and Dad are still on cloud nine. I'm slowly getting used to it.' She played with the engagement ring on her finger, twisting it from side to side.

Dani nodded slowly before sipping her beer. Silence fell between them, conversation suddenly stalled.

'How's the new grinder?' Ashley blurted, desperate for things not to be awkward.

'Grinder? Grinder . . .' Dani repeated, her eyes tilted skyward as she thought. 'Oh, that! The coffee grinder. That was ages ago, but yeah, it's working well. Good having the two so Kirsty and I can work faster.'

What next? Jesus, twenty years of friendship and she

was flailing in a sea of floundering chat. It was like what she really wanted to ask was drowning everything else out, her brain only able to focus on the one thing.

'You okay?' Dani asked. 'You seem preoccupied.'

'Just a lot on my mind,' she lied. 'Weddings involve a lot of planning.'

'As long as there's nothing bad going on at school again.'

It was sweet of Dani to remember. Years and years ago Ashley had had issues with a particularly obnoxious office boss. It was bullying, plain and simple. Thankfully, she was long gone, and Ashley loved her job and her colleagues once more. 'No, no. Nothing like that. Just feeling a little overwhelmed.'

'Is there anything I can do to help?'

Ooft. Dani was pretty much offering her this on a silver platter. 'Actually, there is.'

Dani straightened herself, her eyebrows arched with suspense. 'What can I do?'

Ashley's words were lodged again.

Pleased to find her hand steady, she took a sip of wine. Dani hadn't blinked. This was getting worse by the minute.

Why did this feel so wrong?

'Ash?' Dani prompted.

She wet her lips, buying time. A quick clear of her throat and it was now or never. 'I was wondering—' Dani shifted in her seat and Ashley felt the words slip again. She grabbed them, wrestling them to the tip of her tongue. 'Will you be my maid of honour?'

'Me?' Dani squeaked.

'I don't see anyone else sitting here.'

The world was off Ashley's shoulders, the question finally out there. She'd done the hard part; the ball was in Dani's court now.

'What about Leanne?' Dani asked with a gulp.

'She's busy with the boys and work. Her commitments are crazy. Not that you have loads of free time, but, you know.' Ashley shook her head, realising how this was sounding. 'Not that, you're like, second choice or whatever, but you asked, so . . .' She trailed off.

Dani looked like a gasping fish.

She snapped her mouth shut and tilted her head to the side. 'Me? Your maid of honour? That's like a big deal, isn't it?'

'Kinda. Yes. But that's why I want you. I can't imagine sharing my day with anyone else.'

Dani chewed on her cheek, considering the proposal. 'Will I need to wear a dress?'

'It's a possibility.'

Her face fell, her mouth opening and closing a few times.

'Or not, if it makes you super uncomfortable.'

'No, if that's what you need me to do. It's your day.'

'So, is that a yes then?'

'I guess so.'

Ashley sprung to her feet, rushing round to Dani's side of the table and scooping her close. 'Thank you! You have no idea.' Dani's muscles stiffened as she lightly returned the hug. 'You sure you're okay with this?' Ashley asked, leaning back to check Dani's face.

'Yeah, yeah, of course,' Dani replied with an enthusiastic nod. There was a glaze to her eyes, though. Something wasn't sitting right.

Ashley pursed her lips. 'Hmm. If it's the dress thing I can promise to get you an alternative.'

She released Dani and sat back down.

'Ash, it's your day,' Dani said, her eyes turning genuine. 'You do whatever. I'm just there to help.'

'Okay, but if you're not happy, just say, yeah?'

Dani sipped her beer. Her voice was nearly a mumble when she next spoke, so much so that Ashley had to lean closer to hear. 'I'm really glad you found Hazel. You deserve to be happy.' She cleared her throat, returning to normal volume as she attempted a joke. 'Took you long enough.'

Ashley didn't quite know what to say to that. Dani knew about her past feelings; there was no getting over that. For a long time she'd thought Dani felt the same, but after a drunken holiday kiss everything had changed. Ashley had thought it was finally the start of something special, only for Dani to not remember a thing the next morning. It wasn't special to her, merely drunken banter. Something had just clicked. If she wanted the life she'd always dreamed of she couldn't live in a fantasy world, hoping Dani would come round. It was time to grow up and move on.

She hadn't quite expected to fall head over heels for the first woman she properly met. She'd joined Tinder, but it never sat right. Face-to-face connection was so much better. When Hazel had approached her at a dating event she was caught hook, line, and sinker. How could you not be, with those dreamy brown eyes?

'Good things come to those who wait,' Ashley finally replied.

'So I hear.'

5

'You good?' Kirsty asked, standing outside the trendy west end restaurant.

'Yeah, let's do this,' Dani replied with a decisive nod.

A few weeks had passed without much mention of wedding stuff. Well, that was until Ashley texted saying Dani was expected to attend a celebratory dinner. At least she was given the option to bring Kirsty.

She had no problem with being solo in the company of the Davidsons, but Hazel's family had travelled over from Perth, so they would more than likely be busy hobnobbing with the future in-laws. With Kirsty at her side she at least had one person to talk to.

'After you,' Dani said, opening the door and stepping aside.

She'd forgone her cap again. She still felt a fool for thinking Ashley wanted to meet for anything other than wedding plans. What an idiot she was for dressing up, thinking it would be special, that she should make an effort.

She followed Kirsty into the stuffy restaurant. Summer was sticking around this year and despite being September, the temperature was well above even the most scorchio of July days. Scotland just wasn't equipped for it. No point getting air con when weather like this was as rare as hen's teeth. The sweat on Dani's back made her wish they'd at least plumped for a fan.

The maître d' greeted them before leading them through the packed restaurant and to a private room in the back. This place was proper prestige. You knew a place was good when they had tablecloths. And white ones, at that.

Polite nods and a few mumbled *hello*s greeted them. Ashley briefly made eye contact before returning to conversation with an older woman Dani didn't recognise.

They took a seat opposite Leanne and her family.

'Dani!' Fraser squealed when she sat beside him. The eight-year-old wiggled in his seat, giving her an awkward hug. She gave him a quick tickle in return.

'You gonna behave tonight, trouble?' she asked, trying her best to look serious.

'Yes,' he said, drawing the one syllable out. The glint in his eye said even he didn't believe it, though.

'He most certainly is,' Leanne confirmed. 'You okay beside him?' she quietly mouthed. Dani smiled a *yes* in return. 'He insisted, sorry.'

'There's no one else I'd rather sit beside,' Dani said, more to Fraser than Leanne. He beamed with pride. 'And how's trouble number two?' Dani asked, addressing Seb.

The young boy eyed her with a look that wouldn't be out of place in a horror film. He naturally had those kind of eyes, wild and distant. He tended to zone out, more content in his own wee world than the one surrounding him, especially in crowded places like this. One on one he was a totally different child. She and Ashley had enjoyed some great evenings babysitting them. She'd offer to take him for a walk or something later, give Leanne a break from the cling.

She might welcome a break herself, to be honest.

A sea of familiar faces lined either side of the table. Then, up the top, things got vague. She could make a guess at who Hazel's parents were: she looked just like her mum. Presumably the rest were relatives. Two younger women sat near the very top. Siblings, or here in a similar capacity to Dani? They didn't look like Hazel or her parents.

Was she expected to talk to these people? Ashley had insisted she come tonight, to get to know the immediate wedding party, but it didn't look like she was going to be making introductions any time soon.

'What you thinking?' Kirsty asked, keeping her tone hushed.

'Huh?'

'You kinda zoned out there.'

'Did I?'

'Dani! Do you want to do some colouring?' Fraser asked, not waiting for a reply before he shoved a crayon into her hand.

'Order, order!' Brian joked, tapping a knife against his wine glass.

Eventually, the room fell silent.

He left it a beat too long though and Ashley's Uncle Tam cried out, 'Get on with it then!' Hoots of laughter followed.

When the room finally settled, Brian cleared his throat. 'Thank you for coming tonight. It's brilliant to see our families finally come together.'

Dani gave Fraser a playful poke in the side as he started

to squirm. He'd been good all evening, but suddenly, having to sit still was an issue.

'We couldn't have wished for a better addition to the family,' Brian continued, his eyes misty with emotion.

Dani swallowed down her own lump of resentment.

It was stupid, she knew that. She'd been the one to mess things up, miss her chance, but all of this felt like a slap in the face.

As Brian prattled on about how wonderful Hazel was, Dani took the time to reflect.

Everything would be fine. She'd gone this long on her own. So, Ashley wouldn't be so front and centre anymore? She had Rhona and Trip. Kirsty wasn't about to pop out any kids and forget about her.

The most important thing was that Ashley was happy.

Say it enough, she might start to believe it herself.

Applause stole Dani's attention as Hazel got to her feet. She had on a brown checked suit. Hazel's fashion sense often sparked jealousy in Dani. Maybe it was the tattoos and her always-styled hair, but she just had an edge. Dani couldn't compete, in her navy shirt and grey dress trousers. She lacked pizazz. Some people just have it.

The look Ashley was giving Hazel wasn't lost either. She looked like the cat that got the cream; pure admiration shone from her eyes. She'd never looked at Dani like that.

Sometimes Dani wondered if she'd blown the whole thing out of proportion in her head. So, they'd shared a few good months together when they were seventeen. Was that really enough to hold a torch for a ridiculous amount of years?

Jenny, her therapist, had heard this a thousand times. Whether there had been a spark or not, it was gone now.

Hazel was the downpour that finally extinguished it once and for all.

Hazel thanked the Davidsons for welcoming her with open arms, making her part of the family.

That's what they did, though. Not a bad bone in their bodies. If it wasn't for them Dani probably wouldn't be here. The little lost lamb whose dad died. They never once made her feel pitied, though.

They were the masters of making you feel included.

Except, now Dani felt she was on the outside, watching her worst nightmare unfold without a hope in hell of doing a thing about it.

Jenny had proposed the absurd notion of telling Ashley how she felt. Completely hypothetical, of course.

That had been a fun session. Not.

Too much to unpack.

Too much to lose.

It wasn't worth the risk. Especially not now.

Claps and the occasional whistle signalled Hazel was done.

'Now, go mingle amongst yourselves,' Brian urged. 'Bar is on us!'

Dani didn't need told twice. She turned to Kirsty, who was involved in polite conversation with Leanne's husband, Dave. 'Do you want a drink?'

Kirsty barely broke her stride with conversation, fitting in her answer as if it were just another breath. 'Pinot Grigio, please.'

'And you'll be wanting a pint?' she said to Fraser as she got up. He giggled in response.

The queue to the room's private bar was a few people deep. Nothing like free drinks to get people flocking.

'Dani, hey,' Ashley said, putting a hand on her shoulder to turn her around. 'This is Yaz.'

A girl shorter than Dani greeted her with a smile when she finally turned. She had equally impressive short hair compared to Hazel's and sported an immaculately styled quiff. With her gold chain, T-shirt, and a fair number of rings on her fingers, Dani would bet her last pennies on her being gay too. This had better not be a set-up. She really wasn't her type.

'Hey,' Dani said, unsure.

'Yaz is Hazel's best friend. I figured you should meet since you'll be seeing a lot more of each other on the run up to the big day.'

'Ah, cool,' Dani replied, relief clear. 'So, are you like, Hazel's maid of honour?'

'I'm going down more of a best man route, although I'd prefer something a little more gender-neutral cause I'm enby. If you think of anything fitting, just let me know,' Yaz said with a smile.

Dani thought for a second. 'Friend of honour?'

They all considered it for a second. Ashley's face said it hadn't quite hit the mark. 'Maybe,' Yaz finally replied, obviously being polite.

'Plenty time to work on it,' Dani assured.

'Back in a min,' Ashley said, already beelining for an older couple at the other side of the room.

'So, you excited to be Ashley's maid of honour?' Yaz asked, playing with their chain as they spoke.

'I guess. Big deal to be asked.'

Yaz's eyes flickered with something Dani couldn't quite place. 'It is. So don't fuck it up.' Their words were almost a growl; sincerity weighed each syllable like blocks of concrete, dragging the atmosphere down with them.

An awkward silence descended between them as Dani battled to catch up with the sudden change in tone. Yaz stood their ground, their eyes not moving from Dani. This wasn't banter.

'Where's that come from?' Dani finally asked.

Yaz shrugged. 'Just consider it friendly advice.'

Dani's brow furrowed. 'Has Ashley said something?'

'No,' Yaz replied with a shake of their head and a smug smile.

Before Dani could press things further Ashley reappeared. 'Hey, sorry. They were heading off, I needed to say goodbye. You guys getting on okay?'

'Peachy,' Dani replied through a gritted smile. She'd be civil for Ashley. Today, at least.

6

'And lean closer,' Rhona instructed from behind her camera.

Ashley and Hazel closed the gap between them, their noses now touching. Giggles instantly took over.

'Sorry,' Ashley said when she'd calmed a little.

'No, no, carry on, that's perfect,' Rhona called.

They'd chosen to do their engagement shoot in Queen's Park. It felt only right, given that they'd met because of an event in Shawlands. The park was a landmark in the Glasgow suburb, as much a part of the area as the people.

Right now, they were at the flagpole, Glasgow's skyline tumbling into hills in the background. The weather had been good to them, too. It was strangely sunny for the end of September.

'Someone's phone's ringing,' Rhona shouted, lowering her camera and ducking to the equipment bag at her side. 'That's the second time in as many minutes.'

'Probably me,' Hazel replied, stomping over. After a rummage she pulled her phone out, a scowl already on her face. 'Yep. I'd better take this.'

Ashley wandered over to join Rhona. 'Photos looking good so far?'

'Of course,' Rhona said with a smile.'

'Sorry, I wasn't doubting you, I—'

'I was joking, Ash.' Rhona tilted the camera towards her. 'Want a quick peek?'

'Of course.' Ashley watched as Rhona clicked through the photos on the camera's small rear screen. Even without editing they looked amazing. She'd never been one for getting her photo taken, but with Rhona behind the viewfinder Ashley felt half decent. She was a miracle worker. 'These are great, I don't know how you do it.'

'All in a day's work.' Rhona's eyes flitted to Hazel as she paced back and forth by the treeline, out of earshot. 'Everything okay? She looks stressed.'

Ashley let out a long sigh. 'She is a wee bit.'

'Ah. Not Finola still? Sorry.'

'The one and only,' Ashley replied with a thin-lipped smile.

Hazel was a personal trainer and Rhona had hooked her up with a client just under a year ago. Little did they know she was going to make both their lives a misery. Rhona's only consolation was she had a team to deflect the conflict. Hazel had to ride the storm head on.

Finola was the soon-to-be wife of a Premier League footballer with more money than sense and no idea how normal people lived. She expected Hazel to be at her beck and call 24/7. Her current freakout was over the fact she'd gained two pounds. No amount of explaining about water weight or hormonal changes was getting through. You'd think the wedding was cancelled, for the amount of aggro she was giving Hazel.

'If it's any consolation,' Rhona offered, 'she's still giving us grief too. We've even put a countdown on the wall in the office. T–minus forty days.'

'It's only going to get worse, isn't it?' Ashley asked, putting her hands on her hips as she watched Hazel.

'Probably, yeah.'

At least she was being honest. It was hellish seeing Hazel so stressed. She usually loved her job, but this woman was sucking all the fun out of it. The money was too good, though. Weddings were expensive. Never mind all the stuff they planned to do after.

'Thanks again for fitting us in,' Ashley said, her eyes still fixed on her fiancée.

'My pleasure. It's good to be back home for a while. This summer's been crazy.'

Rhona's job took her all over the world catering to the rich and wealthy. Being a wedding photographer was no job for the lazy. She worked her ass off. Ashley wasn't sure she could be away from friends and family so often. The set-up seemed to work for Rhona, though. She and Kirsty were as strong as ever.

'You're still enjoying it though, yeah?' Ashley asked, to make conversation more than anything.

'Oh yeah. Dream come true.' Rhona fiddled with the buttons on her camera, as if weighing up her next question. 'Spoken to Dani recently?'

Weird question. They lived together. Rhona got to see Dani every day. 'A bit, why?'

'Just wondered. Chet's not been well.'

Ashley straightened. 'Really? She never said.'

Rhona pursed her lips and shrugged. 'I think it's just a hairball, but you know what she's like. She worries.'

Dani told her everything. Or at least, Ashley thought she did. 'I'll text her when we're done.'

'She'd like that,' Rhona said, dropping to a squat by her bag. 'I think we'll use the diffuser next. Move down to the duck pond.'

Had Rhona mentioned Dani on purpose? Was she feeling neglected? It would be fair, to be honest. Wedding prep and work had taken over recently and their messaging was becoming less and less frequent. Sometimes life just got in the way. How could Ashley not know Chet was unwell, though?

She had thought Dani's reply about wedding dress shopping was rather curt. She'd just put that down to a bad mood, though. She hadn't exactly been sunshine and rainbows when it came to wedding stuff.

Hazel made her way back, her face like thunder.

Ashley bit her tongue. If Hazel wanted to talk about it she could. She'd learned the hard way it was better to let Hazel open up when she was ready. Ashley was a born talker, Hazel a natural brooder. She liked to think things over in her own head first, get things straight before spilling her thoughts. Ashley preferred to talk things out, get a second opinion off the bat. The old adage about opposites attracting was true, it would seem.

Their trip to Dunkeld and the Hermitage, where Hazel proposed, had been sorely needed. The closer this high-end wedding got, the more unbearable this Finola woman became. Hazel was distant and grumpy more often than not, and Ashley was struggling, to say the least. She missed the old Hazel. She would be back. Ashley just had to resist the urge to put up her own countdown board like Rhona's staff had.

'Everything good?' Rhona asked, still crouched at her bag.

Hazel shook her head as she ran her tongue along her back teeth. 'I'm near ready to kill that woman.'

Rhona got to her feet. 'I've worked with some real stonkers in my time, but she's taking the biscuit. I get that she's stressed, but the way she talks to us is something else.'

'Tell me about it,' Hazel replied, puffing her cheeks before letting out an unsteady breath.

Ashley kept quiet. It was good for Hazel to let off steam with someone who got exactly what she was going through. They didn't need her pointless input.

Dani's lack of Chet chat lay on Ashley's chest like a fresh weight, gaining pressure the more she thought about it.

She missed hanging out with Dani, but it couldn't be like the old days with Hazel on the scene.

A part of Ashley always felt guilty.

It was like seeing the police in the street. Even though she knew she'd done nothing wrong she still forgot how to act and came off totally suspicious.

It didn't help that Hazel was, to put it lightly, strange about her hanging out with Dani. Ashley had never exposed their tangled past and she was 99 per cent certain no one else had either. But there was always a reluctance when Ashley would say they were hanging out. The usual question of 'who else is going?' didn't go unnoticed. The slight twitch in Hazel's eye that hinted she wasn't quite sold on the idea. Which was ridiculous. She was with Hazel, end of.

Still, her feelings for Dani were always there. Lingering at the back of her mind. Locked away behind a reinforced door. Not quite gone ,but suppressed enough to not be an issue.

It would be great if she could turn them off all together,

think of Dani as just a friend, but they'd never just been friends. Even when they met in school, aged only twelve. Ashley might have been young and a little behind on knowing she was gay, but the pull was there. When the penny finally dropped at fifteen it finally made sense. Loving Dani was as much a part of her as the scar on her right knee. Which, incidentally, was Dani's fault too. Who the hell thinks drinking a bottle of cheap vodka and mucking about in a dark forest is a good idea?

That was the night they'd first kissed. Dani tending to her knee in the pitch black, both of them giggling despite the pain and worry. The scar was obsolete. She would remember that night forever, regardless.

'Hey, Ash,' Hazel said, waving a hand in front of her face. 'We're heading to the pond.'

Ashley shook her thoughts free. 'Yeah sure, I'm right behind you.'

She'd phone Dani tonight or better still, pop round. It was just a matter of choosing the right time to tell Hazel.

7

Dani flicked through the hanging dresses for the second time. She'd never seen so much chiffon in one place. Just the sight of it was making her feel itchy and short of breath.

If Ashley thought she was wearing any of these she was sorely mistaken.

Her first official outing as maid of honour was to accompany Ashley dress shopping. Thankfully, Ash's mum and sister were here too, because Dani didn't know the first thing about dresses.

She pushed apart two dresses, revealing a seafoam number complete with a huge sash ruffle. Dani's face creased in disgust. Thankfully the staff were too busy fawning over Ashley to see.

Debut Desire was a swanky place in Glasgow's west end. Hidden in a side alley, away from the beaten track of Byres Road and Hillhead. Appointment only, don't you know? Dani bobbed her head from side to side, imagining the way the sales women spoke. Nipped, refined, pretentious.

She'd seen the way they looked her up and down. Okay.

So, maybe jeans, a hoodie, and her navy cap weren't the most upmarket clothes she owned. but today was probably going to involve a lot of sitting and a lot of waiting around. She wanted to be comfy. Why dress to impress?

She pushed the offending dress back into place and wandered over to the seating area, sitting down beside Leanne.

A tiny mirrored table with a little bowl of chocolate almonds sat between them. Dani refrained from trying one. This whole place was top to toe white. She felt bad just sitting in the chair. Never mind the threat of melted chocolate.

'See anything you like?' Leanne asked with a cheeky smile.

'Considering one of each. In every colour,' Dani replied, crossing her arms and reclining.

'She's nearly done.'

'Do you think you'll wear a dress?' Mary asked.

Dani pursed her lips. 'It's totally up to Ashley. Although, I can't see Yaz wearing anything but a suit.'

Mary was saved a diplomatic answer by the swoosh of the changing room curtain.

The sales assistant appeared first, her face the epitome of smug.

As she stepped aside, Ashley stole the spotlight.

The air caught in Dani's throat, like someone had her in a chokehold.

She swallowed hard, hoping her senses would return. Right now her brain was short circuiting, all basic functions ceasing to be.

Leanne and Mary cooed and *aww*ed.

Ashley turned, swishing the dress from side to side. 'I'm not sure, if I'm honest.'

'First dress, we've plenty more to see,' Leanne replied. 'Off to a good start though.'

She looked amazing. More than that. Incredible. Inconceivable. Incomparable. Dani's heart continued to flutter. She pulled at the collar of her hoodie, the room suddenly a few degrees warmer.

'What do you think?' Ashley asked, her eyes fixed on Dani.

Words were impossible. She was beautiful. And all without her hair and make-up done. She was normal, everyday Ash; she just so happened to be wearing a wedding dress.

'Looks good.' Dani's tone came out flat and unbothered in her bid to disguise the fact her heart was ready to leap from her chest and there was a slight chance she might be sick.

Ashley's face fell at her response, but there was no way to right it without spilling how wonderful she looked.

Dani would be lying if she said she hadn't imagined what Ashley might look like at their wedding. She knew in her heart it would be Ashley's day; she could have anything she wanted, Dani would just be happy to be marrying her. But she'd daydreamed nonetheless.

Every expectation was topped, though. Nothing could have prepared Dani for how good Ashley would look.

The realisation she would never get her day with Ashley hit like a punch to her gut. This was all for Hazel. She was but a bystander.

Ashley turned to her mother as she twisted to show her back. 'What do you think of the bodice? I like the way it looks like a corset but isn't one.'

The sales assistant moved to Ashley's back, pulling at the laces, making them tighter. Ashley's eyes bulged. Under any other circumstances it would be funny. But Dani couldn't shake the tears that were threatening.

'I like it. Is that the style you had in mind?' Mary asked, getting to her feet to fuss with the skirt.

'I think so. I know I don't want sleeves.'

Leanne focused her attention on Dani and raised a quizzical eyebrow. Dani forced a half-smile in return.

Had someone turned up the heating again? This room was nearly unbearable.

Dani removed her cap, running a hand over her sweaty brow, before repositioning the hat. 'I like the sparkly bits,' she said, feeling it was necessary to add something since she'd let Ashley down with her first impression.

'Yeah, me too,' Ashley replied, her face instantly lightening as she moved the skirt from side to side. It twinkled like someone had woven stars into the material.

'One thousand hand-sewn diamantes,' the sales assistant informed them.

'Hand-sewn?' Mary repeated with a little squeak, the dress's value doubling in her mind. Brian and Mary would get Ashley the moon if it was what she wanted, but Dani could only imagine what it would be like writing the cheque for that. Brian would be sweating bullets.

'There's another three to go. I'll get the next one on,' Ashley said, backing into the changing cubicle.

With the curtain finally drawn, Dani took her chance. 'I'm just going to get some air.'

Her exit was only met with approving nods.

She was in half a mind not to come back. As if firing a warning shot, the universe made sure the door was locked, stopping her in her tracks.

Another sales assistant bounded over, the one who had got Mary a coffee when they'd first arrived. 'Here, let me,' she said, grabbing keys and opening the door. 'Just knock when you want back in.'

The cold air was a slap to the face, in the best possible way. Dani took three long strides to the close's door by the shop and leaned against the cool wall, out of sight.

'Fuck,' she growled under her breath. She opened her eyes wide and stared at the chipped concrete above. She couldn't cry. Not now. Not in front of people.

This was torture. And it was only the first hurdle. There had to be a way to get out of this. Leanne could surely manage and if Ashley was that fussed there was always Trip. She could easily fill Dani's shoes.

She pulled her mobile out from her back pocket and called Kirsty. It was only after the third ring Dani twigged she would be working. Just as she was about to hang up, her sister answered.

'You okay?' Kirsty asked, concern obvious.

Dani took a long breath, surprised at the fresh tears rimming her eyes. If she spoke there would be no holding them back.

'Dani?' Kirsty coaxed. 'You there?'

Her bottom lip wobbled. This was a terrible idea. She wanted words of wisdom or a good excuse to leave. Neither were worth a blotchy face and red eyes.

'Fuck's sake,' Kirsty huffed and hung up the phone.

She'd blame it on a pocket dial.

Dani breathed through her mouth, slowly and deliberately, aware her nose was snotty and blocked.

A passing man made awkward eye contact but thankfully he carried on his way, leaving her in peace.

She'd be fine. She just needed a minute.

Jenny had prepared her for a moment like this. It wasn't her fault. This wasn't Dani's doing. She had no control over it. But she did have control over her reaction.

They'd come up with a plan. It was stupid, ridiculous. If Kirsty ever found out she would mock Dani to kingdom come. But it worked. You couldn't argue with that.

It was all about distraction. Breaking the cycle in her head.

She took another deep breath, her hand on her upper belly, feeling the air fill her lungs.

Then she closed her eyes and imagined a baguette.

A long, crusty, fresh-out-of-the-oven baguette.

Another deep breath and she pictured the baguette being slapped against her cheek. She could almost feel it. Hard, but not harsh. The whack of the perfectly fired outer layer.

That was a good one. Satisfying.

Next was a slice of bread.

Wholemeal. Why not?

It was floppy and soft. Ticklish to a degree.

She rattled through a few more baked goods, focusing hard on texture and sensation.

After picturing a rather fancy cheese cob she finally opened her eyes, letting them adjust to the light with a few blinks.

Was it just Dani Jenny had imagining being slapped with bread, or did all her clients do this? She'd been too scared to ask. Just in case it was some bizarre joke and Jenny laughed in her face about actually doing it. It worked. Dani didn't want to lose her one coping mechanism.

Had she been out here long? No one had come looking for her: that was a good sign. She pulled her phone back out to be greeted with a text from Kirsty. Seven minutes ago.

Good, not too long. She replied with a flimsy excuse about sitting on her phone and stuffed it away.

It was no use talking to Ashley today, telling her she couldn't do this. She'd been so excited on the car ride over here and they were all going out for lunch after. It would only sour the mood.

She'd leave it for today and find the perfect time next week. This had to be done properly. No use blowing their friendship over a relationship that could never be.

8

'How did today go?' Hazel asked, kissing Ashley's cheek before taking a seat at their breakfast bar.

She seemed to be in a better mood today. Ashley's shoulders relaxed.

'Yeah, good.'

Hazel's features creased. 'That wasn't the response I was expecting. You were really excited yesterday. What happened?'

Ashley shrugged and focused on the red onion she was chopping. She'd promised to make them chilli tonight but was in no mood to prep when she got home. Her mind was heavy, the sheer volume of thoughts stopping her from doing anything but lying on the sofa, nothing but a dead weight hugging a cushion and staring at the ceiling.

'Nothing, really. Just underwhelmed.'

Hazel narrowed her eyes. 'Didn't find the dress?'

'It's the first shop. No one finds it first try.'

Her fiancée's eyes remained two dark slits. 'Okay, so not that then. What underwhelmed you?'

Ashley paused the knife, resting the blade on top of the

onion. It was a touchy subject but there was no one else to speak to. She chewed on her cheek, painfully aware Hazel was watching her. She couldn't lift her eyes from the chopping board, scared something in her gaze would give the game away.

'Ash, talk to me.' Hazel reached over, using the bar stool for leverage, and gently grabbed Ashley's arm.

She had to get it off her chest or the weight would crush. 'It's just Dani.'

Hazel's touch stiffened but she didn't sigh or huff or do any of the things she surely wanted to. Instead, she quietly asked: 'What happened?'

Ashley put the knife down with a grunt and Hazel took the opportunity to release her grip and sit down.

'She was so huffy. Like she wanted to be anywhere else but with me.'

Hazel only just caught the smirk pulling at her lips. 'You know how I feel about her,' she replied, raising one eyebrow as if to say *I told you so*.

Ashley sucked on her bottom lip, buying time before answering. She needed to rant but this was no time for freestyling. Every word needed careful consideration.

'I know, but it hurts when she's like this.'

'It's just classic Dani. Doesn't matter that she's meant to be your best friend. She's not into dresses and stuff and doesn't care enough to act like she is.'

'But that's the thing; I don't want her to act. I want her to take an interest.'

'We both know you're wishing on a star with that.'

'I just thought she'd step up her game, you know, cause it's me.'

'Or lower it, cause it's me.'

Ashley cocked her head to the side, her face set. 'What

do you mean by that?' She knew exactly what Hazel meant but couldn't hold back the fury that now coursed in her veins. It was like Hazel wanted to create a divide.

'She's hated me from day one. If you were marrying anyone else it would be a different story.'

Dani hadn't exactly made any effort with Hazel, there was no denying that. But she was civil. *Stand-offish* would be the best word to describe Dani in Hazel's presence. There were layers to it, though. Ashley wasn't an idiot.

'Maybe it would help if you guys did something together.'

If Hazel had been drinking something she would have sprayed the room. The guffaw that echoed in the kitchen seemed to linger.

'I'm not joking,' Ashley added.

'I know.' The smile on Hazel's face hinted she wasn't as serious in her intentions as Ashley.

'It's a lot to ask, I know that,' Ashley assured, picking up the knife and resuming her onion dicing. 'But I think it would make a big difference. You too are similar in more ways than you realise.'

Hazel played with her nails, her attention fully captured by her middle finger. Finally, after what felt like an age, she spoke. 'I know she's your best friend, so I get there's history, but I can't shake the feeling Dani has ulterior motives.'

Ashley's muscles froze, the onion on her board still not fully prepared. Her heart flipped as saliva flooded her mouth. She gulped, steadying herself. 'What do you mean by that?'

Hazel lifted her gaze, snagging Ashley's and holding on tight. 'She likes you. And I know,' she said, waving a hand between them as if flicking Ashley's counter-argument away. 'You've known each other twenty-odd years, there's history, but I swear. She hates me cause she likes you. Loves you, even. Us going for a beer isn't going to change that.'

Ashley's heart rate continued to rise. She went to speak but only a nervous giggle escaped. She composed herself, willing the heat on her cheeks to subside. She was nearly the colour of the pepper she was about to chop. 'Likes me? What makes you say that?'

Hazel shook her head, a silly grin on her lips. 'Call it fiancée intuition. There's more going on here than meets the eye.'

Ashley thought for a moment, finally finishing the onion and moving onto cutting the pepper with such focused attention she might as well have been doing brain surgery.

'And does that worry you? If you're right, which you're totally not.' She added the final sentence in a ramble, like she'd been caught doing something hideous. Could Hazel tell she was floundering? She may as well spell out *I love Danielle Hamilton* with the sodding vegetables, lay the whole dirty truth out on the countertop for Hazel to see.

She could trust herself, though. Didn't matter what her heart felt. She would never act on it.

Plus, there was no way in hell Dani had feelings for her.

Trip said Dani's reluctance to let Hazel in was simply a reaction to sharing her best friend. Which made perfect sense. She'd gone this long with just the two of them; of course Dani was going to be weird when Ashley got a girlfriend. She hated change.

Hazel stood, making the bar stool's legs squeak against the wooden floor. She walked round the counter and hugged Ashley from behind, kissing her cheek before speaking. 'I'm not worried, because I trust you.' Her embrace loosened. 'However, I don't trust Dani one bit.'

Ashley tensed her jaw. Arguing wouldn't do anyone any good. 'Would you rather she wasn't involved?'

Hazel sighed as she leaned her head on Ashley's shoulder. 'She's your bestie. If you want her involved, then that's fine. But don't expect me to go to the pub with her. I need to draw the line somewhere.'

'Fair enough. I understand. I just want you to get along.'

'I know.' Hazel released her with a final kiss on the cheek before returning to her seat. 'You know, I have a client that might be a good match for Dani. Do you think she'd be up for a blind date?'

Ashley's face had contorted before her mind had time to process the idea. It was about as palatable as sour milk. 'Dani really isn't the dating type.'

'Well, maybe that's just what she needs. You never know: if it works out, maybe we could double-date?'

'You think?' Ashley chuckled, raising her brow with scepticism.

'Worth a shot. You ask her, and if she's keen I'll try and set it up.'

It wasn't the worst idea in the world. Maybe Dani would be on board. What worried Ashley was the way her stomach tightened, a new weight forming in her belly, the twisting knot of repulsion growing at the thought of Dani with someone else. Someone other than her.

9

'Is he feeling better now?' Ashley asked as she scratched Chet's chin.

'I think so,' Dani said, plonking herself on the bed and leaning over to pet the cat. 'Just a particularly bad hairball.'

Ashley nodded, her attention still fixed on Chet.

Dani had been surprised when Ashley had texted, wanting to come round to the flat. It had been a long time since it was just the two of them. Never mind Ashley suggesting they watch a film. That was really weird. It almost felt like the old days, pre-Hazel.

Rhona was just back from a trip to Helsinki, so Dani had made the executive decision to give her and Kirsty the living room for a couple's night. She and Ashley were enjoying some time with Chet in her room.

She'd set the laptop up just like they used to: on a chair, by the bed. It wasn't a fancy or complicated set-up, but sometimes simple was best.

'What do you want to watch, then?' Dani asked, leaning forward and hovering her hands over the keyboard, digits ready to leap into action at Ashley's command.

She pursed her lips, thinking. 'I've not watched a film in ages. Far too much going on. It's like I can never switch off. You got any suggestions?'

'Well, tonight is all about giving you some off time. Don't you worry about that.' Dani wiggled her fingers over the keys, as if limbering up. 'I watched this the other day – do you fancy it?'

A few taps of the keys and up popped a film called *Love Uncorked*, a romantic comedy about a woman who inherits a vineyard.

Ashley snorted, her face creased with confusion. Chet jumped at the outburst, only to settle back down like nothing had happened. 'A romantic comedy? You watched a romantic comedy?'

Dani straightened herself, heat searing her cheeks. 'Yes. I like things like that sometimes.'

Ashley sniggered as she playfully grabbed Dani's side, jostling her back and forth. 'Izzy, have you possessed Dani? Blink once for yes, twice for no.'

'Actually, Izzy suggested it,' Dani said through giggles, pawing at Ashley's hand, pretending she wanted her to stop. 'Don't you dare tell her I enjoyed it.'

She mimed zipping her lips shut. 'What's it worth to keep your dirty little secret?'

'I bought you the good wine. Surely that already counts for something.'

'It's a start.' Ashley repositioned herself, getting comfy in the cushions against the wall. 'Right, you better put that on. Let me see the great romance film that melted Dani Hamilton's heart.'

'Oi, I can be romantic when I want to be.'

Ashley raised her eyebrows. 'You've never once been on a proper date the whole time I've known you.'

'True. But that doesn't mean I'm not romantic.'

'Give me an example, then?' The devilish smile on Ashley's face suggested she thought she'd set an impossible task.

It was a bit. Dani thought back to getting Ashley's favourite chocolate when she was at the Co-op for milk, or bringing her flowers because she'd had a bad day. She could hardly use them as illustrations, though.

Never mind the ring she'd bought her five years ago because Ashley had absolutely gushed over it on a trip to Edinburgh. Dani had got the train back the next week, the sense of relief at it still being there second to none. The time had never come to give it to her. And now it would never happen. She really needed to pawn it. Wasn't exactly cheap. No point having a few thou in a box to gather dust.

Dani pulled a face. 'Okay, maybe you're right. But I can at least start learning now.'

Ashley controlled a smug smile. 'Hazel's not overly romantic. But what she does means a lot,' she said as the opening titles appeared on the laptop.

Dani retrieved her vodka and Coke from the dresser and got comfy. She allowed herself a big glug before answering. 'Yeah, what does she do?'

Ashley shrugged. 'Little things. Like, she remembers stuff I don't like.'

'Like sweetcorn.'

Ashley smiled. 'Yes, like sweetcorn. And mushrooms. And she always phones me on her lunch break.'

That didn't seem overly romantic. Dani waited but nothing else came. Time to be diplomatic. 'I guess little gestures are just as thoughtful as grand ones.'

'Exactly.'

'And what about you? What do you do?'

'Not much recently, if I'm honest. This whole wedding thing is stressful.'

'Really?' Dani's attention snapped to Ashley. She'd watched this film a few times, truth be told. She didn't need to see it again. 'Is it not meant to be fun?'

'I guess,' Ashley huffed. 'But there's a lot to juggle.'

'Is Hazel not helping?'

'Oh, yeah, totally of course.' Ashley replied, leaping to her defence. She turned to Dani, Chet the only thing keeping them from touching. 'She's just busy, that's all. Once this nightmare client is done, everything will be different.'

There was a dullness in her eyes that Dani couldn't decipher. Something was up. She stayed turned to Dani, their eyes locked.

Back in the day, before cats and fiancées, it wouldn't be unusual for them to be cuddled up while watching a film. Personal space wasn't really a thing when it came to Dani and Ashley. It wasn't anything sexual, well, not for a very long time, but Dani would be a liar if she said she'd never thought about crossing that line. It would have been so easy.

Suddenly, now there was no way of ever getting the chance again, a thousand missed opportunities stared Dani in the face. How could she have been so stupid?

With a sigh, Ashley turned back to face the screen.

'If I can do anything to help, just shout,' Dani said, her gaze still trained on Ashley.

'It's cool.' The bob of her Adam's apple suggested the opposite. Something was bothering her. The changing light from the laptop screen ghosted Ashley's features. Dani watched, trying to place the energy Ashley was giving off. 'What's up?' Ashley asked with an uneasy chuckle.

'Huh?' Dani grunted and, as if woken from a trance, snapped to face the screen. 'Nothing, sorry.'

Ashley said nothing in return, instead choosing to shoot Dani a half-smile.

They watched the film in silence, but Dani's attention was nowhere near the couple on screen.

Ashley was the one to suggest tonight. She obviously wanted to talk about something. How to get it out of her, though?

Conversation openers flipped through Dani's mind like a conveyor belt at top speed. Finally, she grabbed one to run with.

'So, Hazel is still stressed at work then?'

'Yep,' Ashley replied with a pop of her lips. 'It's making her pretty grumpy, if I'm honest, but it's fine. I know it will pass.'

That didn't sound good. 'Grumpy? Like, towards you?'

Ashley didn't match Dani's eye contact. 'Not exactly towards me. Just in general. It's fine though. Everything's fine.'

'Do you want to say *fine* one more time? Just to be sure?' Dani added a little laugh to keep things on the right side of cheeky.

Ashley didn't take the bait. The dullness was back. 'This woman is a nightmare. I don't blame Hazel for being moody. It's just making certain things tricky.'

'Like?'

'Just stuff.' Ashley took a deep breath like she was working up to something. 'In fact—'

She paused, leaving Dani hanging. 'Yeah?'

'Will you come to a wedding fair with me on Saturday?' Ashley screwed her face up like she'd asked Dani to do something horrible.

'With you and Hazel?'

'Just me. That's why I'm asking.'

Dani nodded slowly, computing what she'd been asked. 'Yeah, sure. I'll need to swap a shift with someone, but I'm sure I can swing it.'

Ashley smiled, her eyes brightening. 'Brilliant.'

'And you're sure there's nothing else?' There was way more to this than Ash was letting on. Maybe more one-on-one time wasn't the worst idea in the world.

'Everything's fine. I'm just tired and periody. Now, shut up, I want to watch this film.'

'Fine,' Dani replied with a snigger, only to have her side grabbed.

Saturday. She'd get the truth on Saturday.

10

The fair was massive. Ashley was glad she'd brought Dani; it would have been intimidating on her own.

She'd not intended to ask Dani to accompany her, but it was all she could think of to cover up the fact she'd completely bottled asking Dani if she'd go on a date with Crissie.

Telling Hazel she'd asked Dani to come was odd. After their pre-dinner spat, talking about Dani was more taboo than ever.

She was fine with it, though. Her crossed arms and tensed muscles suggested otherwise, but her mouth had voiced her blessing, so Ashley could ask for nothing more.

'Where do you want to start?' Dani asked, standing in the middle of the huge centre aisle.

Ashley had only ever been to concerts at the SECC, the huge conference centre in the middle of Glasgow. It was really odd seeing it with the lights on and endless rows of perfectly spaced stands.

A lady grinned manically at her as she walked level with

Dani. She made the mistake of politely returning a weak smile, causing the woman to lunge forward, brochure in hand. 'Would you like a catalogue? Cup of tea and a chat?'

She seemed lovely, but her energy was far too much for ten in the morning. She'd had a coffee on the train over but it had done little to wake her up. Sleep wasn't easy at the moment: too much to think about.

Ashley looked at the sign jutting out from the lady's stand like a road marker. *Sabrina Lowe Photography*.

'We've already got a photographer,' Dani replied, her voice unusually cheery. She'd been upbeat since they met at Crossmyloof station. Thank God one of them was. Dani wandered on, eyes fixed on the brochure they'd got on entry, with the show's map. 'Maybe we should start with food; it's on the far side.' She pointed to the right, putting her weight on her front foot as she peeked down the aisle at a right angle to them.

'Sounds good.'

'Come on, Ash. Get some life in you,' Dani said with a laugh as she shook her by the arm. It was hard not to find her energy infectious.

'Sorry. Bad sleep last night.'

'Any reason why?' Dani asked, her face softening.

It was strange being the centre of attention in a sea of people. Despite the crowds around them she could still feel the eyes of passing exhibitors sizing them up, dying to make eye contact, or better still, strike up conversation. Hazel was in a foul mood this morning because she had a two-hour sesh with the footballer's fiancée at nine. It was hard to imagine her engaging in light-hearted chit-chat with these people. Thank the stars for Dani's unusually chipper mood.

Ashley sidestepped a particularly well-groomed couple before answering. The photography aisle was packed. No one looked as good as Rhona, though. They'd lucked out there.

'It's nothing.'

'Because everything's fine.'

Ashley couldn't help but smile. 'You're not going to drop that, are you?'

'I will when you say it with feeling.'

'Har har.'

'Right, look,' Dani said, coming to a sudden standstill and making Ashley bump into her.

Ashley placed her hands on Dani's hips and leaned against her shoulder, getting a view of where Dani's finger was stabbing at the map. 'A bit of warning, Dan.'

Dani smiled, turning her head so they were just inches apart. Ashley's stomach flipped in a way it most certainly should not have. Especially in the middle of a bloody wedding fair. She stepped back, creating respectable distance.

'Sorry, just a change of plan. Well, kind of. I know exactly what you need to get going.'

'Is it a vat of coffee?' Ashley joked, following Dani like she was a tour guide in a busy city. It was hard to keep up as they weaved through the throng.

'Better than that.'

'Stopping soon,' Dani said, pulling the brakes. Ashley only narrowly avoided crashing into her again. 'What? I gave you warning this time!'

Ashley replaced her scowl with a smile and didn't even have time to tell Dani off before the person manning the stand approached with a friendly smile.

'Ladies,' the middle-aged gent boomed, his Highland accent clear in just one word. 'A sample of our finest gin?'

'Who could say no?' Dani replied, stepping off the white

carpet of the aisle and into his exhibition space. A table topped with a large shelving unit showcased a variety of gins produced somewhere north of Inverness, going by the map on the far wall.

The man passed them both a tiny plastic glass each. Ashley swirled the pink liquid before having a sniff. Alcohol at this time of the morning had never really appealed, but when in Rome.

'This is our signature pink gin, very popular at weddings,' the man informed.

Dani knocked the shot back, taking a sharp intake of breath after swallowing. 'Nice,' she said, putting the empty cup in the bin the man was holding out. 'Sweet, but nice.'

'As I say, our most popular at weddings. A nice alternative to champagne when the guests arrive. When's the big day?'

Ashley gulped the shot down, the heat of the booze settling in her throat like a comforting embrace.

'Fifth of August,' Dani answered as Ashley drank.

'Fantastic,' he beamed, grabbing a brochure off the table. 'Darrel, by the way, and congratulations.' Darrel was talking again before either could correct him. 'Now, that's the pink. Have you considered our heather blend?'

THEY'D BEEN HERE two hours and barely finished the food section. With so many freebies on the go, it was slow going. Cakes were hard to resist.

Dani relaxed on the bench they'd found by the stage. The next talk wasn't for another forty minutes, as speakers broke for lunch, otherwise there would have been no chance of finding a free seat. If it was busy before, it was rammed now.

'I'm so tired,' Dani said, a slight slur to her words from all the free booze. 'Like, totally at your beck and call, but done in.'

Ashley felt the same. Constant chit-chat was hard going.

She was just about to stretch her limbs out when an excited squeal made them both jump.

'Oh my God!' a lady's voice shouted. 'Ashley and Dani! You've barely changed a bit.'

Ashley studied the woman bounding towards them, a bespectacled and perplexed man in tow. Her brain struggled to place her before the penny finally dropped. Alice McGuire from school. They were never in the same social circles, but they'd done Higher Geography together.

'Alice, oh my God, hi,' Ashley said, unable to match the woman's excited energy. She straightened herself slightly, but that was all her body would allow.

Dani sat upright like someone had shoved a rod down her back. 'Alice, wow. Long time no see.'

She came to standstill, one hand on her hip, the other popped to the side to emphasise her disbelief. 'So you finally got together.'

Ashley exchanged a look of confusion with Dani. 'Huh?'

'Shut up! You don't need to pretend now, we're not teenagers any more. The whole year knew you guys were getting it on.'

Dani was redder than the roses on the centre display.

Ashley took the lead on shutting the conversation down. 'Dani's here as a friend. We're not together, engaged, whatever.'

Alice's face dropped but she didn't seem embarrassed by

her faux pas. 'You're kidding. I was really rooting for you guys.'

'Sorry,' Ashley said, the heat flushing her cheeks now rivalling Dani's.

'But you were together in school, yeah? I've not got that wrong?'

Ashley swapped another quizzical look with Dani. There was no harm in being truthful. Before she could come clean, though, Dani spoke.

'No, sorry.'

'Really?' Alice huffed, her lopsided body language saying she didn't buy it one bit. 'Nah, you totally were.'

'No, really. Just best friends, nothing more.'

Why did that hurt? Annoyance balled itself in Ashley's stomach and agitation coursed through her veins, making her muscles tense. She swallowed it down, hoping time would dilute the pain. There was no need to be snippy with Dani, not today, and not about a relationship that didn't matter.

Except it did.

They had been a couple. Okay, so it didn't last all that long, but that was only because of Dani's dad's death. Or so Ashley had thought. Had that been a lie? Had nothing ever been real between them?

Ashley kept quiet. This was between Alice and Dani now. She could spin whatever lies she wanted.

'Okay,' Alice replied, her eyes just slits as doubt pulled them closed. A wry smile ghosted her lips. 'I get it. Well, John and I better be off. We're still looking for a caterer – I don't want the good ones to be fully booked. You know what it's like!' She waggled her head, exaggerating the issue. 'Bye, guys.'

Dani and Ashley chorused their goodbyes and Alice disappeared into the crowd.

'Awkward,' Dani said with a chuckle.

'I'll say,' Ashley huffed, getting to her feet. A wander around the entertainment section would help distract her. *Just leave it. Just leave it.*

She stopped in her tracks, realising she had no idea what direction she should be going.

'Where we headed?' Dani asked, coming to a halt by her side like a faithful dog.

'Entertainment.'

Dani pulled the map from her back pocket and studied it. 'Right,' she said, turning on her heels and twisting the map around. She looked at the stand number to the right, then back to the map. 'Should be over there.' She pointed in the opposite direction to where Ashley was headed.

'Cool.' Bloody hell. Could it be any more obvious she was in a mood? The longer she kept a lid on it the bigger the issue became, a torrent of sentences just waiting to spill, only held back by an occasional gulp.

Maybe it was the free booze making her irrational. That was all it was. She was tipsy and overreacting.

Dani didn't move. Instead, she cocked her head and let her eyes trail Ashley's face.

'What have I done?' she asked, her cheery face falling serious.

'Nothing, it's fine.'

The threat of a smile made the corners of Dani's mouth twitch. She held it together though, obviously sensing how pissed off Ashley was. 'It's not. Tell me.'

She was being silly. The closer the words got to being out of her mouth, the more embarrassed she was to feel this way.

Dani raised her eyebrows, waiting on an answer.

'Come on, let's find some musicians to pester.'

Dani gently grabbed her arm as she walked away.

'Ash. No. Speak to me.'

Ashley turned back to Dani and crossed her arms. This wasn't a conversation she wanted to be having in the middle of a crowd of strangers. Dani wasn't going to drop it, though. She'd brought this on herself.

'We were together, weren't we?' The end came out as a squeak.

Dani's shoulders dropped, her face falling too. She stepped closer, putting her hands on Ashley's biceps. 'Of course. I just didn't want nosey Alice to be yarping onto people from school. I was the main focus of the rumour mill for too long. I don't want to start it again.'

That made sense. Dani left school not long after her dad died, not bothering to finish the Highers she'd started. It was the right decision, but it didn't stop the eternal questions Ashley had got about her friend. And Dani was right: most of them didn't come from a place of empathy. It was sheer nosiness.

'I get that, I just—'

'It's okay. Sorry. I didn't mean to upset you.'

'I'm not upset. Just being silly.'

'No. I told a lie that involved you. You're allowed to have an opinion about it.'

Having such a calm conversation born of agitation was a breath of fresh air. If this was Hazel, they'd be having an argument now.

'I just, I wanted to know. Just to be sure.'

Dani tilted her head to the side as if thinking. It was an odd thing to say, but it was the truth and Dani deserved that.

'Ashley, we dated for like, a year,' Dani said with that stupid goofy smile that always put her stomach in knots. She rubbed her hands up and down Ashley's arms. 'We good?'

'Yeah,' Ashley replied, nodding with conviction.

'You really think I'm going to write off the only girlfriend I've ever had? Without you I'm just some sad weirdo who can't find a date. Come on, let's find these musicians.'

Dani was off before Ashley could reply. She weaved past a stationary couple and fell into step. 'Do you want to date? I thought you weren't into that.'

Her answer came as a shrug. 'I'm a work in progress.'

Ashley had never heard Dani talk like that. Usually it was an instant spiel about commitment and not wanting to be tied down. 'What do you mean?'

'I want to focus on myself for a while. Then we'll see.'

This was huge. Dani had changed a lot in the last year or so. It was subtle to start with, but as time charged on monumental moments like this happened. With anyone else, this would be nothing. But Dani didn't do relationships. She did sex. Nothing more.

Dani's lacklustre and callous approach to sleeping around had near killed Ashley on occasion. It had soon become easier to turn a blind eye. Ignorance was bliss. She didn't ask Dani about it and Dani didn't tell her. It was an unspoken rule.

But even that had stopped. In fact, Dani had let slip recently that she hadn't slept with anyone for a year. Another monumental moment shared in the queue for Greggs. She really picked her moments.

'So, you do want to date eventually?' Ashley asked, seeking clarity.

'I guess. I don't really know.' Dani politely declined the offer of cheese and cracker samples from a passing stand before turning back to Ashley. 'I'm trying to be more open-minded. I guess if I met the right girl I would give it a bash.'

The lightest gust of wind could have floored Ashley. This wasn't just monumental. It was flabbergasting, mind-blowing, absolutely what-the-fuck.

'Where's this change of heart come from?'

Another shrug. 'Getting old, Ash. Time to grow up.' Her tone suggested it wasn't the most exciting concept to have graced the planet, but it was true. Ashley had felt similar when she'd gone to Lovefest and met Hazel.

Why couldn't she have had this revelation a couple of years ago? Why now?

The thought stopped Ashley dead in her tracks as she unpicked what she was really implying.

Fuck.

'You okay?' Dani asked, suddenly realising Ashley wasn't keeping pace.

She shook her thoughts free. 'Yeah, yeah. Sorry, just looking at these—' She scanned the stand to her left. Jesus, what section were they cutting through now? 'Wigs.'

Dani joined her, cocking her head to the side as if to get a better angle. 'You don't need a wig. You have lovely hair.'

'You're right, silly idea.' She trudged on before the owner of the stand could pull them in.

They rounded the corner and were back at the booze aisle.

'Are we lost?' Ashley asked with a giggle.

'No! Course not, I know exactly where we're going.' A cheeky smile told the truth.

'Right, well hold up,' Ashley said, taking Dani by the arm and diverting her to a vodka stand and an aproned assistant giving out generous samples. 'I want to try some of these.' She passed one to Dani. 'Down the hatch.'

They clicked the plastic cups together. 'Cheers.'

As the booze nipped the back of her throat Ashley took the liquid courage in a chokehold, refusing to let it slip this time. 'If you fancy a date, I know someone.'

Dani coughed, a mixture of strong alcohol and surprise. She took the empty cup from Ashley and chucked them in the bin before thanking the vendor.

'Did you hear me?' Ashley asked as they walked away.

'I did. It's not Yaz, is it?'

'Jesus. No. Yaz is definitely not your type. Why did you instantly think it would be Yaz?'

'Dunno, just, how many single people do you know? And Yaz does not like me at all.'

'No?'

'Nope.'

'Why do you think that?'

'Doesn't matter. Who's this girl, then?'

She'd press for Yaz details later. Now was the time to continue holding the bull by the horns. 'She's one of Hazel's clients. Really pretty. Very femme. Just your type.'

'So, I have a type now?' Dani joked.

Ashley was sure they'd just skirted past the edge of the wig section again. She snagged Dani's glare with a knowing look. 'I've seen enough women over the years to have a fair stab at what you might find attractive.'

Dani paused, chewing on her cheek as she fiddled with the fur on a sporran. She kept her eyes fixed on the leather accessory as she spoke. 'You think we'd get on? Like, you want me to go?'

Ashley stood level with Dani, like she was also admiring the traditional Scottish garb. Luckily the stall holder was engaged with someone else. 'If you want to go, then I can arrange it.'

Dani lifted the furry piece hanging from the front of the garment, akin to two handcrafted furry dice but a heck of a lot more sophisticated. She dropped it, letting it flop back into place. 'Yeah, sure. Why not?'

11

Dani swigged her beer before placing it back on her bedside table and flopping onto the bed beside Chet. She ran her hand down the length of his soft fur and he purred in return. 'Can I just stay in with you?' she asked him, giving his head a good scratch.

He meowed, but it didn't sound like a convincing argument to bail on her date.

Crissie sounded lovely but Dani really wasn't in the mood to woo. Especially someone she'd never met before. She trusted Ashley's judgement, but it was strange. She'd been on plenty of 'dates' with girls she'd met on Tinder, all thinly veiled precursors to sex. And she'd brought even more home from bars and clubs. But a blind date? It felt wrong.

She wasn't nervous. Far from it. She just couldn't be arsed. Plain and simple.

Plus, there was the small matter of already knowing there was no future. Why lead the poor woman on?

At the risk of sounding like a complete sad sack, when

Dani pictured a future it was either with Ashley or on her own. No one could fill her space. It just didn't compute.

She flopped onto her back and stared at the ceiling. Eight billion people on the planet and Dani was set on Ashley Fiona Davidson. A blue-eyed blonde with a penchant for jumpers paired with shirts, and vanilla milkshakes. She'd known since she was a teenager. No going back now.

But how to cancel? She didn't even have this woman's number; it was all through Ashley. No excuse seemed good enough.

A knock at her bedroom door made her heart lurch.

'You are going out, yeah?' Kirsty asked, poking her head in the door when no protest came.

'Yeah. Soon. Probably.'

She didn't need to lift her gaze to know her sister's eyes were narrowing. 'You don't look ready.'

'Getting there.'

The door opened wider with a creak and before Dani knew it, Kirsty was perched beside her on the bed. 'What's up?'

'Nothing.'

A pause filled the air, expanding with every passing beat of Dani's heart.

'You don't have to go,' Kirsty said, her voice low, like she was delivering mind-blowing news that needed time to be digested.

'Ashley really wants me to.'

'Okay, but Ashley isn't the one going on the actual date, with an actual real-life human.'

Dani pressed harder into the mattress, wishing it would just swallow her up. It was a few hours, tops. Maybe she'd have a good time. Maybe conversation would be a struggle.

Whatever happened, it was finite. She would be home before she knew it. 'I'll be fine.'

The mattress bounced as Kirsty shifted. 'You doing okay with the whole Ashley-Hazel thing now?'

'Of course.' The words came out like bullets, hard and fast, without room for remorse.

'Good, because I'm not cleaning up your sick again if you get steaming tonight.'

Dani's cheeks reddened at the thought. When Ashley had first got with Hazel, alcohol had seemed like a good coping mechanism. Enough hangovers (and therapy sessions) and she soon saw the flaw in her plan.

'I'll be a good girl, promise.'

'You want me to tell Ashley I'm ill?'

Dani propped herself up on one elbow. 'What? So ill that me and Rhona need to assist you? She'd never believe that.'

Kirsty put a hand on Dani's thigh and gave it a jiggle. 'Right, well. We're not drinking tonight: if you need me or Rhona to come pick you up, just shout. Give the signal and we'll form an escape plan.'

'I'm sure she won't be that bad.'

'You never know.'

'Thanks,' Dani said, voice dripping with sarcasm. She grabbed her pillow to whack Kirsty but she was too fast. Chet jumped off the bed at the sudden action. 'Oh, Chet, baby, I'm sorry.' It was too late. Without even a look he was out of the room, a chuckling Kirsty not far behind.

Time to get ready. It couldn't be put off any longer.

∽

Dani stabbed at her phone as the train passed through Pollokshields. One more stop to go. No messages. No disasters or emergencies. Guilt squeezed her chest. *Be careful what you wish for.*

It was a few hours with a so-called hottie. No family emergency was worth bailing. Not if it wasn't real, anyway.

She swallowed down the anxiety welling in her chest. The thought of speaking to someone wasn't getting to her; it was the thought of lying to this poor woman. She didn't want to go. Sitting here now, in an almost empty carriage, she knew it was already a no. Was her date waiting on her, excited, thinking about a possible future? Maybe it made her a narcissist to be thinking so highly of herself. Perhaps her date wasn't fussed either.

The train slowed as it crossed the bridge over the River Clyde. Lights from the neighbouring flats and offices shimmered orange streaks across the water.

Dani felt sick.

She gulped, trying and failing to ignore how wet her mouth now was.

After what felt like an age, the train pulled into Central Station.

They were to meet in a bar just off Buchanan Street.

Only a few short days had passed from Ashley asking to Dani stepping onto the platform. They'd been a whirlwind of work and Christmas prep, but now, as December's icy chill wrapped its arms around her, the nerves that had been coiling inside pinged open, spreading far and wide within, suffocating her insides and piercing her skin. She clenched her jaw and hugged her jacket tight.

One drink.

A gaggle of women, dressed in sequined outfits and already three sheets to the wind, sauntered past. Probably off to an office party. They never did a Christmas night in the café; they always waited until January. Far too busy during the festive season. Much better to wait until everyone could enjoy it.

Snails, turtles, and sloths could have beaten Dani in a race. Her trainers were slowly becoming one with the tarmac.

She let out a ragged breath as she presented her ticket to the gate. It swallowed it and the gates magically opened.

Was anything worth getting this worked up over?

As Dani neared the station's infamous clock, laughter pierced the air. A real hoot: someone was having a great evening.

It was enough to reset the thoughts in Dani's head, a sudden buffer to the record that had been scratching all day.

She didn't need to go.

The world wasn't going to end because she stood this poor woman up, but her evening would be a damn sight better if she did.

At the crossroads of the clock and accessibility centre, Dani veered left instead of right. She ignored the busy exits taking her to Union Street and George Street. Five minutes' walk that way and she would be with her date.

Instead, she let the icy air of Hope Street steal her breath.

She was here; might as well enjoy a drink before heading home.

This side of the station was mainly offices and small takeaways, geared up for workers in suits, not grumpy lesbians in denim jackets. Well, maybe there was a slight crossover in the Venn diagram of life. The thought made Dani smile. She was already starting to feel like herself again.

She rarely ventured into town, never mind Hope Street, so it was an adventure deciding where to go. It wouldn't do to risk going near Fletchers, where they were meant to meet, despite the abundance of familiar pubs.

At the sight of the green man she took her chance and crossed the road, feeling even a few metres of extra distance would make all the difference. A few short strides later it was like being in no man's land. The bank on the corner had closed years ago, the space never to be refilled, and the surrounding buildings were all offices plunged in darkness.

There was no point heading up the adjacent road: she knew Bath Street from getting the airport bus. Not much there to entertain her.

She carried up the steepening hill. A whisky bar came into view. Probably not the right place for a solo woman like her. Lovely, surely, but just not Dani.

Another set of lights and a more promising row of shop fronts came into view. Smack in the middle a group of smokers lingered. Tattooed, grungy, and most of them bearded: this place felt a little more her. Okay, on the sliding scale of style she was poles apart, but she felt safe with grungy, much more so than whisky-sipping old men.

She cut through the smokers without even a second look from them and located the entrance. An A-board outside told her the place was called Micky Hugh's, and if she wanted, twenty wings were hers for the meagre price of £5. She just might.

The bar was muggy and surprisingly empty for how many office parties seemed to be on the go in town. It was mid-week, though.

Dani gave a decisive nod before heading to the bar. Yeah, this place would do nicely. She'd Goldilocks-ed herself into finding a wee gem in Glasgow city centre. It lacked the pre-loved charm of her favourite Southside place – Bar Orama – but the place still felt homely. Records and whisky posters decorated the walls, with a well-used dartboard in the corner. Its dark lighting was just what Dani needed tonight: here she could lay low, keep to herself.

She leaned against the wooden bar lined with empty bar stools, all neatly positioned, untouched and unmoved from when staff had presumably laid them out before opening.

It didn't take long for an attractive barmaid with vivid purple hair and a cropped band tee to serve her.

'What can I get for you?' she asked, flashing snow-white teeth.

Dani eyed the beer pumps. A neon badge with an illustration of a lady riding a rocket, done in the style of old cigarette cards, caught her attention. She read the name twice before committing. 'Pocket Rocket?'

The barmaid smiled. 'Good choice. Brewed just up the road by a female-only team. Boss Brew. Best beer in all of Glasgow,' she informed her as she poured the foaming booze.

Dani's mouth watered at the sight. She paid, and picked a stool at the end of the bar. Her eyes closed as she sipped the beer. It was like a delicate kiss with the power to drag you off to bed and have you grinning for days. *Damn.* No need to guess where the name came from.

Dani turned her phone off and slipped it back into her pocket.

∽

TWO BEERS LATER, the urge to check her phone was strong. Plus, the thought of needlessly worrying Kirsty was niggling her. She should have at least told her about the change of plans.

She stared at the reflective black screen as it sat on the sticky bar. Right now it was Schrodinger's phone. Ashley was mad. Ashley was worried. Ashley would never talk to her again. Ashley was glad she didn't go.

As her final thought stuck its talons into the fibres of her brain she caught the barmaid's attention and ordered a shot of whisky. The notion had been sitting at the front of her mind since seeing the bar. A nice, warming shot was exactly what she needed before facing the wrath of real life.

All too quick, the shot was placed in front of her.

'Hard night?' the barmaid asked, with comforting eyes.

'Not really.' Dani considered how much she could be bothered sharing. She'd just sat for an hour and was now staring at a dead phone while ordering shots of whisky. She probably owed a sliver of an explanation at least. 'I was meant to have a date.'

'But they stood you up?' Sympathy grew with the creases around her eyes.

'Other way around. I know, I'm a dick.'

Her features didn't shift as she leaned against the bar. 'Not necessarily. Did you have a good reason not to go?'

Dani held a single finger in the air, signalling she needed a moment. With one swift move she downed the booze, giving her head a shake like a wet dog. Jesus, that was strong stuff. The barmaid waited patiently, an amused smile now pulling at her lips.

Finally, when the alcohol's heat had stopped spreading across her chest, Dani spoke. 'It was a set-up. A blind date. I didn't want to go in the first place.'

The barmaid turned and retrieved the bottle of whisky

from its place on the wooden shelving. Without a word, she topped Dani's glass up. 'So why did you say you'd go?'

'Thank you,' Dani said, looking at the fresh shot. 'Erm, I guess I didn't want to let my friend down.'

The woman pursed her lips, hiding a smirk. 'And this is better, how?'

Dani lolled her head back with a chuckle. 'I failed to think my plan through. You've got me there.' She righted herself, choosing to play with a cardboard coaster rather than make eye contact. 'Let's just say it was a last-minute decision.'

'Ah.' She looked at Dani's phone. 'What's your friend saying about it?'

'I'm not had the balls to turn it back on yet.' The woman's snigger made Dani lift her gaze, finally connecting eyes again.

'How about you turn it on and sort your friend out, and as a reward I can put my number in it?'

Dani raised one quizzical eyebrow. 'Oh, really?' Bold. A few years ago, after a come on like that, they wouldn't have made it out of the pub before taking things further, let alone actually exchanging numbers.

'Sound like a deal?'

'I suppose.'

This wasn't how she saw the evening going, but the ego boost and rush of dopamine was a welcome pick-me-up.

With a devilish smile the barmaid walked away to serve, not before stopping to introduce herself. 'Caroline,' she said, running her tongue over her teeth.

Dani responded with a smile. She was pretty. Her skinny black jeans looked like they'd been sprayed on and her heeled boots ticked all the right boxes. Perhaps this wasn't a terrible idea after all. Why hadn't she ventured up Hope Street before?

After a final glance at Caroline, she returned her attention to her phone. She held the side button down, turning it on, and downed her second shot as she waited for it to load.

It felt like an eternity but finally the screen jolted to life and a stream of missed calls and messages flooded her lock screen.

Her heart tripped into action.

This was nauseating.

Or maybe that was the booze.

First, she dealt with Kirsty. They were easy messages to read. She was worried, as Ashley had got in touch saying she was a no-show. She fired off a quick text letting her know the situation.

Then it was time to tackle what she was dreading. Dani drained the remainder of her pint first.

The texts started out concerned before growing agitated and ending in straight-up exasperation.

There were two voicemails. How much of a glutton for punishment was she? Maybe it was an apology for the texts.

Ashley never got angry. Not at Dani, anyway. She chewed on her bottom lip, disappointment sinking into her bones like water to a sponge. She could have just gone for one drink.

Now Ashley was mad because she'd made things awkward for Hazel.

So Hazel was mad.

And Hazel being mad made Ashley madder.

The first message was a simple enquiry as to where she was. Ashley's tone was neutral, concern lightly lacing her words.

The next was a completely new person to Dani.

Tears pricked her eyes as she listened. '—one drink, Dani. Did you ever have any intention of going? Do you know how awkward this is going to make things for Hazel at work? That's one of her clients. I thought you wanted this. If you didn't want to go you could have just said. Why are you always so selfish? Could you not have thought of me for just once in your life?'

The rant continued but Dani had heard enough. She stabbed the delete button and put the phone back on the bar.

Her shot glass was filled before she even had to ask.

Despite being mid-week, the Polo Lounge was packed, mainly with straight-looking office workers, but Dani didn't mind. The busier the better, it made hanging out on the sidelines easier.

She clutched her pint glass, swaying slightly.

The Polo was a Glasgow institution: the huge gay bar and club stood proud in the middle of Glasgow and it was every Glasgow gay's right of passage to have been here at least once.

Dani was no stranger, but it had been a long time since she'd visited.

As promised, Caroline had put her number in Dani's phone, telling her to get in touch so they could meet when her shift ended. Always good to have a backup plan.

Despite her spinning head, Dani surveyed the dancefloor, hoping to catch someone's eye.

A woman in a tight purple dress who looked to be about fifty locked eyes and shot her a nervous smile. She was definitely one of the office crew. Dani averted her gaze. She was in no mood for a challenge or, heaven forbid, being someone's Christmas fling. Been there, done that. They had a habit of being disgustingly clingy afterwards.

Jenny, her therapist, had told Dani she used sex as an avoidance technique. The words flared through her mind like a neon sign that refused to go out, no matter how many times she pulled the plug. It was harder to act out when she knew the motives. Before, it was just about feeling good. Now her brain had a tendency to spiral. Guilt was usually the main culprit for pulling the brakes. That, and the coping mechanisms Jenny had provided.

Tonight, though, alcohol was doing a great job at spurring her on.

The closer it got to Ashley's wedding, the harder it was getting to cope. She'd spoken to Jenny about it numerous times but there was only so much talking could help. Sometimes she wanted to smash stuff and throw a temper tantrum. Other times she wanted to cry. Most of the time she just wanted to scream until her throat was raw.

What was the harm in booze and sex if it took the edge off a little?

Jenny had never been through this. How could she really know what the best way of coping was?

Dani sipped her beer, her gaze still taking in the room. No one stood out.

There was a fine line between looking flirty and coming off as a predator. Dani was anything but the latter. She gave women a good night; she wasn't out to hurt people.

A cute girl in a cream vest bumped into her, almost spilling both their drinks. Dani gave her a charming smile. She blushed in response.

It didn't incite the usual numbing relief inside Dani.

In fact, she felt worse.

The girl disappeared into the crowd and Dani stayed put.

Maybe her band-aids were losing their healing ability. She'd pushed them so far the power was gone.

She checked her phone. Nothing.

After another shot, she'd texted Ashley a simple *Sorry*. Hours later, it was still left on read.

She was trying. Really trying to do the right thing these days. Whether it was dress appointments or answering questions about colourways. Wedding fairs or second opinions on venues. She did it. She stepped up. Made her want to tear her skin off, but she did it.

A little slip-up was allowed.

She was only human.

Ashley's voicemail played on repeat in her mind, like a terrible earworm. It couldn't be shaken off. Selfish, she could live with, but did Ashley really think she never put her first? All Dani did was put Ash first.

How long had she felt that way? A reel of their friendship showed in her head and she tried her best to see things from Ashley's point of view. Right: there were some instances Dani wasn't overly proud of, but on the whole, she did it to protect Ashley. It was the only way.

Her bottom lip wobbled so she steadied it with the rim of her glass. Crying in the club. That would be a new one.

It was near midnight and Ashley would have work tomorrow. She couldn't call her.

She'd need to sort it another way. The question was: how?

12

'Quiet one tonight?' Doreen asked, clicking the button on her monitor to switch it off.

'I suppose,' Ashley replied, stifling a yawn. She'd be glad to get home: she was feeling all kinds of weird. Her eyes felt glassy, her throat strange, and her temperature off. Most likely due to lack of sleep.

The office had been a hive of activity today. The teachers' big night out had been at the weekend and the hot goss had taken a few days to sift down to clerical staff. They had it on good authority that Mr Benson of the maths department had shared a cheeky snog with Miss Wilkes of English. The only problem? Mr Benson had a wife.

Scandal of the highest kind.

No one liked a cheater. How could you? Didn't matter if you were drunk or whatever, it was still cheating.

Julia had tried to even out the verbal assault on Mr B with 'maybe he's unhappy in his marriage' only to be shot down in flames. It was like working with a flock of hens; the noise and rabble could have drowned out a jet engine.

Ashley had done her best to avoid the chat despite,

agreeing with most of it, because, regardless of motive, Mr Benson's extramarital relations were none of her business. Sometimes things were complicated and most of the time the whole truth would never be known. Who was she to judge without having the entire picture?

Dani had occupied her mind a lot more than she would have liked today. She was mad, yes, but she would get over that. In fact, she felt bad for being so harsh. She never should have tried to set Dani up. There was no other way for it to end but in failure. Sure, she hadn't expected Dani to ghost the poor woman, and it did make things awkward for Hazel, but they'd all forget the disaster with time.

What really bothered Ashley was the relief she'd felt. Like someone had been standing on her chest and suddenly disappeared. She'd lain in bed, wide awake, turning the feeling over and over in her mind, trying to shift it, attempting to rationalise it.

As soon she stepped into the office it was nothing but Mr Benson chat and she couldn't help but think the universe was having a laugh at her expense.

Or maybe it was a warning.

She needed to get rid of these feelings, fast. She was getting married soon. It didn't matter if she acted on it or not – fat chance, the last twenty years had shown there was no possibility of that – but she couldn't marry Hazel and harbour feelings for Dani.

She was mad at herself for feeling that way and being stupid enough to take it out on Dani. She didn't deserve the things Ashley had said. Her cheeks burned red at the thought. She'd call in to Café Odyssey on the way home, apologise. Things like that were best done face to face.

After a few final goodbyes, Ashley clicked her own monitor off. She'd half expected Trip to call by today; she loved a gossip. Although, she was an English teacher. Maybe too close to home.

She stood up and stretched, putting her hands on her lower back for a better arch. Sitting at a desk all day did nothing good for her joints. She was putting on her jacket when a gentle cough from the doorway caught her attention.

A sheepish Dani hid behind the biggest bouquet of flowers Ashley had ever seen. Ashley's mood instantly lightened, her nipping throat a mere memory.

'Hey,' Dani said, her voice as shy as she looked.

'Hey,' Ashley echoed.

'I, erm, these are for you.' Dani thrust the flowers towards her as she crossed the office floor. 'Figured you'd want me to wait until the end of the day. I know you don't like to be the centre of attention.'

'Forget where I live?' Ashley joked, temporarily forgetting her manners. 'And thank you.' She sniffed the closest bloom: a bright orange chrysanthemum.

Dani's cheeks darkened. 'Figured Hazel wouldn't be my number one fan. And I wanted to have a chat. Thought I could walk you home.'

'Yeah, you're not exactly flavour of the month. You didn't need to get me these, though.'

'I did. Sorry for being an arsehole.' Dani stepped aside, giving Ashley room to lead the way.

They were in the corridor before Ashley raised enough courage to speak. 'I'm sorry for that voicemail. It was harsh. I was just mad.'

Dani tensed her jaw, the muscles in her face flexing. 'I deserved it. It'll be the last time I let you down. Promise.'

The cold air stole their breath, giving her time to process Dani's words. She hugged her jacket tight, the film of the flowers crinkling loudly. 'When else have you let me down?'

Dani shrugged. She looked tired, her eyes red. 'Too many times to count.'

Ashley stopped, keeping her distance from the lingering pupils by the gates. 'You've been crying.'

Dani's gaze flicked to the abandoned pub on the other side of the road. She worried her back teeth with her tongue, a nervous smile fighting to appear. 'No. Hungover to fuck, though.'

Ashley wasn't convinced but she kept her mouth shut. 'You went out, then? Make any new friends?' The question was out before she had time to weigh up the connotations. Was it obvious she cared?

'Only with the toilet bowl this morning. I don't know what I was thinking yesterday. Maybe it was nerves. I dunno.' Her voice trailed off as she scuffed her trainer across the painted white line on the tarmac.

Dani scratched the back of her neck before adjusting her beanie, like she didn't quite know what to do with her hands. Ashley wanted to scoop her into a hug and tell her everything was okay. It was a stupid misunderstanding on both sides. The fact that she was carrying half a florists wouldn't allow it, though.

The whole thing was better forgotten: a clean slate for both parties.

Ashley made a show of sniffing the flowers as they passed through the school gates. 'These are beautiful. Thank you again.'

'It was the least I could do. I didn't really know what to get Hazel but I figured you'd both enjoy flowers.' She waved a hand between them. She'd never seen Dani so awkward. Hangover or not, something was up.

She couldn't invite her back to the flat. Hazel would be home soon and that would only cause issues. She'd ranted most of the evening, her dislike of Dani stronger now she finally had something tangible to latch on to.

'Was that all you wanted to chat about? To apologise?' Ashley asked as they waited to cross Moss-side Road.

A kind man in an Audi stopped to let them out and Dani raised a hand as a thank you. 'I guess.'

Ashley raised her eyebrows. 'Dani. Spill.'

Dani's eyes flitted to the sky, as if she'd spotted something life changing on the slate roofs of the neighbouring flats. 'Just, I know you have a lot of wedding stuff on just now so I don't want to be a burden or anything, so like, totally don't worry about me—' She paused for breath and Ashley kept her mouth shut, despite being desperate to reassure her. 'But I've a lot going on in my head just now. Well, like, forever, I guess, so I'll help as I can, but Kirsty says I'm to go easy on myself.'

'If Kirsty's saying that it must be serious,' Ashley said, trying to lighten the mood. The smile on her face didn't match how her heart was thundering. Dani didn't do emotion, she didn't do vulnerable. Things must be bad if she was saying all this. And sober. How could Ashley not have known something was up?

'Exactly,' Dani replied with a thin-lipped smile.

Ashley never knew what to say in situations like this. Especially not when the person reaching out was Dani. This was brand new territory. 'Anything I can do to help?'

Dani shook her head.

She'd known that was too vague, even as she said it. 'Want to hang out this weekend?' Hazel would need to suck it up. Dani needed her.

'I'd like that.'

Much better. Maybe if they stayed in and watched a movie or something Dani would open up. What could be wrong? She'd never mentioned anything before.

Before they knew it they were at the back of the Co-op and the side of Café Odyssey greeted them like a fork in the road. No point in Dani going any further; her flat was in the opposite direction.

'Want me to walk you home?'

Ashley considered it. Hazel would already be in. Her PT sessions were short today. Was it worth the risk of her seeing her with Dani?

She was making this into more than it was. So what if her lifelong friend walked her home? Why did her head insist on creating an issue that wasn't there? Still, she went with the safe option. 'No, it's fine. You get home, it's freezing. I'll text you about a movie night.'

Dani's eyes smiled and her mouth twitched a hint of appreciation. 'Sounds good.'

'I'M IN THE KITCHEN, BABE,' Hazel called as Ashley pushed the flat's door open with her foot.

Usually she would take her jacket off at the door and hang it on the coat rack, but today her hands were too busy with Dani's massive bouquet. She padded through to the kitchen instead. It took a hot second for Hazel to clock what she was holding, her attention fixed on the boiling pot in front of her, but when she did her eyes grew as wide as saucers.

'Are they for me?'

Ashley laughed, half from nerves, half from the

absurdity of her next sentence. 'In part. They're from Dani, a sorry for last night.'

Hazel's eyes rolled so hard she should have pulled a muscle. She mumbled under her breath, her focus back on stirring the mince.

'I didn't quite catch that?' Ashley prompted, keeping her tone level. She was far too tired and ill to argue. The cold air had only made her throat feel worse and her temperature was like having a faulty thermostat. She didn't know whether to shiver or sweat.

'I said, too little too late.' Hazel's tone was biting but Ashley ignored it.

She put the bouquet on the counter and pulled a bar stool out, not even bothering to take off her mac before sitting. She rested her head in her hands and let out a long, weary sigh.

'You okay?' Hazel asked, her attitude changing in an instant as she sensed Ashley wasn't a hundred per cent. She scooted round to her side.

Ashley took a deep breath. 'Just not feeling right. Probably just tired.'

Hazel cocked her head to the side, her eyes searching Ashley's face. She held her palm to her fiancée's forehead. 'You're really clammy.'

'I'll be grand.'

'Nope, no. You get your comfies on, lie on the sofa. I'll get you some tablets.' Ashley was being guided by the elbow before she could protest. 'And when you've done that, I've something to show you.'

'Show me?'

'Yep, now, get,' she replied, giving Ashley's bum a satisfying smack.

. . .

Cosy on the sofa, Ashley only felt worse. She pulled the thin, velvety blanket closer. Despite being all kinds of sweaty she was shivering like she'd ventured to the Antarctic with nothing but a jumper.

Ibuprofen had taken the edge off, but with every passing minute her throat tightened and the notion of being able to make work tomorrow got further away.

'How you doing?' Hazel asked, squatting level with Ashley's face. She ran a hand over Ashley's damp hair without even a flutter of disgust.

'Not good.'

'My poor girl,' she said with a pout. 'This has come on quick. What do you think it is?'

Ashley had a sneaking suspicion but didn't want to properly consider it, for fear of making it reality.

She'd long suffered with tonsillitis, so much so that her doctor had wanted to take the tonsils out. It had been a while since an attack, though and she'd thought, or rather hoped, to have grown out of it. It had almost been inevitable: the stress of the wedding and other things was running her down.

'It'll be my tonsils,' Ashley said, her voice raspy. 'It happens sometimes.'

'What can I do for you?'

Ashley shook her head. 'You've done all you can. I'll go to the doctors tomorrow. It'll be fine.' Each word was like agony and swallowing was akin to eating glass. Antibiotics would see her fit but tonight would be no fun.

Hazel kissed Ashley's forehead. 'Just shout if you need anything.' Her eyes snagged Ashley's and a smile formed on her lips, making her dimples pop. Ashley loved her dimples; there was something about them that made her heart flutter.

The same way Dani's appearance had made her feel better today. She winced. Comparing them now?

'You okay?' Hazel asked, her smile replaced with a frown.

'Just sore.'

'This might cheer you up.' She lowered herself onto her knees and pulled her hoodie over her head, leaving her short hair ruffled. Next, her top was lifted.

'What's going on?' Ashley asked, flinching at the pain in her throat as she chuckled. She was in no mood for sex.

'Just you wait and see.' Hazel stopped at her chest, gearing up for a reveal. 'You ready?'

'I mean, I'll never say no to boobs,' Ashley replied with a grin. She wanted to add that it couldn't go further, but words were too much. Until she got some antibiotics in her Hazel was going to have to enjoy the peace and quiet.

Hazel bit down on her bottom lip, excitement buzzing around her. 'Right, here goes.' She lifted her T-shirt, exposing her sports bra. It was the clear film above her left breast that caught Ashley's attention, though.

There, right over her heart, was a new tattoo: the letter A in a serif font and just a little bigger than a thumbnail.

Ashley's breath caught in her lungs, her sore throat no longer the reason for her lack of words.

'Is—is that for me?'

Hazel's dimples appeared again. 'Who else would I get it for?' she asked with a quiet laugh. She lowered her top and then gently placed a hand over the tattoo's spot. 'Over my heart, cause it belongs to you.'

Tears rimmed Ashley's eyes. Her lip wobbled.

Hazel held Ashley's hand between hers. 'I know I've been difficult recently, so I wanted to get you something.'

'Engagement not enough?' Ashley joked, tears still clouding her eyes.

Hazel bowed her head, hiding a shy smile. 'Just a little extra. Show you how much you mean to me. You can take a ring off, but not this,' she said, jabbing a finger to her chest and wincing a little. 'This is permanent. Like us.'

Ashley gulped and razor-blade pain seared down her throat, almost matching the pain in her chest, guilt holding her heart in a vice-like grip. She was happy. Truly. But why did disappointment sit heavy on her chest, with visions of Dani playing in her head?

13

Dani held the keyring in her teeth and pushed the flat door open with her back, grasping her bulging shopping bags as she awkwardly tumbled into Ashley's flat. Her biceps ached. It was a short walk from Morrisons to Waverley Gardens, but she'd gone a little OTT with her shopping.

When she'd found out Ashley was suffering from tonsillitis and Hazel had been called away for work, she couldn't bear the thought of her bestie being alone. She'd only managed to get to the doctors this afternoon, and when Ash's tonsils were bad, they were horrendous. She'd nearly been hospitalised twice. Now was the time to keep her fluids up and make sure she was eating.

'Ash, it's me,' she called, heading straight to the kitchen to dump the bags.

She was rarely here now Hazel had moved in. It felt familiar but jarringly different. The odd print and trinket stood out like sore thumbs, like a bad game of spot the difference. Other things were more subtle: the hoodie on the back of the bar stool; the St Johnstone mug by the sink. Little hints Ashley was no longer alone.

There was no time to reminisce.

She put the bags on the kitchen island and set to work creating piles: freezer, fridge, or cupboard.

A noise from the doorway distracted her from the task in hand. There stood Ashley, living up to her name. Her face was grey, her eyes hooded. She hugged her fluffy dressing gown tight around her waist.

'What's all this?' Her voice was like sandpaper.

Dani rushed to her side, trying in vain to direct her back to the living room. 'You shouldn't be up, missus. Let's get you back to the sofa.'

But Ashley wasn't for being told what to do. She wandered further into the kitchen, running a hand along the counter as she took in Dani's haul. Her eyes grew wide as she clocked the assortment of drinks and food. 'This is a lot.' The final word was almost inaudible as emotion caught her off guard.

Dani scooped her into a fierce hug. 'Hey, come on.' She squeezed tighter. 'It's just food. Got to keep you strong.'

Her reply was a loud sniff as Ashley burrowed into Dani's shoulder. 'Sorry.'

'What for?' It was rhetorical. She'd had a similar reaction to seeing Dani the first time it got really bad. Her tonsils were so swollen she couldn't even manage water and the doctor wanted Ashley in hospital, to be put on fluids. She'd convinced her mum to give her one more night on antibiotics. Another dose of them and a night cooried up with Dani watching terrible TV had thankfully done the trick.

Dani leaned back, her hands on Ashley's hips as she snagged her gaze. 'Now, let me talk you through this feast.'

She released Ashley and moved towards the island. 'Don't feel you need to have it all – I just figured I should get a little of everything. You can pick and choose then. Had plenty fluids?'

'Some water. Hazel's going to bring me home some Lucozade later.'

Dani resisted the urge to scowl. Instead, she produced a large bottle of the sugary juice from one of the bags. 'Ta-da. I also got you this milkshake thing, diluting juice, and, erm—' She rummaged in the bags, looking for the final item. 'Aha. And yeah, hot chocolate.'

Ashley smiled, her eyes still misty.

Dani continued her walk through. 'So, food. Got you ice cream, potato waffles, cheesecake. Those stinking 12p noodles you like when you're ill.' She pulled a face. They were cheap, nasty, and smelled like chemical chicken, but if they got Ashley to eat she would suffer the smell. 'Yoghurt, cream cheese, and mashed potato.'

Ashley's smile widened. 'You didn't have to get all this.'

'Did too. Okay, now close your eyes, and put your hands out.'

'Is it Babybels?' Ashley asked, following Dani's instructions and holding her hands out, palm up.

Dani's face fell. She hadn't got much cheese. 'It's not. Do you want them? I can go back out.'

Ashley's cheeks were like rosy apples. 'I'm just messing.'

Dani's shoulders relaxed. 'Feeling better already. Good,' she joked as she pulled the little box of pills from her denim jacket's pocket. She placed it in Ashley's hands. 'Dissolvable aspirin from the chemist. I know it helped to gargle it last time.'

Ashley's eyes widened, her brow firmly knotted. 'That was ages ago. How did you remember that?'

Dani shrugged. 'I do pay attention, sometimes.'

Before she knew it Ashley had her in a bear hug. Her heart about gave out when a kiss was planted on her cheek. Her skin burned hot where Ashley's lips had touched.

'Thank you.'

'Anything for you, Ash.' Was that too much? It was out there now. Ashley didn't seem phased; she was studying the medicine box like it was covered in ancient hieroglyphics that needed careful consideration. 'Now, you get back on the sofa. I'll make you some noodles.'

NOODLES CONSUMED at a snail's pace, but, most importantly, eaten, they'd now relaxed into watching TV. Dani didn't really care for what was on – Angela Lansbury was causing mischief in a classic *Murder She Wrote* – because her mind was firmly fixed on Ashley. Her breathing sounded okay and her temperature was gone. Hopefully the tablets were going to work quickly this time.

Ashley shifted her position and rearranged the fleecy throw that was covering them both.

'Thanks again for buying all that stuff,' she said, twisting to face Dani.

'Any time. We need to get you better. Can't be ill at Christmas.'

Ashley sighed. 'You're too good to me.'

'Hardly.'

Dani did a tiny jump when Ashley tapped her arm, indicating she wanted to swoop under it for a cuddle. Her heart danced to a new rhythm, one where Ashley was cosied hard into her chest, her hands pulled close as she balled herself up. The thought of doing this with anyone else was monumentally wrong.

She had a therapy session tomorrow and couldn't wait to tell Jenny about her disaster date. There was so much to unpack she felt like she was drowning under the questions. Was she regressing or progressing? It was hard to tell. Sometimes it was two steps forward, one step back.

'This is nice,' Ashley mumbled.

Dani gave in to her screaming inner voice and rested her chin on the top of Ashley's head. 'Think the tablets are kicking in?'

'A bit, yeah.'

'Can I do anything else?'

'Just this.'

Dani's insides heated with pride. Looking after Ashley made her heart sing. It was just a shame she felt so crap. Another day off work and she'd be grand, though. Dani inwardly groaned at the thought of doing a double shift tomorrow. She'd had to swap with Kirsty to get time off today. Never mind. Was worth it.

'What about a bath?' Dani asked, daring to flit her fingers back and forth over Ashley's upper arm. It was an innocent move, but since Hazel the simplest of actions felt all kinds of wrong.

Ashley's muscles stiffened and Dani worried she was going to be told off. Instead, she lifted her head, her eyes defiant and a smirk plastered on her face. 'You saying I smell?'

'Wee bit,' Dani replied, only just keeping a straight face.

A tickle attack followed. It was a good sign the tablets were working their magic. It wasn't that Dani didn't trust Hazel's nursing ability, but she'd been through this so many times, nobody knew what Ashley needed better than her. Not even her mum.

Attack abated, Dani took a moment to catch her breath. Ashley held her gaze, not even blinking, her own chest heaving. How can someone be so ill, unwashed, no make-up, hair a frizzy mess, and yet so ridiculously pretty? Ashley Davidson was in a league all of her own.

'Do you want your cheesecake now?' Dani asked, fearing she might do something silly if she didn't remove herself from the sofa soon.

Ashley considered it. 'Yeah, sure, why not? Hmm, well, maybe.'

Dani cocked her head to the side. 'Yes or no will suffice.'

'Will you share a slice with me?'

'Deal.'

It didn't take Dani long to return with a plated cheesecake slice and two forks. She placed it on the blanket between them.

'Remember that time you vommed soup into my lap cause you took too many painkillers and antibiotics at once?'

Ashley paused her fork. 'Why would you bring that up at a time like this?' She chuckled. 'And yes. Of course I remember. I was mortified, and it was also dangerous. Never again. Big lesson learned that day.'

Dani shook her head. It hadn't been that bad, but it was a core Ashley-and-Dani memory. They were in Ashley's childhood bedroom and it wasn't long after they'd properly hooked up for the first time. It was then, her leg covered in chicken broth soup, that she knew she'd marry Ashley some day. If you can get over soup spew, you can get over anything.

She wanted to go back and shake that girl. She only had

a few months before everything went to shit: she should have proposed then and there. Made it official so she couldn't back out.

'Good cheesecake,' Dani said, stuffing a forkful into her mouth. Vanilla, classic, unbeatable.

'Hazel hates stuff like this, being a PT and all.' Ashley twirled her fork in the air as she spoke. 'So, we'd better demolish it all before she gets back.'

'When will that be?'

'Dunno. Back-to-back sessions today, so maybe seven-ish. I'll need to have her tea ready anyway.'

Dani snorted. 'Eh, I don't think so. You need to rest. You tell me what to cook and I'll do it.'

'You're going to cook?'

'I can cook!'

'You can microwave,' Ashley retorted, pulling a face.

In fairness, Kirsty did handle most of the complicated dishes in the flat. Dani was more into pre-made sauces and pizza deliveries. Baking, though? Her mum had shown her all that a long time ago. It came hand in hand with the café. She was never one for enjoying the kitchen, but if her mum needed help throwing the scones together she was on it. A Victoria sponge wasn't going to cut it tonight, though.

'Let me help at least. What's on the menu tonight?'

Ashley pursed her lips. 'Some chicken thing.'

'Some chicken thing?' Dani repeated with a rueful smile. 'Sounds easy.'

14

Flustered wasn't the right word, but Dani was definitely over her head. It was sweet to watch her as she read the recipe over and over again, her face gaining seriousness with each sweep of the page.

Ashley rested her elbows on the kitchen counter and leaned her chin against her palms. 'You're absolutely certain I can't help?'

'All under control!'

The smear of tomato puree across Dani's white T-shirt told a different tale.

The weight of Dani's actions today laid heavy on Ashley's chest. She had been beyond sweet. It wasn't just buying the food or swapping her shift. It was the thoughtfulness of getting her exactly what she needed without being asked. Even Mum hadn't had time to pop round yet. She would after work, but without Dani, Ashley had been left to fend for herself today.

It had taken the doctor about two seconds to look at her pus-filled throat and prescribe antibiotics. She'd felt so tired and rough that the thought of shopping for throat-friendly food was too much. She was going to make do with what was in the house. Which had turned out to be very little.

Then, in the blink of an eye, she had a supermarket aisle's worth of grub to choose from.

Dani was as close to an angel as you could get.

'Tahini?' Dani asked, her tongue wrapping round the word like she'd only just learned to speak.

'Top left cupboard.' Ashley directed her with a bob of her head.

Tahini-marinated chicken wasn't top of her list for things to eat tonight but Hazel was on a strict diet, carefully planned and prepared. She couldn't just go changing stuff and ruining her fiancée's macros for the day. Whatever they were. Ashley was still a little clueless when it came to dietary stuff. It wasn't that she didn't care enough to learn, more that it was super complicated and had a habit of going over her head.

She watched as Dani stirred the chicken through the thick paste. 'So, this needs to go in the fridge for a few hours. Then it's just a case of skewering them and popping them under the grill. Will you be okay doing that?'

'I think I can manage to put the grill on,' Ashley joked. 'Anyway, Hazel will be back by then.'

Dani gave her hands a good wash and put the chicken away. In the process her top gained a new smear.

'That'll stain if you don't soak it,' Ashley prompted, still perched on her bar stool. It was like having front row seats to a bizarre cooking show.

Dani looked at her top, pawing at the offending marks. 'Nah, it'll be good.'

'Paprika and tomato paste, trust me. You'll never be able to wear it again.'

With a loud sigh Dani pulled her top over her head and flung it in the sink, turning the cold tap on full.

Ashley had to grip the counter for fear of falling off her stool. She didn't expect that to happen. If Hazel came home early this would be a tricky situation to explain.

She opened her mouth to tell Dani to grab one of her tops but words were hard. Didn't matter anyway, Dani was already one foot out of the kitchen, taking matters into her own hands.

Dani in a sports bra. Now there was an image she wouldn't forget in a hurry.

It wasn't like she'd not seen Dani in a bikini or less, if she really wanted to cast her mind back, but a repeat performance certainly wasn't on the agenda today. The way Ashley's heart was pounding against her ribs was a concern. Hazel's A tattoo lodged itself at the forefront of Ashley's mind, a blaring warning sign.

She was her friend, in clothing. Kim wore the skimpiest bikinis ever when they were in Ibiza. But she never got Ashley flustered like this.

Dani returned, now in one of Ashley's hoodies, and her heart ached for a new reason. She looked damn cute.

Before she could chastise herself Dani was at her side, a hand on Ashley's forehead.

'You okay? You're very red.'

'Tablets must be wearing off. I'll be fine.'

Dani didn't look convinced. She looked at her watch. 'You can't take any more for another two hours. You want a cold flannel or something?'

Ashley shook her head. Hoping her erroneous thoughts would disappear with the motion.

She loved Hazel but it was impossible to look at Dani

and not have feelings. After twenty-odd years it was as much a part of her as the freckles across her nose.

'I think I just want to get to bed, if I'm honest.' Anything to be alone.

'You get to bed and I'll finish this. I still need to boil the bulgy wheat.'

Ashley bit back a laugh. 'Bulgur wheat. And it's fine, that doesn't take long. Hazel can sort that when she gets in. It was marinating the chicken that really needed done.'

'Only if you're sure. Can I get you any more food? Juice.'

'I'm good.'

Dani crossed the kitchen to the sink and wrung the water from her top. 'Guess I could have just done this at home. I'll need to steal your hoodie – that okay?'

'Can't have you done for indecent exposure,' Ashley replied with a wink.

Dani turned, her body slumping as she came to a halt. 'You sure you're okay? I don't want to leave you if you're not feeling right.'

'I just need a sleep. Hazel will be home in a few hours. I'll be fine.'

'Only if you're sure.' Dani chewed on her cheek, her eyes betraying her reluctance to leave.

'If I need anything I'll text. Promise.'

Dani's arms were wrapped around Ashley before she had time to react.

'I hope you feel better soon, Ash. Text me if you need anything.' With a final squeeze she was off.

As the flat door clicked shut Ashley let out a breathy sigh.

There was no magic feeling to anchor herself to. A hug from Hazel was as good as a hug from Dani. So why couldn't she be content with just Hazel? Why did her mind have to wander and play silly beggars with her heart?

This was bad.

Very bad.

The easiest way would be cold turkey, ghost and move on, but their lives were so intertwined it would be impossible.

There had to be a way. A way to create distance and never see Dani again. The thought made her want to retch.

ASHLEY WAS STILL HALF-ASLEEP when she felt the mattress bounce as Hazel perched beside her. She clicked on the bedside lamp and planted a kiss on Ashley's head.

'How you feeling?' Her tone was quiet, her words wrapped in comforting concern.

'Bit better.'

Hazel's eyes narrowed. 'Have you been crying? Your eyes are all puffy.'

Shit. Tears had been shed but she'd hoped enough time would have passed to rid her of any evidence.

'Just not feeling good,' Ashley lied.

Hazel ran a hand over Ashley's hair. 'Tablets not working?'

'A bit,' she replied with a shrug as she propped herself up on her forearm.

If only there was a pause button she could hit on life, give herself space to breathe and get her thoughts in order. Instead, every waking moment brought up new thoughts and feelings, forever compounding until it felt like she was suffocating.

Hazel cupped Ashley's jaw in her hands. 'I'm starving.

Let me get tea on and then I'll come back through for a cuddle.'

Food wasn't on Ashley's radar. 'I might skip tea, just have noodles or something later.'

'Noodles? No nutrition in them; you need to give your body the ammo to fight this thing.' She leaned back, taking Ashley in. 'It won't be ready for a while yet. See how you feel when it's cooked.'

There was no point in arguing. 'Okay.'

Ashley slumped into her pillow when Hazel left the bedroom and ran her hands down her face. What was worse? Tonsillitis, or the thoughts whirring about her head?

She grabbed her phone. A text from Dani: *how you feeling? X*

Ignoring her mum's messages, she put the phone back on her bedside table, leaving Dani on read. Maybe they could move somewhere, away from Glasgow, just her and Hazel. Start afresh.

She liked her job, though. Her friends. Her family.

Bit extreme, Ash. This was an unrequited crush, not a case for witness protection.

Ashley swung her legs out of the bed and grabbed her dressing gown, pulling it tight around herself like a much-needed hug, as she stood. She padded through to the kitchen. Hazel greeted her with a smile as she started on the bulgar wheat.

'Your mum's been, then.'

'Huh?'

'All the food.'

'Oh.' Ashley's cheeks burned fiery red. 'Dani popped round with it. She didn't stay long.'

Hazel's face stiffened. 'That was nice of her.'

'Very.'

An icy silence blanketed the kitchen. Ashley felt the need to break it, lest she blurt out any other lies about Dani's visit. *She took her top off!* flashed boldly in her head. 'Can I do anything to help?'

'All under control, babe. You go sit down. I'll make you a lemon and honey drink.'

'Thanks,' Ashley replied, happy to leave the kitchen and Hazel's palpable distaste of her best friend.

She didn't want food or hot drinks. She wanted Hazel to hug her on the sofa until her bones cracked. She wanted her to say everything was going to be alright.

Tonsillitis could be solved with a tablet. If only the same existed for matters of the heart.

15

'Is she for real?' Rhona asked with a hearty chuckle as she and Dani watched Trip.

It was Dani's favourite time of the month: whenever Rhona's work allowed, the trio went bouldering. For someone that did little to no exercise, Trip was surprisingly good at it. Although Dani suspected she enjoyed the other aspect of their visits a little more: getting numbers from pretty girls as she waited for her turn on the wall.

Trip's newest interest flashed a pearly white smile, her eyes gleaming as she laughed at a joke. After a quick goodbye, Trip joined her friends.

Dani pulled a mock face of surprise and annoyance.

'What?' Trip giggled. 'She was having trouble getting the right amount of chalk, so I helped.'

'Aye, I bet you did,' Rhona replied, hands on hips.

Trip's ego didn't need inflating, but Dani was forever impressed. It had been so long since she'd chatted someone up without an app or alcohol she doubted she'd be as successful.

'Who's going now?' Trip asked, humbly wanting to move the conversation on.

'Me,' Rhona said, walking towards the wall. 'But I wanted you to spot me on the jump.'

'Got it,' Trip replied, getting into position.

It was good to hang out with her friends, get out of her head a little. It had been a strange two weeks.

As if reading her mind, Trip spoke: 'What's up?'

'What do you mean?'

'You're super quiet today.'

'Am not.'

'Dani. Come on. Share with the class.'

Dani sighed as she pretended to watch Rhona ascend the wall. 'Ashley's being weird. Have you noticed anything odd?'

Trip stuck out her bottom lip as she thought. 'Not that I can think of. Weird how?'

'I think she's avoiding me.'

'Avoiding you?' Trips eyebrows nearly touched.

Dani's eyes darted to a crease in the crash mat; she traced it as she shook her head. 'I'm just being silly. Forget I said anything.'

Trip closed the gap between them. 'Nah, tell me what's happened.'

Rhona scaled the wall with impressive speed and for a second Dani hoped it was enough to distract Trip, but her steely gaze was like fire on Dani's skin. 'She's been leaving me on read. Which is fine. She's busy. But I asked her to come Christmas shopping with me, go to the market in town, like we usually do. And she kept fobbing me off with excuses. I gave up in the end.'

Trip nodded assuringly. 'She's maybe just busy with

wedding stuff. You know she gets stressed. Plus, she was ill. Probably got loads to catch up on.'

Dani chewed on the inside of her cheek. They were plausible answers, but Dani knew in her heart they weren't the real reason. She'd done something. Or maybe Hazel had finally seen through her charade and asked Ashley to distance herself. Whatever it was, it felt like a stab to the heart, an ever-growing weight around Dani's neck that only got worse each day.

'Yeah, you're right,' Dani lied. She might as well have said the sky was purple, her tone was so unconvincing.

Rhona called to be spotted and she managed the metre-wide jump with ease. It wasn't long before she stood beside Trip and Dani. Her proud-as-punch smile faded in a heartbeat. 'What's up?' she asked, slightly out of breath.

'Nothing.' Dani shrugged.

'Nah. You were quiet last night as well.'

The look Trip exchanged with Rhona was hardly subtle.

'I think we need a drink,' Rhona said, clapping her hands together with a cloud of dust.

BAR ORAMA WAS QUIET, which was no surprise given how grim the Scottish weather was today. The usually bustling LGBTQ+ hub of the Southside was reduced to just a handful of patrons tonight, despite owner Kev's attempt at a happy hour deal. Some you won, some you lost.

Rhona had taken full advantage and soon returned to their booth with six beers, plus a packet of salt and vinegar crisps dangling between her teeth. She divvied them out before sliding onto the seat beside Trip.

'Have you done anything for Hazel to think you've

overstepped?' Rhona asked, tearing the crisps open and placing the bag in the centre of the table.

'Not that I can think of. Last time things were normal was when she had tonsillitis and I went round.'

'You didn't say or do anything unusual?' Trip asked, taking a long draw of beer.

Dani shook her head. 'After twenty years I've perfected the knack of not doing or saying anything unusual around Ashley.'

She was glad Trip had cajoled the issue out of her. She needed to talk. She'd considered speaking to Kirsty and Rhona a few nights this week, but quickly chickened out. Her head was flip-flopping between making a mountain out of a molehill and this being the biggest issue on the planet.

'And she's never done this before?' Rhona asked.

'Nope. I mean, she's got quieter since seeing Hazel, but nothing like this. This is straight-up avoidance.'

'She might just be genuinely busy,' Trip offered.

'I know the difference.' Dani played with the label on her beer bottle, picking the corner until it was tatty. 'It's a feeling. This is more than being busy.'

'Fair enough,' Rhona said, grabbing another crisp.

'Want me to talk to her?' Trip asked.

Dani sprung to attention. 'No, no, no. Definitely not.'

'I could be subtle.'

Both Rhona and Dani shot her a look that couldn't be argued with.

'Please don't say anything,' Dani pleaded. 'Whatever I've done it will probably make it worse. I just wish I knew how to make it better.'

'I know you don't want to hear it,' Rhona said, with a wince more than a smile. 'But you probably just need to give her space. Let her work out whatever's going on in her head. You're Dani and Ashley, you always work things out.'

'I know you're right but it's Christmas and, like . . .' Dani cut herself off with a shake. She was on the verge of making a fool of herself.

'Pal, it'll be fine. See how things are in a week.'

'We were meant to have a dress fitting next week and she's cancelled it.'

Trip clicked her tongue to the roof of her mouth. 'That is a bit odd. What was her reason?'

'School stuff.'

'School stuff?' Trip repeated, pulling a face that made her chin nearly touch her neck. 'What kind of office work means you can't go to a dress fitting?'

'See,' Dani yelped, her eyes wide.

'Right, I'll give you that.'

'Weddings bring out the crazy in everyone,' Rhona assured. 'She'll have got in her head about something other than you. Sometimes we need to withdraw to focus on stuff. She'll be back before you know it.'

'But what if she's not?' Dani asked with a pitiful squeak.

16

'Ashleeeey!' Trip announced, using her hands to make a funnel and boom her voice over the office.

A few people looked, but most ignored her friend; they were used to her popping in. 'Trip, to what do I owe the honour?' Ashley asked, smoothing the back of her skirt down as she stood. She leaned at the end of the counter separating them.

'I've got a free period and wondered if you could come help me with something?'

'Me? Help you? During office hours?' Ashley looked around the office for clues, as if this might be a massive prank or gotcha moment. No one batted an eyelid.

'Just for fifteen mins. Is it okay if I steal her, Doreen?' Trip shot Ashley's manager an award-winning smile. It wasn't returned.

'I suppose it is the end of term. But fifteen minutes, that's all.' No one messed with Doreen. Kids, parents, staff: if Doreen said jump you didn't ask how high, you kept your mouth shut and leaped like your life depended on it. Do anything wrong and it did.

With a cautious sigh Ashley crossed back to her desk. 'Lemme just finish this.' She clicked through her spreadsheet, tying up loose ends as she wracked her brain about what Trip could want. This had ulterior motives written all over it.

Trip was literally bouncing on the spot by the time she finished. 'Come on, Ash. Time is of the essence.'

'Alright, alright. Calm your ham.'

They left, to Doreen's distant reminder not to take long.

'How are you today?' Trip asked, as they rounded the corner to the corridor by the library.

'I'm good.' Ashley's words dripped with scepticism. If you twisted them they would wring out like a sopping towel.

'Good. Good. That's what I like to hear.'

Their footsteps echoed as they reached the edge of the Maths corridor. Another sharp turn and they were on the stairs up to the English department.

'Not long until term finishes,' Ashley said, hoping small talk would not only fill the silence but also hit upon what Trip really wanted.

Trip rolled her eyes as she held the heavy double door open for Ashley. 'I know. Can't come soon enough.'

'Tell me about it. I need a holiday, stat.'

Something flickered in Trip's eyes. It was quick and Ashley nearly missed it as she focused on where she was going. But it was there. A little twinkling diamond in the rough. 'Feeling the strain of wedding planning, or . . . ?' Trip trailed off.

Ashley shrugged, waiting for Trip to unlock her classroom door. 'Bit of everything, I guess. This is always a busy time.'

The light faded in Trip's eyes. Whatever Ashley had sparked was now extinguished. 'You?'

'Ah, you know how it is. Dad and I never really do Christmas. Right, in you come,' she ushered, gesturing Ashley into her room.

This all felt a little to lamb-to-the-slaughter for Ashley's liking. She half expected people to leap out from behind the empty desks shouting 'Surprise!'. There was nothing though. Just an empty classroom. The noise of boisterous students in the neighbouring rooms filled the heavy air.

'Something's going on.'

Trip's eyes narrowed. 'So you admit it?'

'Huh?' Ashley grunted.

'Something is going on?'

'What?'

'Something. Is. Going. On.' She said each word carefully, like they would be front page news tomorrow, groundbreaking stuff.

'Are you feeling okay?'

Trip leaned against her desk, her eyes now mere slits. 'Are you okay?'

'Trip, you're scaring me. Why did you call me here? What's going on?'

Ashley jumped when her friend sprung to her feet, like someone had put a coin in her back and given her new life. 'I need your help with that,' she replied, striding up the narrow gap between desks to the back wall and a limp piece of tinsel hanging off the otherwise neat display.

'That?' Ashley asked, doing a double take and pointing to the decoration. There couldn't be more than a foot hanging down. One well-placed staple and it would be fixed.

'Yeah, please. I've got a staple gun. If you go on the table, I'll spot you.'

Ashley snorted with laughter. 'You being funny?'

'I should certainly think not,' Trip retorted, indignant.

'Trip! You're six foot without shoes. You could sort that yourself.' Ashley crossed her arms, certain this was some weird joke or trick.

'Further to fall then, if I come off the table. You really want me to break my neck?'

It was Ashley's turn to narrow her eyes. 'No. Something's going on. Tell me. Then I'll help.'

Trips eyes darted between the tinsel and Ashley. Then back again. 'I'm scared of heights.'

'Trip.'

'Tinsel smells funny.'

'Trip.'

'Fear of the staple gun. What if I get distracted and staple my hand?'

'TRIP.'

'Why are you avoiding Dani?'

The question was like an ice cold shower. The blood drained downward, her breath caught, and her heart stuttered. 'I, erm, I'm not.'

Trip raised her eyebrows. It was her turn to play the name game. 'Ash.'

'Did she say something?' Her heart fought to return to normal by making up the lost beats at a dizzying rate.

'She'd be mortified if she knew I was asking this, but yeah, it was mentioned when we went bouldering.'

Ashley stared at the dropping Christmas decoration. 'I'm not.'

'You're not avoiding her?'

'Right.' Trip considered her next words she fiddled with the staple gun on the desk. 'So why you being rude?'

'Excuse me?' Ashley asked with a nervous chuckle.

'Leaving her on read, telling her you can't do stuff. She's your oldest friend. Why are you suddenly over being pals?'

'I'm not.'

'Well, you are. She told me, showed me your messages.'

'I mean I'm not over being friends.'

Trip nodded slowly. 'So, what's up?'

Ashley groaned. This wasn't the time or the place for this conversation. 'Do we really need to do this here?'

'Well, according to your messages you're too busy to see anyone, so where else could I talk to you but work?'

It was a fair point. 'It's just—' Ashley stopped herself, pondering the best way to put this. Trip knew her and Dani's history better than anyone. The amount of heart to hearts they'd shared was impossible to count. But saying it out loud, now she was with Hazel, was dangerous territory. She would trust Trip with her life, but this? Once the words were out they couldn't be stuffed back in. 'I—' Her lip wobbled.

'Whoa, whoa, hey,' Trip soothed, scooping her into a comforting embrace. 'You don't have to say anything you don't want to.'

Ashley nodded into her friend's shoulder, willing the tears to disappear before they started and worrying she was getting foundation on Trip's white shirt. Too late now.

After a while, Trip spoke: 'Want to come to mine tonight? Get a pizza? If you want to chat, fine. If not, hey, I got a pizza.'

She couldn't help but smile as she pulled back from Trip's hug. Ashley ran a finger under each eye, hoping to tidy herself up. 'I'd like that, yeah.'

∽

After two glasses of wine and three slices of pizza, Ashley finally felt brave enough to share the mess that was swirling around her head. The issue was how to bring it up. The words were there, just not the natural segue in the conversation.

Trip's focus was on the TV and the romcom she'd shoved on. It wasn't Trip's bag at all and Ashley was grateful for the compromise. She needed light and upbeat, not Trip's usual action and adventure films.

'So,' Ashley began, and Trip's head snapped toward her, pizza slice in mouth.

'So?'

This was as torturous as coming out to her mum. The dread. Impending doom. The words growing in her chest until they became so big she popped and spilled everything.

Short. Sweet. Nothing to it.

'I'm not avoiding Dani. Per se.'

'Per se,' Trip repeated, shifting her position on the couch so she was now cross-legged and facing Ashley. She polished off her slice with ease. Sometimes Ashley could swear that woman had hollow legs: no matter what she ate she was always like a rake.

'I just—'

Trip cocked her head, waiting. When nothing further came she coaxed Ashley again. 'You just?'

'I love Hazel. And I wouldn't have said I would marry her if I didn't—'

'But?'

' I can't stop thinking about Dani. Which I know is stupid. Nothing will ever happen between us, but it's like an illness, a disease. I just can't stop.'

Ashley resisted the urge to pant. That was close to running a marathon.

Trip sucked on her top lip as she thought. 'And, purely hypothetically, if something could happen, would that change things?' She clicked the sound down on the TV as she spoke.

Ashley thought, catching the words *did she say something?* before they blurted out. 'I dunno.'

'But it would make a difference, yeah?'

'Yeah.'

Trip nodded. Where was this going? 'Well, then you need to ask yourself what you want. You're giving yourself space from Dani, so does that mean you've chosen Hazel?'

'Choosing anyone makes it sound like a competition.'

'It kind of is,' Trip replied with a cheeky grin.

'I'm not a prize or an object.'

The smile disappeared. 'No, no, I didn't mean that. I just mean, if your heart and your head are wanting different things, you need to follow one path. You can't have both.'

How Ashley wished she could have both. Her heart felt big enough for the two of them. It wasn't practical in the long run, though. 'I hate ignoring Dani but it seems the right thing to do.'

'So, is that it? You don't want to see her again? If that's your final decision I'll support you. I won't pick sides. All is fair in love and war.'

Ashley imagined her future without Dani. It was barren, but morally right. She could be happy with Hazel. A kid or two. Hazel really wanted a dog. It wouldn't be a bad life. Still though, something paramount was lacking.

'It's ridiculous though, Trip. She doesn't have feelings for me. I think Hazel's just got in my head.'

'What do you mean?'

'She thinks Dani's holding some kind of torch for me and it's got my head spinning in ways I'd got over years ago. I dunno.' It was like wading through pond water. All the shit and misguided feelings she'd let settle on the bottom were being dredged up, wreaking fresh havoc.

'Have you ever told Dani how you feel?'

Ashley shook her head. 'She knows.'

'Because you've spoken about it . . .?'

Ashley's face was deadpan. 'You really think I'm going to make a fool of myself? It's been twenty years, Trip. That's insane. If she felt anything towards me something would have happened.'

'You kissed in Ibiza. Is that not something?'

The wind left Ashley in a silent puff. She took a hot second to compose herself. 'Are you – how do you know we kissed?'

Trip's cheeks burned crimson as her eyes widened. 'Just guessing that it's maybe happened over the years.'

'Jesus Christ, Trip. Please, just be honest with me.' There was no malice to her tone, just sheer desperation.

'Dani told me.'

No matter what Ashley did, air wouldn't stay in her lungs. She got up and paced the room, a hand to her forehead as she thought. 'She remembers?'

'Of course.'

'Fuck.' Embarrassed didn't cut it. She'd had a sneaking suspicion Dani had remembered but she'd feigned being too drunk, claiming the night was a blur. If she remembered then that settled it: there was nothing between them. Ashley was nothing but a laughing stock and lovelorn fool. What a fucking idiot.

'Why are you acting like this is the worst news in the world?' Trip asked, so unfazed she had the audacity to grab another slice of pizza. Ashley wanted to bat it out her hand and ask for a little respect.

She stopped pacing. 'When she told you, was it like, to make fun of me? Or like—'

Trip cut her short. 'Make fun of you?'

'Yeah, like, you'll never guess what that stupid idiot Ashley did?'

'Course not.' As if twigging what Ashley was thinking, Trip put her nibbled pizza back in the box. 'Look, don't tell her I told you, but Dani trusted me and only me when that happened.' Trip's features betrayed how bad she felt at telling Ashley, but she continued regardless. 'Fuck. Right. Jesus. Sit down.'

Ashley's heart lurched as she sat. 'What?'

'You need to talk to Dani.'

'Why?'

'Just talk to her.'

'If you're saying what I think you're saying...'

'And what if I am?'

No. There was no way. 'Hypothetical bullshit. Look, either you tell me what you know or this evening is over.'

Despite the TV being muted, Trip clicked it off with the remote. The air shifted as the atmosphere gained weight. For a second, Ashley wondered if this was Trip signalling for her to leave, but finally she spoke, her voice quiet. 'It's you. It's always been you. That's all I'm saying. And you tell Dani I breathed a word, I'll never forgive you.'

Ashley was numb. The world was a blur as she passed by Trip and headed for the kitchen. Before she knew it she had a glass in her hand and had the cold tap on full.

Her hand trembled as the glass filled.

'Ashley.' Trip prompted. She sounded a thousand miles away, despite standing behind her.

She turned the tap off but her grip wouldn't allow her to

actually take a drink. She slammed the glass on the drainer instead.

'How long have you known?'

'I, erm, I . . .'

'Have long have you known?' Ashley asked again with more purpose.

'A while. A long time. I dunno.'

Ashley took a long breath, her abdominals aching from holding things together. 'This isn't some stupid throwaway crush, Trip,' Ashley replied, her hands gripping the edge of Trip's wooden counter. Her legs were jelly, her knees wanting to buckle given the slightest chance. 'I've had feelings for Dani as long as I've known you.'

'I . . . but it wasn't my place to say anything.'

She couldn't bear to face her. 'The chances I've passed up because of her. The pain she's caused me by sleeping about. You saw all that—'

'I know, but—'

Ashley finally found the courage to look Trip in the eye. She looked as hurt as Ashley felt. 'All this time you knew. You knew. And you didn't even think to say something? Anything?' Her voice was loud now. So loud Trip winced. 'When I got with Hazel, did you not think to say then?'

'I thought you'd moved on. What am I meant to be? A mind reader?'

Ashley pushed past her and into the living room. Scooping up her boots, aiming to leave as soon as possible.

Trip was hot on her heels. 'Ash. Come on. See things from my point of view. This wasn't my news to tell. Dani should have told you.'

A tear rolled down Ashley's cheek and she swiped it away. 'No. You knew. All these years you knew and you never once said a word. You waited until I was getting married and

—' she held up her finger and thumb to indicate a tiny space '—this close to getting over Dani. Finally being free of this mess. And now you tell me.'

She stood, surprised her legs held without even the slightest wobble, and scooped up her jacket.

Trip's jaw tensed as she searched for what to say. It was no use. Nothing could make this better. Ashley was in the hall in record time. 'I thought better of you, Trip. Seems I didn't know you at all.'

17

'Trip,' Dani said, surprised to see her friend at the end of the bar on a Friday evening. It was nearly closing time, and boy did she need it. Today had been non-stop.

'Dani.'

She paused her tongs over the final scone in the cabinet, plate in hand, ready to complete her latest order. 'Why do you look so guilty?'

Trip chewed on her cheek.

Dani placed the scone on the plate as gently as it were a bomb, then rang the bell, letting her cousin knew it was ready to be served. All the while never taking her eyes off her friend.

'Christ. What have you done?' Dani asked with a laugh. 'Got a girl pregnant?' she joked, hoping to lighten the mood.

'Heard from Ashley lately?'

Dani's stomach dropped. 'Has something happened to her?'

'What? No, no, no. It's just—' Trip fell silent as Dani's cousin Heather collected the tray and walked it back to the seating area. 'I don't think I'm her favourite person at the moment.'

Dani put the rag she'd been using to clean her station down on the counter and eyed Trip with hesitant suspicion. 'She's ignoring you too?'

Trip grimaced. 'Yeah, but I know why. Are you free for a drink after this?'

'Yeah, of course. Kirsty's just talking Mum over some rota changes. I can get her to close after I do these drinks.'

Trip already looked like a weight was off her shoulders.

The weather was too wild to traipse the twenty minutes to Bar Orama, so they settled for drinks in Dani and Kirsty's flat. After a sweaty, difficult day, Dani was in no mood to go where any of her customers might be, so Shawlands was out of the question.

'Right, what have you done?' she asked, returning from her room to find Trip draped over her armchair, her eyes closed, and the beer she'd opened untouched.

Trip groaned. 'I've fucked up.'

Dani took a seat on the sofa. 'Should I be worried?'

She opened one eye and chanced a glance at Dani. 'Yes.'

Her heart leaped into action. 'Trip, what the fuck have you done?'

Doe eyes weren't going to help, but Trip tried anyway. 'In the long run, I think it will be a good thing. Well hopefully, you'll see it that way, after a bit of time, at least . . .'

'What have you done?' Dani repeated, taking a long, slow draw of beer. Something told her she wouldn't be so calm in a minute.

'Ashley came round to mine.'

'Uh-huh.'

'And she was freaking out.'

'Freaking out?'

'Okay, maybe not so much freaking out. Not before – well, she was worried.'

'Worried?' Another sip of beer. This was like getting blood from a stone. 'The abridged version please, Trip.'

'Right, so. She was telling me why she's been avoiding you.'

Dani's blood ran cold, like the slushy rain currently battering the windows. 'Okay.'

'And, I might have, kinda, well—'

The door to the flat swung open with a thunk, followed by a cheery hello from Kirsty. Trip stopped in her tracks.

'That was quick,' Dani snapped, not meaning for it to be so nippy.

Kirsty put her bag on the kitchen counter. 'Yeah, it was.' She didn't sound impressed. 'What's going on?'

'Trip's done something stupid.'

Kirsty couldn't contain the stupid grin contorting her face. 'Sarah Gordon's done something stupid. So unlike you, Trip,' she teased, taking a seat before leaping to her feet. 'No, no, wait. I want a wine for this.'

Trip looked relieved at the reprieve. She eyed Dani with silent unease until Kirsty retook her seat.

'Spill,' Dani urged, her words holding more weight than a cannonball.

'I told Ashley you had feelings for her.'

Kirsty choked on her wine. Dani's heart stopped for a few seconds as her mouth hung open.

'You did what?' she finally blurted.

Kirsty was a choking mess, so much so Chet got off the sofa with an angry meow and left the room.

'Look, look, see, it just kind of happened, and I had to! She's having second thoughts about Hazel.'

Well, that was a game changer. Dani gave her sister a hard thump on the back. 'Second thoughts? Really?'

'She still likes you, Dani. I had to say something.'

Dani twisted the beer bottle between her palms with no intention to drink more. What was already in her stomach sloshed about with every breath.

'What did she say to that?' Kirsty asked.

'She was mad,' Trip replied, pulling a face.

'Mad?' Dani blurted.

'At me. She thinks I should have said something years ago.'

Dani stood, itching the back of her neck as she paced behind the sofa. 'When did this happen?'

'Yesterday.'

Kirsty locked eyes with Dani. She didn't need to ask the question to get an answer. 'I've not heard from her.'

'She probably just needs time.'

Dani bobbed her head as a poor attempt at a nod, her eyes fixed on the window but nothing in particular. What was she meant to do with this information?

The air in the room was electric, as if everyone wanted to speak but daren't utter a word.

Dani broke the silence, but only because if she didn't speak she was going to jangle so much with nerves she'd be sick. 'So, what do I do?'

'She's still with Hazel, yeah?' Kirsty added.

Trip sat up, placing her fingers together and tapping them to her mouth as she thought. 'I think her head's a mess. Give her time. She needs to weigh things up.'

'Weigh things up?' Dani groaned, punctuating the sentence with a puff of air. 'Me against Hazel, wow. Absolutely cracking.' She crossed her arms on the breakfast bar and lay her head down.

'That's not what I meant.' Trip defended herself.

'Kinda is,' Kirsty replied. 'Look. This is massive. The two of you have been a mess since you were seventeen. You can't expect her to just come running.'

'Yeah, but, like, should I tell her I know, or . . . ?' Dani asked, twisting her head to face the living room.

Trip considered it. 'Not yet. Give her a week. Let her get her ducks in a row. If you don't hear anything after that, get in touch. Casually, like.'

'And if she doesn't reply?' Dani already knew the answer.

'I'll go speak to her.'

'I think you've done enough,' Kirsty scoffed, and narrowly missed a swat to the knee from Trip.

'I couldn't not say anything, Dani.'

'I know,' she replied, standing straight. She lifted her cap and ran a hand over her hair. 'Fuck. This is horrible.'

'Good horrible?' Trip asked.

'I don't want to break a couple up. That was never my intention,' Dani said, retaking her seat by Kirsty. Trip gave her knee a reassuring jiggle.

'I know,' she said, removing her hand and grabbing her beer. 'Me neither. But I couldn't let her say all that stuff and not let her know the whole picture.'

'So, she still likes me?' Dani couldn't hide the smile pulling at the corner of her mouth. The sick feeling in the pit of her stomach was slowly being replaced with jubilation.

'Dan, you idiot,' Kirsty chided.

'Hey!'

'When's she ever not liked you?' Trip added with a look to Kirsty.

'No idea why,' Kirsty retorted.

Dani grabbed Kirsty's side and only stopped when she

realised how precarious her wine was. She'd paid for half this couch and Chet had done enough damage already.

'Imagine,' Dani beamed, a fresh grin forming.

'Alright, alright. Don't get ahead of yourself,' Trip said, making Dani come back to earth with a bump. 'Spare a thought for Hazel in all this.'

'She already hates me.'

'It'll be fine,' Kirsty said, lying through her teeth. 'You've waited this long: what's a while longer?'

A week might as well be a lifetime when the possibility of Ashley choosing Hazel was on the line. But what else could she do but wait?

18

Ashley bounced her leg up and down as she waited on the sofa for Hazel to come home.

It had been nearly a week since Trip had dropped the bombshell that Dani had feelings for her. Six torturous, anxiety-inducing days of mental acrobatics. If her thoughts were a mess before now they might as well be on a spin cycle. She was exhausted.

Strangely, the biggest obstacle to overcome was Hazel's tattoo. That tiny letter A, only a few centimetres tall, was like a searing brand. But she couldn't stay with Hazel purely over a little ink.

She'd never asked for her to get something so permanent.

It didn't stop Ashley feeling like a monumental dick, though.

Plus, it was Christmas. Not exactly perfect timing.

She let out a ragged breath. Every passing second made her more nauseous. Christ. This was horrible.

She wanted to pace but her legs weren't up for supporting her.

There was no way she could marry Hazel and have the thought of Dani forever looming over her. Was she completely settled on being with Dani? No, not entirely. But she couldn't flip-flop through life with these emotions, her wedding creeping closer by the day. She needed to hit pause with Hazel and get her head in order.

The sound of the flat door opening made her jump.

Saliva flooded her mouth and her palms became sweaty. She pulled at the sleeves of her jumper for something to fiddle with, anything to stop her shaking.

'Hey,' Hazel said with a cheery grin as she popped her head into the living room. She doubled back. 'You okay? You're as white as a sheet.'

Ashley couldn't speak. Even nodding was taxing.

'Are you ill again?' Hazel asked, taking Ashley's hand in hers. 'You're really clammy.'

'No. Not ill.'

The room was ten times smaller than usual.

'Okay.' Hazel's voice was unsteady.

The tension between them was crushing. Ashley wanted to push Hazel's hand away, leave the flat, and never look back. The feeling of her skin against hers was like fire.

'We need to have a chat.' She couldn't bear to make eye contact.

Hazel removed her hand and Ashley could finally breathe again.

'That doesn't sound good,' Hazel replied with an uneasy chuckle.

'Erm,' Ashley started. She'd mentally rehearsed this a thousand times in the last few days. Actually doing it was another matter. She couldn't even eat her breakfast today for thinking of what was to come. Her insides were a vibrating mess of nerves and guilt. It had to be done.

'Ashley, you're worrying me.'

Eye contact still wasn't possible. 'I – fuck – I never planned for this.' She took a deep breath. 'I just, I need space. To think about something.'

These were not the carefully chosen words she'd scripted.

'What?'

'It's nothing you've done wrong, I just need time to myself. It's not that I don't love you, of course I do, it's just—'

'Ashley, what the fuck? Where is this coming from? Did I do something? Say something?' Hazel's voice cracked. It was a wonder Ashley was being so stoic.

'No. No. Like I say, it's all me.'

'Look at me,' Hazel said, pawing at Ashley's face. 'Look at me.'

Finally their eyes met and the tears that had somehow been kept at bay fell with force down Ashley's cheeks. 'I'm sorry.'

'Is this a joke?'

Fuck. The look in her eyes imprinted onto Ashley's heart. Pure devastation.

'You really think I'd make a sick joke like this?'

Hazel swallowed hard as a tear rolled down her face. 'But, we're getting married. I don't understand what I've done wrong.'

'You've not done anything wrong.'

They sat in silence for a moment and Ashley wondered if the conversation was over.

That was until Hazel got to her feet with such force the sofa would have moved had it not been against the wall.

Her voice had a fresh layer of venom to it. 'Is this to do with Dani?'

'Why would Dani have anything to do with it?' A wave of nausea washed over Ashley.

'I . . . have—' Hazel paced by the coffee table as she ran a hand through her short hair. 'Have you cheated on me?'

'What? No!' Ashley yelped. 'Of course not.'

Hazel nodded with the force of a dashboard toy as she chewed her cheek. 'But this is to do with Dani, yeah?'

'I told you,' Ashley replied through gritted teeth. 'This is about me. I have stuff going on in my head that I need to get straight.'

Hazel fell to her knees by Ashley's side and placed her hands on her fiancée's. 'Ash, tell me what's wrong. Whatever it is. We can fix it. Together.'

There was no going back now. The words were out. This conversation would forever change things, regardless of how the future turned out. 'This isn't the end. Please. I just need time.'

'I don't understand.'

'Neither do I, really.'

'So, that's it?' Hazel asked with a gulp. 'Do we cancel the wedding?'

'Not yet, but I guess we might need to postpone things, yeah.'

Hazel's gaze dropped to Ashley's shoes and silence filled the room once more.

What was she meant to do now?

She'd never broken up with anyone before. Heck. She'd never even really dated anyone.

Did she just get up and leave?

Ashley focused on her breathing and Hazel remained at her feet.

'I'm going to stay at my mum's tonight,' Ashley said, breaking the silence like a sledgehammer to a pane of glass.

'Okay. Then what?'

There was no clear answer. 'I'll see how things go.'

'What about Christmas?'

The issue had occurred to Ashley. It was a tough one. Spend it together and pretend everything was okay so Hazel's parents were none the wiser, or stick to her guns? 'We'll need to have a chat about that.'

'Well, are we together or not?'

Ashley swallowed any biting remarks that might have lingered on the tip of her tongue. 'Just give me a few days to think about it.'

Silence again.

It was time like this Ashley wished they had a pet. A visit from Chet would be good about now. Something to break the tension.

'How long have you felt like this?' Hazel asked, still rooted to her spot on the hardwood floor.

'A while. Not long. But long enough.'

'There's really nothing I can do?'

'Just give me space, it's all I need.'

Hazel stood and Ashley's heart ached once more at the sight of her. She wasn't usually a crier but now her eyes were damp and her cheeks blotchy.

None of this was fair. Ashley was happy. Why did these stupid intrusive thoughts have to rear their head?

'So. Okay. You going now?'

'I guess, yeah.' Anything to get out this flat.

'Can I ask you one last thing?'

'Yeah, of course.'

'Did Dani know you were going to do this?'

'Hazel.'

'Ashley, please. Just be honest with me.'

'No, no,' Ashley said, shaking her head. 'She knows nothing about this. And I don't want her to.'

Hazel nodded slowly. 'This is just a blip. It's normal to get cold feet if you're getting married. I've heard about it loads.'

'Yeah. Just a blip.'

They held each other's gaze for a few seconds before Ashley broke contact and went to the bedroom to retrieve the bag she'd packed. Enough clothes for a week at least. The less she had to return here the better, Hazel or not. The place felt dirty, tarnished: the memory of this conversation would forever play in the living room like a terrible projector film.

Hazel stood in the kitchen doorway, her eyes red and puffy.

Without another word Ashley opened the flat door and stepped into the close. Only when the door was safely clicked shut did she allow a strangled sob to escape. It was no use breaking down here.

She took the steps as fast as she could. Her parent's wasn't far away. Only, her head wasn't leading her there. She had somewhere else to be.

19

Dani padded to the intercom set with groggy eyes, still half asleep after being woken up from a nap.

The buzzer sounded again, its shrill wail like a banshee.

Kirsty was out with Rhona tonight, celebrating her return after a few nights away in Greece. Bit early for them to be back.

The buzzer rang again just as Dani went to lift the receiver.

She was in two minds to leave Kirsty outside. 'Impatient cow.'

The weather was minging, though. Wouldn't be fair to soak Rhona.

'Hello?' Dani grunted.

'Hey, it's me.'

Didn't sound like Kirsty or Rhona. 'Who's me?'

'Ashley.'

Without another word Dani clicked the door release button. The loud ringer was only drowned out by her heart.

Radio silence and then she turned up at her door unannounced. What did that mean?

Dani ran to the bathroom and made sure she was presentable. No hat. No time. A knock at the door signalled Ashley's arrival.

She let out a sharp breath and locked eyes with her reflection in the bathroom mirror. 'You've got this.'

They'd done this a thousand times, but opening the door to Ashley today felt big. Like, start-of-something huge. Which was stupid. She was maybe just here to kill some time, pretend like nothing weird was going on.

Dani knew she was wrong as soon as she saw Ashley. Even though she was drenched from head to toe it was obvious she'd been crying.

'Hey, hey, what's wrong?' Dani asked, stepping aside to let Ashley in.

She dropped a heavy rucksack to the floor and opened her mouth to speak, but only a pitiful sob escaped.

Dani scooped her up, holding on for dear life as Ashley cried.

'What's happened? Are your parents okay?'

Ashley nodded against her shoulder.

'Hazel? She okay?'

Another nod.

She could go through Ashley's entire inner circle but decided to give up and be a literal shoulder to cry on instead.

They stood for what felt like hours but was probably only minutes.

Finally, Ashley pulled back, her face a snotty mess.

Dani wanted to wipe the tears away, kiss her on the forehead, and tell her everything would be okay, whatever had happened. The gesture would be loaded, though.

'Okay?' she asked.

'Yeah,' Ashley replied, her breath hitching.

Ashley snagged Dani's gaze and the weight of her anguish hung between them, boring into Dani. She'd never seen Ashley like this. The pain in her eyes was almost unbearable, but Dani held steady, determined not to break the connection. Tonight she was the strong one. Whatever Ashley needed of her, she would provide.

With a deep sniff Ashley stepped back, picked up her bag, and headed to Dani's room.

Guess I'm to follow.

She slumped backwards onto Dani's bed like a half-arsed Fosbury flopper and covered her eyes with her hands as she let out a low, guttural moan.

'Bad day at the office?' Dani asked as she sat on the edge of the bed.

That got a little smile. Good.

'Do you have any booze?' Ashley asked, still covering her eyes.

Okay, it must be bad. Dani was the drinker, not Ash.

'Tequila for sure. Kirsty might have some wine we could steal. I can always go buy you some if you want.'

Ashley sat up. 'Tequila will do.'

'Tequila, okay. Will I bring it here?'

Ashley nodded with gusto. 'Yeah, please.'

She looked possessed. Filled with fresh vigour, her wide eyes and uneasy smile were a strange juxtaposition to her tear-stained cheeks and wild hair.

Dani didn't dare ask questions. She returned minutes later with the three-quarters-full bottle. Ashley about took her hand off as she snatched it away.

'We've no limes,' Dani said as Ashley took a gulp. Her face crumpled, but only for a moment; soon she was swigging back more.

She let her take another glug before speaking. 'Are you going to tell me what's going on?'

Ashley focused on doing another mouthful of tequila before putting the open bottle on Dani's bedside. She wiped the back of her hand over her mouth.

Dani was quiet, patiently waiting for an answer: there was no sense in rushing her.

'Right, I—' Ashley began before puffing her cheeks out and huffing air. 'I broke up with Hazel.'

Dani froze. Inside, her heart was doing cartwheels; upstairs, her head was in disbelief. 'You did? Why?'

Ashley reached for the tequila again but instead of taking a swig she held in between her hands, her eyes trained on its neck. 'Just, things weren't feeling right, I guess. I need space.'

Dani nodded. *Fuck.* This had to be because of her. There were no such things as coincidences.

Guilt lay heavy in Dani's stomach. This was the outcome she wanted, though: it couldn't happen any other way.

If Hazel didn't hate her before, she certainly did now.

'Anything you want to talk about?'

Ashley shook her head. 'Not today.'

'Come here,' Dani said, opening her arms wide. Ashley didn't need asked twice. She scooted over and leaned her head against Dani's chest. Dani mumbled into Ashley's still-wet hair. 'If and when you want to talk you know where to come, yeah?'

'Of course.'

Ashley's jacket was just as wet as her hair and squelched under Dani's fingertips as she gave her shoulder a reassuring squeeze. She looked at the wet patch on her bed. It would dry.

Dani kept her chin rested on the top of Ashley's head. The sudden proximity was a welcome relief after a tortuous week. She knew in her heart Trip was right about giving Ashley space, but still, it was horrible. She couldn't eat. She could barely sleep, hence today's nap. She'd not even wanted to touch alcohol. The thought of consuming anything made her stomach lurch.

And now? Now she wanted to do laps around the house, shouting for joy.

Ashley shifted her position and her hand skirted under Dani's top. She quickly retracted it and placed it on Dani's waist, holding a handful of T-shirt to pull her closer, get comfier. It was an obvious mistake, but Dani's skin wasn't to be fazed. Goosebumps flushed over her, the spot where Ashley had touched now a beacon of desire, pulsing hot like she'd been licked by fire.

'You okay?' Dani asked, surprised how low her voice was.

'Yeah. Thank you.' Ashley sounded sleepy. If she fell asleep Dani would treat her like she did Chet: you stay until they wake up, no matter how uncomfy you are.

Comfortable silence enveloped the room.

If only you could pause a moment, enjoy it a little longer.

'Dan?' Ashley asked quietly.

'Yeah?'

'Can I stay here tonight?'

'Of course – you know you can stay whenever you need to.'

'Good.' Ashley took a deep, ragged breath. 'I was going to stay at my parents' but I can't be arsed with all their questions. It's going to be hellish.'

'Stay as long as you need.'

'I'm going to have to tell them sooner or later.'

Ashley pawed at her face as fresh tears quietly fell. Dani looped her fingers together, bringing Ashley closer. Any nearer and she would be in Dani's T-shirt.

Sometimes Dani wished you could hug someone so hard that all the love you had inside you would jump into them, filling them up and pushing the hurt away. The Hamiltons weren't a huggy family, but when Dad died it was the only comfort that worked: no words felt right, so days passed in silence. Only well-timed reassuring squeezes kept them from falling apart completely. Hugs were emotional currency, and for Ashley, Dani had an unlimited fortune.

'Let's not think about it tonight,' Dani reassured her. 'How about I run you a bath? Get you out of these wet clothes. You can have a glass of wine.'

'Sounds good.'

Dani gave in and kissed the top of Ashley's head. There was no recoil. 'Then we can get cosy and watch a film. You've been through a lot tonight, let's just take things easy.'

'Where's Kirsty and Rhona?'

'They're out, so we can please ourselves. I'll text Kirsty, let them know you're here.' Dani paused, a thought occurring. 'Can I tell her why? Or do you want to keep it on the DL for now?'

Ashley huffed. 'Just tell her. Might as well.'

Another gentle kiss to the head. 'Okay.' Dani leaned back, freeing herself from Ashley's grip. 'Now, get those clothes on the radiator and steal my dressing gown. I'll get the bath on.'

The pain in Ashley's eyes hadn't budged, but now another emotion clouded them. She snagged Dani's gaze with such tenderness that she wanted to lock her hands round Ashley's face and snog her into oblivion there and then. Hardly appropriate behaviour, given the shitemare Ashley had endured today.

'Thank you,' Ashley said quietly.

'It's nothing.'

Ashley gave a thin-lipped smile in response.

'Right, back in a min.' Dani's heart lurched into action as she entered the hall. She could pinch herself. This was really happening. *Fuck.* She needed to do something to dispel all this nervous energy. Wine. There was a good excuse. She'd pour Ashley a small glass of Kirsty's dregs then pop to the shop for a fresh bottle. It was Friday; no harm, no foul.

Bath on, she popped to the kitchen and poured the wine with a shaky hand. Her veins buzzed with adrenaline. It was like her chest was full of bees. She let out a puff of air before returning to her bedroom to find Ashley in her gown and inspecting her face in the mirror.

'What a mess,' she said, as much to Chet as Dani.

'I've seen worse. Your wine.'

Ashley smiled as she wasted no time in sampling Kirsty's plonk. 'That's hit the spot, thank you.'

'Can I get you anything else?'

'You've done enough.'

'Doesn't feel like it.'

Ashley opened her mouth but had second thoughts before starting again. 'Right, I'm going to enjoy a nice warm bath.' She stopped in the doorway and turned on her heel, catching Dani's eye with the same affectionate gaze as before. For a brief second Dani thought she was going to ask her to join her. 'Thanks again.'

She was gone, and Dani felt her heart might explode from longing. Sleeping in the same bed was going to be tough. But she'd gone this long: what was one more night?

20

'More prosecco?' Mum asked, hovering the bottle over Ashley's glass.

She was pretty squiffy already, but why not? It was Christmas Day. 'Go on then.'

Mum smiled as she topped up Ashley's glass but her eyes were still full of pity. The whole day had featured an invisible guest: the unspoken hanging over them, begging to be addressed, but neither parent would bring it up. Poor Ashley, without Hazel.

Telling them hadn't been too bad. Yes, there had been the inevitable ten thousand questions and they totally didn't get Ashley's reasoning, but it was okay. As good as it could be.

She was still being stubbornly vague. The thought of mentioning Dani was sickening. It also still felt like cheating. It was too soon. Even sleeping in the same bed had felt incredibly wrong.

Ashley watched her mum remove the brandy glass from Dad's drooping hand. He always fell asleep first after dinner. Guaranteed, though, if either one of them tried to change the channel from the current action movie, he would sit up faster than a jack-in-the-box.

They exchanged a look as Ashley sipped her fresh booze. It hadn't been a bad Christmas Day.

Leanne, Dave, and the kids were still here, presenting a very welcome distraction. They were currently playing with their new pogo stick in the garden. It was far too cold for Ashley. She was happy to miss out and heat herself with bubbles.

'That you done?' Mum said in the kitchen, her voice followed by the stomping of boots.

Leanne's voice came: 'Well, I am. Bloody freezing.'

'Language.'

'Honestly, two kids of my own and still being told off,' she joked, finishing her sentence in the doorway to the living room. 'Brandy in the conservatory, wee sis?'

Ashley looked at her nearly full glass. In for a penny, in for a pound. Plus, Leanne never asked her to do solo stuff; this needed investigating. Although, Ashley could bet her savings on what the topic might be. As she'd learned so often recently, best to get things done and out of the way.

'Sure, why not?' Ashley replied, getting to her feet. A little more unsteadily than she would have liked, but an afternoon of drinking will do that, no matter how much food you consume.

Leanne grabbed the bottle of brandy from the counter and Ashley got two glasses; not a further word spoken.

Still nothing was said after they'd sat in the quiet conservatory and Leanne had poured two generous measures.

'Cheers,' she said, lifting her glass to clink Ashley's.

'Cheers.'

It only took one sip before the atmosphere was pierced

with a single, quiet word. Short but powerful, it was the king of awkward conversation openers: 'So.'

'So,' Ashley repeated.

'Heard from Dani today?'

It was an innocent question but Ashley knew what was hiding behind it. Her insides squirmed. 'She wished me Merry Christmas, yeah.'

Leanne nodded, her eyes trained on their reflection in the dark windows. 'She keeping well?'

Ashley scrunched her face up. 'Since when are you ninety? Who says "keeping well"?' she asked with a chuckle.

Leanne joined in her laughter. 'Alright, alright. Let's not beat about the bush. Your break-up has something to do with her, yeah?'

Time to be brave. 'In part, yeah.' Phew. That wasn't so bad. It was out now, no going back.

'Does she know?'

'Know what?'

'That you like her, doy!' Leanne mocked, putting on a voice.

'Obviously. Well, I've not told her, but she has to know.'

Leanne nodded with vigour. 'You're right. After all, she's not blind.' She hid a smug grin behind her brandy glass and narrowly avoided Ashley's swiping hand.

'Fair, I guess.' She took a swig of her brandy, allowing the booze to give her a fresh wave of courage. 'Trip told me she has feelings for me.'

'The fuck?' Leanne blurted, a little too loudly, and instinctively turned her head towards the kitchen and Mum. No telling off. 'Trip has feelings for you?'

Ashley waved a hand between them. 'No, no, noooo. Lord. No. Imagine. Dani has feelings for me.'

Leanne pulled another face. 'Oh my God. Is this news to

you? Honestly, the two of you drive me insane!'

'It's easy to say you knew once you know,' Ashley huffed. Did that make sense? Brandy and prosecco maybe weren't the best combo.

'Twenty-odd years I've had to watch you two goofballs waste time. Just tell her, like, actually physically tell her. Please? For me? It will be the bestest Christmas gift ever.'

Ashley sighed. 'It's too soon. What about Hazel?'

'What about her? It's only words. I'm not saying jump into bed with the poor lassie. Just tell her how you feel. Sometimes what's obvious really isn't at all.'

Ashley took a deep breath. The idea made her stomach ache.

'If I'm not wanting anything to happen, why would I risk putting myself out there?' Ashley twisted her glass, swirling the liquid inside, surprised at how close it was to being finished.

'Do you want to waste another twenty years pussyfooting around each other?'

'That's never going to happen.'

Leanne's eyes flicked to the half-melted snow on the conservatory roof, tracing a slushy pile as she thought.

'Nothing is ever going to happen if the two of you don't start communicating.' She looked at her watch. 'Look, it's just gone seven. Text her, go for a walk. Do something. It's Christmas.' She emphasised her last word with a squeeze of Ashley's forearm.

Ashley scrunched her face up.

'Ash, ple—' A shriek from the garden cut her short. No prizes for guessing it was pogo stick-induced. 'Shit. Be right back.'

Alone, Ashley pondered her sister's words. It wouldn't hurt to tell Dani. Get all her cards on the table.

She pulled her phone out and was surprised to see a message from Hazel on her lock screen. Two little words – *Merry Christmas* – felt like a punch in the gut. Especially since she'd got her phone out to text Dani.

The thought of texting Hazel had crossed her mind this morning, but the signals were too mixed. It would be rude not to reply, though. She fired off a quick message.

The wind was out of her sails now.

It was just a walk.

They could go round Queen's Park; it wasn't far from Dani's mum's house.

Just a walk.

The distant crying had faded from the garden now. Leanne would be back soon, nagging her to take action.

Nothing like a bossy older sister to spur you on.

She kept it low-key to start, planning to work up to meeting her.

Hey, had a good day?

The reply was almost instant: *Hey! I have! Baby was sick on Kirsty, she is fuming, hah. Wbu?*

I bet she was! Good thing he's cute. I've had a great day. Want to go for a walk? She took a deep breath before stabbing at the send icon.

The reply wasn't so fast this time. Ashley chose not to dwell on it. Dani wasn't a mind reader, she could hardly know what she was planning... could she?

Kirsty wants to come too, that okay?

Bloody hell. How to reply? No, not really. Ashley clicked her phone off and placed it on the table between the arm chairs.

The only option was to say yes, lest she look Dodgy McDodgy. But Kirsty would ruin the whole thing: no point going out in the freezing cold for an actual walk.

Fuck.

Yeah, sure. Of course.

Another quick reply: *Awesome. Meet by the bowling green in 30?*

Not ideal, but better than nothing. Plus, she'd missed Dani the past few weeks. Never seeing her again wouldn't have worked. It was like planning to give up food or sunshine. There might be alternatives, but nothing beat the real thing.

Ashley trudged through to the kitchen to find Leanne tending to a scuffed Fraser. She was currently pawing at a bloody graze on his chin with one of Mum's good wash cloths, dripping water on the floor. His squeals told Ashley it wasn't the most pleasant of experiences.

'Any broken bones?' she asked, locating the prosecco she'd left earlier when getting glasses. She finished it off in one swift gulp.

'Thankfully not,' Leanne answered for him. 'Pogo's seen better days, though.'

Fraser grunted. Nothing fazed him. He'd probably be back outside in five minutes.

'I'm heading out.'

Leanne snapped her head towards Ashley, her child's chin still gripped in her hand. 'Oh really?' she chided, raising a singular eyebrow.

'Yep. To meet Dani. And Kirsty.'

Pursed lips, then Leanne returned to scrubbing Fraser. 'Well, have fun. Don't stay out too late.'

'You know me,' Ashley replied, watching Fraser wince. Any more scrubbing and she'd hit bone.

'That's the problem. Live a little, take a chance. It's Christmas.'

21

'I still can't believe Bobby was sick on me,' Kirsty said, stuffing her hands in her jacket pockets as they traipsed up Kilmarnock Road. She had on Mum's jumper, which was about six sizes too big; it looked quite comical. Dani was surprised she'd wanted to come out. Kirsty wouldn't leave for work if her hair wasn't spot on. Although, given a choice between a house with a highly-strung two-year-old and a newborn, Dani had been quick to choose the park too.

It had been a good day. Christmas was extra special now her nephews were here to centre attention on. It was even better now Louis was getting old enough to know what was going on. Another few years and Christmas would be full on magical.

'All part and parcel of being an auntie,' Dani joked. 'Still don't fancy one?'

Kirsty shot her a look. 'No way. Rhona agrees. They're much better when you can give them back.'

'Fair enough.'

'You going to get Ashley up the duff?'

Dani dug her elbow sharply between Kirsty's ribs. 'Enough!'

'What?' Kirsty gibed, rubbing at the spot Dani had attacked. 'It's pretty much a given you'll get together now.'

Dani didn't reply. It was too much pressure. Much easier to think in the present: they were friends, nothing more. Not a jot had changed.

Anything further and Dani's chest got tight, air suddenly in short supply.

'You want kids, though?' Kirsty asked as they stood at the traffic lights before Langside Hall and the entrance to the park.

'Of course. You know that. Why the twenty questions?'

Kirsty shrugged. 'Being with kids all day gets you thinking. I might ask Santa for a poncho next year if I'm going to have to hang out with more babies.'

Dani chuckled. 'I think you'll be safe for a few years yet.'

They walked in silence past the hall and down the slushy pavement towards the side gate where Ashley had said to meet. Dani pulled her hat as far as it could go over her ears.

'Fucking freezing, isn't it?' Kirsty said, hugging her jacket tighter around her torso.

'Probably going to snow.'

'As if you can tell.'

'I can smell it.'

'Alright, Lorelei Gilmore. Far too cold for snow.'

'Just you wait.' Dani was saved further argument by the sight of Ashley at the gates. She gave a little half-wave and Dani's heart tripped over itself. Didn't matter how many times she saw Ashley, the reaction would always be the same. The cold was no longer responsible for the goosebumps flushing over her skin. Ashley was Dani's personal central heating on a cold day, a mug of steaming hot cocoa when you got in from a long walk. It could snow all it liked with Ashley by her side.

'Hey,' Ashley said, looking suspiciously sheepish.

'Hey,' the sisters chorused.

Dani swooped in for a quick hug. 'Merry Christmas.'

Everything felt so awkward between them recently. If it wasn't the threat of Hazel, it was the weight of the unspoken snuffing normal interactions out. Every gesture felt loaded, every sentence had a double meaning, and every look could be conveyed as something else.

The trio set off, Kirsty the piggy in the middle.

'Will we go up by the greenhouse then swoop round to the pond?'

'Sounds good,' Ashley agreed.

Dani didn't mind. At this time of day Queen's Park was all trees. The impressive park boasted a few duck ponds, allotments, 19th-century greenhouses, a golf course, and other sporty endeavours. But in the dark? It was all the same to Dani. She wasn't here for the swings.

The steep hill up to the greenhouses was slippy today, so Dani let Kirsty carry the conversation as she focused on not going arse over elbow. They exchanged pleasantries about the day and stories about excitable children. Nothing groundbreaking.

When they reached the top of the hill Dani breathed a sigh of relief, her breath coming out like a plume of smoke.

'Seems like an age ago I was walking up this hill asking Rhona to be Kat's photographer,' Dani puffed, surprised to find herself out of breath. She should have brought her inhaler out. Too late now.

'God, yeah, that's a throwback,' Kirsty agreed. 'I was so mad you did that.'

'Really?' Ashley asked with a shiver.

'Relationships are scary at the start.'

'You've never told me that,' Dani said, raising her eyebrows with so much scepticism they were lost to her woolly hat.

'Believe it or not, I do not articulate every waking thought to you, dear sister. But yeah, I really went round in circles with Rhona. It could have gone either way.'

'What changed your mind?' Ashley asked.

Kirsty shrugged. 'It just felt right. I figured I owed it to myself to give it a chance.'

'And now look at you,' Dani chided, only just keeping a lid on a silly voice.

'Hoi! It's nice to be happy.'

'True. But I'm losing the use of my living room tomorrow because of you.'

'What?' Ashley asked with a giggle.

'Rhona's in Queensferry, so we're doing Christmas tomorrow.'

'I saw Kirsty kissing Saaaanta Claus,' Dani sang, running ahead so she could loop her arms around her back and mimic snogging. A swift whack to the back of the head put a stop to her antics.

'I think you should stay with Ashley tonight. Stop you carrying on,' Kirsty said with a grin.

'I dunno, it's pretty manic at Mum's,' Ashley blurted, a little too defensively.

'Relax, she's joking.' Dani replied nonchalantly, but the response stung like a slap on the cheek.

'Will do her good,' Kirsty continued, unaware of the snub. 'It's about time Dani took notes on being romantic.'

Dani shot Kirsty a look that was colder than the water in

Queen's Park pond. She was getting a bit lairy, her comments getting too close to the bone for Dani's liking.

'I should hang out with Izzy, then. Have you heard from her recently?' Dani asked Kirsty, desperate to change the conversation.

'Yes,' Kirsty groaned. 'The eco retreat was a bust. Nicole dumped her on the bus back home.'

'Yikes.' Izzy was the most romantic woman Dani knew. She could be a character straight from a romance novel. But fuck, did she have the worst taste in women.

'That sucks,' Ashley echoed. 'She's still coming out for New Year though, yeah?'

'That's the plan. Just don't mention tofu.'

'Did anyone pick up the tickets from Kim?' Dani asked, having a panicked lightbulb moment.

'Not yet,' Kirsty replied. 'But it will be her or Travis on the door; they're hardly going to deny us entry.'

'Dunno. You know what Kim's like,' Dani said, joking, and got a fresh chuckle.

Their favourite bar, conveniently where their friends worked, was hosting a big Hogmanay bash to mark going into their twentieth year. It was hard to imagine the bar being there that long. Well, maybe not when you looked at its fixtures and fittings: they didn't look like they'd been updated since opening.

The catch was: you had to go as an 90s icon. Dani was planning to recycle her monkey outfit from years ago and bung a red, heart-shaped tag around her neck. *Boom*. Beanie Baby.

'Shit,' Ashley huffed to no one in particular.

'What?' Kirsty asked, looking for the issue.

'Nothing, it's okay.'

'Nah, tell us. Need to be somewhere?' Dani guessed.

Ashley breathed out slowly, engulfing herself in white air. 'Hazel and I were going together and now I'll be a Garth without a Wayne.'

'Ah,' Dani said, not sure if she should console Ashley or offer alternatives.

'That's a toughie,' Kirsty concluded.

Silence filled the air as much as their foggy breath. No one spoke until they reached the bottom of the hill, where the road forked towards the flagpole or down to the golf course. Without a word they all instinctively took a sharp left. No one wandered near the golf course at this time of day.

'Do you think Hazel will still go?' Kirsty asked, her voice unsure.

Ashley looked like she'd just been whacked over the head with one of the putting flags. 'Surely not.'

'Had you not considered it?'

Dani kept out of it. The less she said about Hazel, the better.

'I guess, but no one would be that gallus. Surely? Bar Orama is my place. Our place.'

'Still.'

'Shit.'

Silence again. Kirsty exchanged a quick look with Dani, cringing. She'd put her foot in it.

'The place will be so packed you won't even notice,' Dani said, knowing fine well it was a lie. Bar Orama was tiny. You could barely avoid a fart, never mind a person.

Ashley said nothing, just gave Dani a half-assed smile.

'Can't you text her? Like, test the waters?' Kirsty asked with a shimmy of her shoulders.

'Dunno,' Ashley replied, sighing the word more than saying it. 'She texted *Merry Christmas* and I replied. If I ask her if she's going, does that not start to sound like I want a conversation? Or even worse, for her to actually come?'

The words made Dani's heart flutter. So things were definitely over between them? She'd got the impression from Trip it might not be so cut and dried.

'You're right,' Kirsty agreed. 'Leave it and let fate take its course.'

As they rounded the corner of the path the chatter and laughter from a large crowd was obvious. And yet, there were no people to be seen. The tree line hid the park beyond and Glasgow's skyline was nothing but pinholes against the black sky. Even the stars were skipping tonight.

'Is there something on?' Kirsty asked, craning her neck.

'Not that I know of,' Dani replied.

Up here, they were more exposed and the chilly air nipped at Dani's skin. No doubt her cheeks were rosy and her nose glistening.

'Whatever it is, sounds fun,' Ashley said, also trying to peer through the trees.

It didn't take long for them to reach the bottom of the hill, but the source of the noise was still nowhere to be found. The occasional person had passed them with a friendly *hello* or *Merry Christmas*, but nowhere near enough people to be making such a racket.

'Do you think we should be worried?' Kirsty asked, only half-joking.

Dani sped up, managing to gain a few metres on her sister and friend. It wasn't until she properly crested the hill that she saw it.

The boating pond had frozen over and the people of Glasgow's Southside had flocked to enjoy it. Those that weren't skating (or what resembled skating, most only had on boots) were sledding on the muddy hill leading down to it.

The atmosphere was alive with happiness.

Just being near it was like walking through a force field. You couldn't help but smile too.

'Oh my God, guys,' Dani called over her shoulder.

'What is it – oh wow,' Kirsty cooed.

'That's insane,' Ashley added.

Dani couldn't remember it ever freezing over before.

'Can we go play?' she asked, not waiting for an answer. There was no way she was missing out on this. It could be once in a lifetime.

She left the path and crossed the grass, not worrying how muddy her boots got. There was no time to waste.

Up close it was even more magical. The entire pond was frozen solid, the usually mobile artwork in its centre locked in time.

Her first thought was to wonder where the ducks had gone. Did they go in trees? It was too stupid a question to ask out loud. She made a mental note to look it up when she got home.

'Coming?' Dani asked.

Kirsty pulled her phone from her pocket. 'I think Rhona will be back soon, so I'll pass.'

'Do you think it's safe?' Ashley asked, eying the ice with lashings of uncertainty.

Dani skimmed her eyes over the pond. 'Doesn't look like anyone's gone in. Come on, it'll be okay.'

'Have fun, girls,' Kirsty said with a smile, leaving before Dani could protest.

She was going whether Ashley joined her or not.

Still, she toed the edge of the ice with trepidation.

A woman on actual ice skates whizzed past.

'Let's go to the quiet end,' Dani said, hoping Ashley would follow her.

Away from the crowds was much better. There were only the three giant, plastic ducks to keep them company, all frozen at odd angles like they were trying to break free.

Again, Dani toed the ice.

It felt okay.

She grinned at Ashley as she leaped onto the ice. Breaking through wasn't the problem. The two yards she slid was the issue. She windmilled her arms and was grateful when she came to a halt.

'Is it safe?' Ashley asked, arms crossed as she watched Dani from the safety of the path.

'As houses.' She tapped her foot to prove the point and nearly slid again. These were not the boots for ice. She extended a hand in Ashley's direction.

'Okay. I trust you.' Ashley smiled coyly as she stepped onto the ice, managing to keep her balance a heck of a lot better than Dani. Slowly, shuffling like a heavy penguin, she made her way to Dani.

Not even a foot away she slipped, only to hold onto Dani for purchase.

'I've got you,' Dani assured her, holding not just Ashley's forearms, but her gaze too.

For a moment it was just the two of them. The noise of the world filtered to nothing as Dani's vision centred on Ashley.

As if to cement the memory forever, the universe added the ultimate Christmas gift: snow.

It was light at first, then huge flakes fell, resting on Ashley's hair, shoulders, and nose like fluff balls.

Dani tilted her head skyward and stuck her tongue out.

'Emember when -e used o do is as ids?' she said, only managing half the syllables she intended.

'Es,' Ashley giggled as she joined in.

They were barely kids, mind. Fourteen or fifteen maybe. It felt like lifetimes had passed since then. Not just twenty years. If only teenage Dani could see her now.

'Did you catch one?' Ashley asked, lowering her head. Her hands stayed locked around Dani's arms.

'I think so.' She kept her grip on Ashley as she watched the skater whizz by, a good distance from them this time. She was definitely a professional. It was the 360° spin that gave it away. 'This is amazing, eh?'

'Has it ever done this before?'

'Not that I can remember.'

They locked eyes again and a snowflake settled on Ashley's nose. She giggled, stepping back to shake the flake, only to lose her footing.

It happened in slow motion. Soon, her legs were gone from under her and she was tumbling back, taking Dani with her.

They landed with a thud.

'You okay?' Dani asked, slightly winded from landing on Ashley.

She winced. 'Yeah, I'm fine.'

Through all that and Ashley was still holding on, despite Dani now being between her legs, their faces now just inches apart.

She had to kiss her: the moment was too perfect. She gulped, calling on all her courage.

Just as she was about to close her eyes, though:

'Why did you lie about kissing me?' Ashley blurted, looking like she instantly regretted asking.

'Huh?'

'In Ibiza, you said you were too drunk to remember the night before. Trip said you told her we kissed.'

Dani pushed herself upright, allowing Ashley's words to filter through as she sat on the ice with a fresh thump. God, it was freezing. Ashley mirrored her position. Just two girls sitting on a frozen boat pond. One of them so dumbfounded she couldn't speak.

'Why didn't you say you remembered?' Ashley asked again, her voice less certain this time.

Dani brushed at the snowflakes settling on her knee, buying time. 'Does it matter?'

Ashley's eyes flashed with agitation. 'Of course it matters. I finally get the balls to kiss you – okay, I was wasted,' she exclaimed, flapping her arms about, 'but it meant a lot to me. Then the next day you acted like nothing happened.'

'I wasn't – look, it doesn't matter,' Dani grunted, slowly getting to her feet. Storming off wasn't an option; she had to take it easy unless she wanted a repeat performance and a bruised arse.

Why bring this up now? The past was the past. Ashley didn't need to know every little nuance of her emotional baggage. It would only scare her off.

Ashley shuffled after her. 'Dani, please, let's just talk.'

'There's nothing to talk about.'

'Just tell me why you lied.'

An eternity later, Dani was finally back on the pavement surrounding the pond. It had felt slippy before, but compared to the temporary ice rink it was solid. She picked up speed.

'Dani,' Ashley pleaded, taking her by the elbow.

She pulled herself free. 'Ash. Just drop it, okay?'

'As if. Now I really need to know. There must be a reason

you've held back all this time. Waiting to see if you got a better offer?'

Dani didn't bother to answer such a stupid question. What should have been an unforgettable moment had descended into chaos.

She couldn't tell Ashley the truth. It was too much. Who would want to be with someone so messed up? She already knew Dani better than anyone else, was that not enough? Why did she expect access to her deepest darkest thoughts as well?

'Dani, just stop walking will you? I want to talk.'

'Yeah, well, I don't.'

'Jesus. Why are you overreacting like this?'

'I'm going home.'

'That sounds like a good idea.'

'Merry Christmas, Ash.'

At the fork in the path they went their separate ways and Dani held her breath, scared tears might fall before she even reached the exit to the park.

Merry fucking Christmas, indeed.

22

'Out tonight?' Mum asked, taking a seat on the sofa opposite Ashley's. She'd just made a fresh brew, and although Ashley had said no to one, now she could see it her mind had changed. Who the heck said no to tea? Decisions were not her forte right now.

'I think so,' Ashley replied with a sigh.

'You don't sound too excited.'

She'd reluctantly sourced a new costume: Baby Spice, from the popular 90s band the Spice Girls. Possibly weird to go without accompanying band members, but the look was easy to pull together and her hair was easy to style into bunches. Job done.

'It's just complicated.'

'Hazel?'

Ashley winced internally. Mum had barely said her name in the last few weeks, but every time she did it made Ashley tense with guilt. It was one thing dealing with her own problems, but a whole other when family was involved. Mum had liked Hazel: they'd got on. She'd even helped

Mum sort space for Fraser's birthday bouncy castle in the spring. No mean feat when an azalea has to be moved.

'And the rest.'

Without looking she could feel Mum's face shift. 'Want to talk about anything?'

'Not particularly. I need to go sort my outfit.'

She left before Mum could ask more questions and lumbered up the stairs to her bedroom, where she flopped onto the bed.

Dani hadn't spoken to her since Christmas Day, despite a few messages. Ashley had bitten her tongue, though, and resisted the urge to be snippy. Dani could be huffy all she wanted. She'd quiz Trip tonight. A few shots and Trip would be easy to get info out of. She would be a terrible spy.

Ashley traced the lines of the wallpaper on her ceiling with her eyes. The place hadn't been redecorated since the 80s and the strips were starting to curl at the edges, making the seams obvious.

She shifted, trying in vain to get comfy, springs digging into her back and arms. The sofa bed was horrendous to sleep on: that felt like punishment enough for her self-inflicted relationship crisis. The room was anything but comforting, too. Most of her possessions had gone to Waverley Gardens when she moved out but, given her current predicament, the mundane ones had migrated back: perfume, toiletries, her jewellery box.

The place could do with a freshen up. It was only natural the paper would start parting at the seams after so long without adequate TLC. She knew how it felt. A fresh start would be ideal. *New year, new me.* That's what people always said.

She grabbed her phone from the dresser and checked

Messenger, despite having no notifications. Still nothing from Dani.

She hadn't planned on asking her about the kiss. In fact, there was a moment, a spark in the air, like Dani was going to kiss her right there and then on the pond. She should have kept her mouth shut. Instead she had to blurt out a stupid question and ruin the whole thing.

Still though, it lingered. Why had Dani lied?

It niggled even more given how evasive Dani had been. What was she hiding?

There was a message from Kirsty, asking if she was still coming. At least one Hamilton was still speaking to her.

Apparently, Dani was closing the cafe but would be home by six. Did she want to just come round then and they could all get ready together?

Did Dani want that, or was Kirsty taking control?

Irrelevant. She couldn't avoid Dani, so why not? It would be better than breaking the ice in Bar Orama.

Ashley fired off a quick reply saying she'd be there, then dumped her phone onto the bed.

She'd held off going into Café Odyssey. She didn't want to press Dani for an answer, but breaking the tension was paramount. Would she be huffy tonight, or act like nothing had happened?

She checked her watch. Four o'clock.

Weird to do that, or not?

Maybe Trip would join her, make it seem more casual. She'd slowly forgiven her for the Dani fiasco. Not entirely, but the hatchet was buried enough to allow conversation. Maybe now was a good time to finally put it fully behind her. No one wanted to go into the new year with grudges.

She fished her phone from the bed and hit call.

'Ashleeey!'

'Hey, Trip. How are ya?'

'So-so.' The sound of outside filled the line.

'Everything okay?'

'Always. What can I do for you?'

She'd heard kids more convincing with their lies for playing truant. 'I wondered if you wanted a coffee, but you sure you're okay?'

Trip huffed into the phone. 'Don't laugh.'

'Okay.' Ashley smiled, already on the edge.

'I'm lost.'

'Lost? How can you be lost? Where are you?'

Indistinguishable words prefaced Trip's reply. 'If I knew that I wouldn't be lost!' She punctuated her sentence with a chuckle but panic laced her words.

'When you say lost . . . how lost?' Ashley kept her tone neutral, unsure how serious the issue was.

'Okay, so, I know where I am cause of my phone, but I don't know how to get back. There's no trains and I can't find a bloody bus that goes to the city centre. And some jakie told me they all end in thirty minutes, but I dunno if that's true or not. He'd clearly already been on the bev.'

There was no point asking how or why just yet. 'So, where are you?'

'Milton of Campsie.'

It rang a bell. A very distant one, at least – geographically as well as internally. 'Where the heck is that?'

'Arse end of nowhere.' Another huff. 'Way out the north of Glasgow.'

'What are you doing there?'

'Things.'

'Trip.'

'I was at the Polo last night and—'

Ashley cut her off. She'd heard enough. Trip could explain more later. 'I'll come get you.'

'Are you sure?' Not even the hint of protest, just relief flooding from every pore.

'Yeah, course. I've got nothing better to do.'

MILTON OF CAMPSIE really was miles away. It took Ashley nearly an hour to get there. She'd still been hoping to call by Café Odyssey later, but there was no chance now. She'd need to wait and see Dani at her flat.

The village was tiny and picturesque, with old sandstone houses and lots of trees. She could see Trip's predicament, though: Ashley had only passed two shops and a church so far. There wasn't much else to the place. On a day like today it would be early doors for transport.

She turned onto the unassuming street her iPhone was directing her to and was greeted with a soggy and sad Trip.

Two seconds later she was in the car, no doubt soaking Ashley's seat.

'Aw, Jesus. Thanks, pal,' she said, running a hand through her sodden locks.

'Trip, what the hell? How did you end up here?'

'I met this girl in the Polo. Elle? Ella? Something like that. And I guess I wasn't paying proper attention to how the long the taxi was back to hers.'

'I'll say. You don't even know her name? Trip!' Ashley jokingly scolded.

'What?' Trip yelped. 'She had a good time. We both had a good time.'

'Oooh! Going to see her again?'

'As if. Not if she lives out here. That's some commute.'

'Poor Elle, Ella, Eloise. Snubbed because of her postcode.'

'I've heard worse excuses.'

'You've said much worse.'

Trip leaned her head against the headrest and closed her eyes, a smile creeping onto her lips. 'I owe you big time. I thought I was going to be stuck here for Hogmanay. I was this close to going back to hers,' she said, signalling the tiny distance with her fingers.

'Did Kirsty call you?'

'It's not cancelled, is it?' Trip asked, springing to attention. 'I was trying to save battery and not look at my socials.'

'No, no, don't worry. She wants us to have a drink at hers, get ready there.'

'Phew,' Trip sighed, a hand on her chest. 'I'm really looking forward to tonight. Can't see in the new year without doing something.'

'Too right.' Ashley took a deep breath, kidding on she was focused on joining the motorway. 'So, heard from Dani recently?'

'Nope. How come?'

Ashley shrugged. 'No reason.'

'Ohh, has something happened between you guys?'

'Not in the way you think.'

'Ah.'

'We've kind of fallen out.'

'Shit. How come?'

Ashley chewed on her cheek. 'Do you know why Dani lied about kissing me in Ibiza?'

Trip squirmed in her seat. 'It's really not my place to say.'

'But you do know?'

'Yeah.'

Ashley kept her eyes on the road. Thankfully the weather wasn't bad. The sky was heavy and laden, but no snow or rain. Yet. 'You owe me big time for today. How about a little clue?'

Trip fidgeted again. 'Honestly, Ash. It's not my place. And I think I've done enough damage with my big mouth this year.'

'Is it something bad?'

'It's personal.'

'Dani-personal, or something to do with me?'

'Dani-personal.' Trip fiddled with her thumb ring. 'Look, if Dani wants to tell you she will. It's, look, okay, you'll get it if I tell you this. It's to do with her dad.'

Fuck. That explained the reaction. Shit. Shit. Shit. How was she to know, though? 'Ah. Okay. I'll drop it.'

'Thanks.'

Silence filled the car as Ashley's brain whirred into action. It didn't matter what Dani's reasons were now, Ashley couldn't push it. If she'd had the slightest clue she wouldn't have asked in the first place.

Guilt twisted her inside into knots. SHIT.

She'd have some making up to do tonight.

'Got your costume ready for tonight?' Trip asked, breaking their bubble of peace.

'Yep, Baby Spice. You?'

'Brendan Fraser from *The Mummy*.'

Ashley whistled through her teeth. 'Wow. You are going to kill it tonight.'

Trip's face contorted into the definition of smug. 'I know, right? It's going to be mega.'

'So, you'll come to Kirsty's first?'

'Course.' Trip looked at her watch. 'In fact, if you swing by mine I can grab my stuff and just shower at Kirsty's.'

'Deal.'

Trip drummed on the passenger dash, excited energy taking over. 'So: going to steal a New Year's kiss?'

'I should be so lucky.'

'It'll be fine between you two. A few drinks and all will be forgotten.'

Ashley half-smiled and kept her eyes on the Ford Focus cutting across the lanes, sending a fan of slush their way.

Trip was right, though: a few drinks and the tension would ease. Hogmanay wasn't the time for carrying baggage. Tonight, no matter what happened, Ashley was getting her kiss.

23

'Takeaway only now,' Dani said, not even bothering to look up from the cake she was plating up.

'Actually, it was you I was hoping to see.'

Dani's head snapped up to place the familiar voice.

Hazel.

'You finish soon, yeah?' Hazel continued when Dani failed to make anything past a squeak.

She mentally pulled herself together. 'Yeah, well, I need to get these out and clean, but yeah. Door is getting locked in two minutes.'

Hazel nodded. 'Cool, I'll just go take a seat. See you in a bit.' With that she was off, through the doorway and into the seating area.

The fuck?

As if only just realising what was happening her heart sprung to life, rattling furiously against her ribs.

Why was Hazel here?

She fished her phone from her back pocket. No missed calls or texts. Ashley would have warned her if she'd known.

Although, Dani had done a grand job of distancing herself this week.

She was going in circles with what to tell Ashley. Honesty was always the best policy, but was it really necessary when it was in the past? Especially when it was so bloody heavy and depressing? Dani had worked hard to move on. Yes, it would help Ashley understand her reluctance all these years, but aside from that, shouldn't you be judged on the merits of your present and not the skeletons of your past?

On the advice of her therapist she'd drafted Ashley a letter, explaining the whole sorry mess. It was meant to be cathartic, for Dani's eyes only, but she'd kept it in her top drawer, wondering if actually giving it to Ashley might help her see sense and leave Hazel.

But it was never meant to be read. And breaking up a couple was never an option.

Things were different now, though. Would opening up to Ashley help or hinder their fledgling relationship? She deserved answers.

Dani plonked the final piece of carrot cake onto a plate. The couple it was going to had been in all afternoon, and despite Dani saying they'd be turfing everyone out in fifteen minutes they'd insisted on a final hurrah. So much for doing takeaway only and getting a quick finish.

She made herself an espresso and considered making something for Hazel, but had second thoughts. She didn't want to encourage her to stay longer than needed. Hopefully, this was a flying visit. Although the way she'd made herself comfy next door didn't scream haste.

She downed the coffee in one swift move.

It was four fifty-nine. Who would argue about sixty seconds on Hogmanay? Dani passed through the kitchen, which had stopped serving food an hour ago, and found Mum at the sink, giving her hands a final wash.

'Looking good in here. That you done?' Dani asked, not breaking her stride.

'Oh, aye! I'll help you clean now. Just table six to go?'

'Thereabouts.'

As she pushed the double doors to the serving area open Hazel visibly flinched, her muscles stiffening as she sat straighter.

Dani shot her a thin-lipped smile and pumped her eyebrows as if to say *with you in a min*.

The layout of the café could be a pain in the arse when you were on your own. There was no other way to get from the bar and cake fridge to the customer side. It was a trek and a half cutting through the kitchen, seating area, and then back to Dani's domain. Thank God her cousins were usually here to serve.

She retrieved her tray and gave them to table six, reminding them they only had ten minutes to scoff it.

Hazel didn't take her eyes off her.

'What's up?' Dani asked, trying to sound unfazed. She didn't bother to take a seat.

'Sit down,' Hazel urged calmly.

There goes that plan. Dani pulled the seat out, trying her best to keep her nerves at bay. It was impossible, though. Her mind was running through the ten thousand reasons for Hazel's visit, each a blinding flash of possibility.

'So,' Hazel began. She looked more nervous than Dani felt. Bags lined her eyes and her skin looked blotchy. 'How are you?'

The question threw Dani. It was the last thing she'd expected Hazel to ask. 'Erm, okay, I guess. Looking forward to getting home. You?'

Hazel shrugged. 'Been better.'

The sound of the chattering couple and busy forks filled the air.

'Do you need me for anything?' Dani asked, wishing she'd worded the question better. But all she wanted was for Hazel to leave so she could get home and sink a beer.

'Have you seen Ashley lately?'

How to answer? Mum walked through the double doors with the broom and instantly caught Dani's eye. She did her best to mould her face into something that said *everything's fine.*

'Erm, yeah. I saw her on Christmas Day for a bit.'

'She okay?'

'Yeah. I think so. We didn't really chat.'

'No?' For such a short word, Hazel's tone gave it a thousand layers.

'Not, like, because, we were—' Dani coughed, shoving her nerves into her chest, damning further rambling. 'We went for a walk. With Kirsty.'

'Ah.'

'So, yeah. She's okay, from what I know.'

Hazel thought for a moment, avoiding Dani's eye contact.

Couldn't this have been a text or private message? Anything but this awkward shitshow.

'She's not mentioned me at all, then?'

'She's kinda kept to herself, if I'm honest.'

'Hmm.' Hazel sat forward, setting her clasped hands on the table. 'Can I just be frank with you?'

'Of course.'

'I don't know what is or isn't going on with you guys, but I love Ashley. You know that—'

'Of course.'

'—I need her back, Dani.'

Dani nodded, her lips pursed. 'I don't know what you want me to do about that.'

'I know her leaving me had something to do with you.' She lightly raised a hand off the table to stop Dani protesting. 'I just need you to be honest with her, tell her nothing can happen. Put in a good word for me.'

'A good word for you?' A little snort of laughter escaped, but it could have been worse. Her first reaction would usually have been a belly laugh.

Hazel blushed. 'I know we've never seen eye to eye. But, look, you could have anyone. I've seen you in action on a night out. I need Ashley. You see that, right?'

Dani's insides itched with second-hand embarrassment. Hazel was one step away from getting on her knees and begging.

Mum passed their table with a quick glance, beelining for the couple and telling them their time was up. Surprisingly, they went with little protest, and it wasn't long before it was just the three of them remaining. Dani was glad this wasn't a normal shift. Usually there would still be a few kitchen staff and servers closing the place down. This conversation didn't need an audience.

Before Dani could deter her with another reassuring look, Mum was at the table.

'You girls okay?'

'Yeah, just finishing up,' Dani replied.

Mum gave a knowing look. 'Right, well, I need your help in five. You know I can't be late tonight. Five minutes, okay?'

She had nowhere to be but at home with a glass of chilled prosecco and her stepdad knew better than to touch that, no matter how late she was. What a gem that woman was.

Dan sighed, wondering how best to tie this up. 'I get why you want my help. Ash is my best friend, after all, but it has to come down to her. She makes her own decisions. If you want her back, you need to talk to her.'

Wait. Was that really the encouragement she wanted to give? No, don't go talk to Ashley. Not yet. Not when Dani hadn't had a chance to talk to her. *Shit.* Too late to backpedal.

Hazel puffed out her cheeks with a long, low sigh. She reclined in her seat.

Just take the fucking hint and leave!

'I know you're right,' she said, poking at a mark on the table, 'but it's easier said than done. How do I get her back, Dani?'

Jesus Christ. Did she want her hand held through this? 'I have no idea. Given my track record with dating Ashley, I think I'm the last person you should ask.'

'You dated?'

'Yeah, when we were teenagers.' Dani's voice lifted, as if she was unsure herself. Had Ashley never mentioned it?

Hazel's eyes narrowed. 'She said nothing had ever happened between you guys.'

Ah. Shit.

'It was nothing. Just two freshly out lesbians, experimenting. It was no good. We're better off as mates.' Dani's subconscious grabbed her megaphone, wondering what the chuffing hell she was feeding into Ashley's web of lies.

'Was it for long?'

Dani shrugged as sweat bloomed across the back of her neck. 'Honestly, I don't really remember. Just fooling about.'

That didn't look like the right thing to say. Hazel's muscles stiffened.

'So, something did happen.'

'Yeah, like twenty years ago.' Dani's cheeks burned red. Where was Mum? If only she could catch her eye and find an excuse to end this shitshow.

'Nothing since?'

'Nothing,' Dani lied, with a slow shake of her head.

Hazel chewed on her cheeks, still showing no signs of leaving. 'Do you want something to happen?'

Holy fuck-a-moly. Dani's mouth flapped open once, twice.

'So, that's a yes.' Hazel answered for her.

The jig was up. Why bother lying? 'Yeah. I'm in love with her.' All this time bottling her emotions and the sentence came out so easily, you'd think she said it every day.

The smallest puff of air could have tipped Hazel over. Her face was emotionless, her body rigid. 'So the truth finally comes out.'

'No sense in lying. But if Ashley wants you, I understand that. I want you to know I've never acted on it. Never. And certainly not when you guys were together.'

'What's weird is, I believe you.' Hazel considered her next question. 'Does Ashley know?'

'I've never told her.'

'Let's keep it that way.' Was that a threat or a menacing way of giving advice?

As if sensing the tension, Mum appeared out of nowhere. 'Sorry, Hazel. I really need to get going. I have tickets for a Hogmanay bash at The Fabled Lion tonight.'

Hazel's face lifted, sweetness and light filling her features. 'Of course; no problem. See you, Dani.'

Her chair squeaked as she stood but Dani stayed seated. What was she meant to do? Shake the woman's hand or something?

With a piss-poor wave she was off and Dani let out a loud sigh of relief.

'What was that about?' Mum asked as she locked the door.

'Ashley.'

'Well, I guessed that! What about Ashley?'

'She wants her back.'

'What's that got to do with you?'

'I think she sees me as an obstacle to that happening.'

'Anything I should be worried about?'

'Not much we can do, if it is.'

Mum's brow furrowed. 'I've got some whisky in the office. Let's have a drink as we clean; we can chat once we're done.'

Mums. They always knew what to do.

'HONEY, I'M HOME!' Dani called into the flat as she swerved into her room. The door was closed. Weird.

She soon found out why.

A chorus of *hello*s from various rooms was drowned out by Dani walking into a half-dressed Ashley in her bedroom. 'Whoa, whoa, sorry!' she yelped, backing out with a hand over her eyes.

She wandered through to the kitchen to find Trip leaning against the kitchen counter, beer in one hand, phone in the other.

'Why did no one say Ashley was in my room?'

'Late Christmas gift,' Trip replied with a smirk.

Dani blushed. 'But seriously, what's going on?'

'Kirsty's wanting us to get ready together.'

Dani looked at Trip's ensemble. Untucked blue shirt,

jeans, trainers. Wasn't a 90s icon she was aware of. 'And you are?'

'I'm waiting to get a room.'

'Ah.'

'Beer?'

'I'll get it. Where's my sister?'

'In her room. With Rhona.'

The look Trip gave suggested they might be a while yet. At least someone was having a good day.

The buzzer sounded and Trip dashed into the hall. 'That'll be Izzy.'

Dani put the beer bottle into the opener on the fridge and pulled the cap off with a satisfying hiss. She glugged back half the bottle before a sharp pain in her stomach made her stop. Thankfully, she managed to burp before Izzy's excited squealing filled the hall. Two seconds later she was in the kitchen giving Dani a hug.

Tall, blonde, classically beautiful: Izzy could wear a bin bag tonight and still turn heads.

Dani always felt like a troll in her presence.

Not that it mattered. She was Kirsty's best friend and Dani always felt relaxed around her. Had done since they met, when Izzy had briefly worked in Café Odyssey.

'Dani! Long time no see!' Izzy exclaimed, dumping her bag on the sofa. 'How the Dickens are ya?'

'Good, good. Tired from work, but okay.'

'I've got something that will help that,' she replied, ducking into her bag to produce a bottle of tequila.

Trip punched the air with excitement. 'Izzy! Always my favourite,' she joked.

'Shots, Miss Hamilton?'

After the day she'd had, the bottle would be better. 'Oh, go on then, you've twisted my arm.'

She was so focused on Izzy pouring stomach-churning measures that Dani didn't see Ashley enter the room until she was right behind her.

Her heart stopped dead before rushing all her blood south.

Fuck.

Ashley looked incredible.

There was no point hiding the way Dani's eyes dragged up Ashley's body. It was done before she could process it.

If she were a cartoon, Dani would have bulging eyes popping out of her head and she'd be wolf whistling.

The sneak peek she'd got before didn't do it justice.

Ashley had on a form-fitting pink dress with white trainers and knee-high socks. She'd finished the outfit by styling her hair into two cute bunches.

She was anything but cute, though.

Ashley was smoking hot.

Wow. Wow. Wow.

Dani needed a cold shower, not tequila.

'Dani,' Trip said, waving her hand in front of Dani's face. 'Your tequila. Ashley, want one?'

'Sure, why not?' Ashley agreed, slotting into place beside Dani at the counter.

'You look incredible,' Dani blurted. She ignored the quiet titter of laughter from Izzy.

'Thank you,' Ashley replied, her cheeks now the same colour as her dress.

The four of them clinked glasses before licking salt off their hands, downing the shot, and sucking on a wedge of lime. Dani grimaced. Didn't matter how often you did it: tequila was a bastard to drink.

She put the glass on the counter and turned to Ashley. 'Can we have a quick chat? In private.'

'Oi, oi!' Trip whooped.

'Not like that,' Dani assured her, never taking her eyes from Ashley's.

'Yeah, sure.' Her eyes narrowed with a flash of nerves.

'Nothing bad,' Dani said, leading the way to her room. 'Okay, well, maybe.'

'What?' Ashley replied in a squeak.

'Look, just take a seat and I'll explain.'

Ashley did as commanded and Dani closed the door. She puffed out her cheeks, psyching herself up. 'I had a visitor at the café, just before I closed.'

'A visitor?'

'Hazel.'

Ashley's face fell. 'What did she want?'

'She wants you back, Ash.'

'And what? You're going to help her?' She rolled her eyes.

'To be fair, I think that's exactly what she wanted me to do.'

Ashley grunted in response, her jaw tensed so hard she might break a tooth. 'What did you say?'

Dani shrugged as she leaned her back against her dresser. 'That you were the one to talk to, not me.'

'And was that it?'

'I guess.'

'You guess?'

If the tequila could work its magic about now, that would be great. A little courage would go a long way. Dani scratched the back of her neck. 'She asked if anything had ever happened between us, and if I had feelings for you.'

Ashley lifted her head and Dani couldn't tell if she was mad or shocked. 'And you said?' she asked, low and slow.

'She put me on the back foot! I didn't know what you'd

told her.' Dani rambled as she started to pace. Heat rose up her neck.

'So, you said?' Ashley repeated, even slower than before.

'The truth, obviously!'

Had she just admitted that she had feelings, or was it not obvious? She'd never actually said it out loud to Ashley. Everyone in the group had heard her utter the words but Ashley.

'How did she take that?' Ashley asked, her eyes just slits once more.

'She told me not to tell you.'

'Not tell me what?'

'That I love you.' The air in the room grew still and Dani fought to right things. Shame damage control was never her talent. 'Oh yeah, by the way, *nota bene*, that's a thing. Has been for a while.' Dani stopped her pacing and studied Ashley. She was as stunned as a deer in headlights. Dani couldn't even see her chest move. Was she even breathing? 'Jesus, say something, Ashley.'

'Okay.'

'Okay?'

'I'm, just, like, can I—'

'Dani!' Kirsty shouted, barging into the room. 'Izzy, wants to kn—am I interrupting something?'

'What happened to knocking?' Dani snapped.

'Sorry, excited,' Kirsty replied with an exaggerated pout.

'Look, it's cool,' Ashley said, standing up. 'We'll talk later.'

Dani thumped the top of Kirsty's arm. 'Thanks.'

'Ow,' she whined, rubbing at her sore spot. 'Get your outfit on. We need to drink.'

She'd never agreed with her sister more.

24

'Do you want another drink?' Dani shout-whispered into Ashley's ear.

She'd never seen Bar Orama this busy. Halloween was always packed, but nothing like this. Kev was really pushing capacity tonight.

It was a good excuse to stand as humanly close to Dani as possible. She looked cute in her monkey suit, although the tail kept whacking people.

Ashley put a hand on Dani's waist and pulled her closer. 'Go on, then.' She held on for a moment longer. Even just the proximity was enough to settle flutters in her core.

Dani loved her. An admission of feelings would have been enough, but she'd gone straight for the L-word. It was like having her personal firework show. Ashley was on cloud nine. The words fizzed in her chest and made her heart sing, but not just a song: a whole bloody concert. She could live off this vibe for days. Bottle it up and get it on the black market and she'd be a millionaire.

She turned to Izzy as Dani weaved into the crowd. 'You having a good time?'

'Of course!' Izzy replied with a smile. Her lips were doing the right moves but her eyes were flat. Her last break-up had hit hard: Ashley almost felt guilty for feeling so good.

'There's a cute masc at the bar who's been checking you out all night.' It was only eleven o'clock and Izzy had already turned more heads than Ashley had in a lifetime.

Izzy flashed another go at a smile. 'I saw. They're really not my type, though.'

Ashley knew that fine well, but figured a distraction might be in order tonight. She scanned the room for other potential suitors and her heart dropped.

Hazel. Coming through the bar's entrance with Yaz.

Talk about having guts.

'What's up?' Izzy asked, obviously having seen the colour drain from Ashley's face. No doubt her cheeks now matched her socks.

'Hazel at the door. But don't look.'

It was too late: Izzy stole a quick glance. 'Shitting fuck. You going to say hi?'

'I suppose I'd better.' This ruined everything. The whole evening she'd been daydreaming about kissing Dani at the bells, building up her courage, steeling her nerves. Now it was like a bucket of ice cold water had been dunked over her head.

She should have had the sense to look away, but hindsight is a wonderful thing. Her eyes locked with Hazel's through the crowd and the grin that split her face broke Ashley's heart. She gave a little wave in return.

There was nothing. Just the searing disappointment that she wouldn't be able to kiss Dani.

Shit.

A fresh vodka and Coke was thrust in front of her and Ashley instinctively found space that wasn't there before.

Dani wasn't daft.

'What's up?' she asked, concern ghosting her features.

'Hazel,' Izzy replied as she accepted her drink from Dani.

'Here?'

'Just come through the door,' Ashley said, downing half her drink in one swift motion.

'You okay?'

'Ish.'

'Want to go?'

Ashley shook her head. 'It'll be fine.' Famous last words.

'You might want to pop to the loo,' Izzy hissed in her ear.

'Huh?' Too late. Hazel was meandering through the crowd, beelining straight for her, Yaz in tow.

Ashley's muscles stiffened as if someone had zapped with her a stun gun. She braced herself.

'Hey,' Hazel said, smile on full beam.

'Hey,' Ashley replied, trying to match her friendliness.

Yaz stood behind her, like some bizarre bodyguard. Ashley was sure if you could read their thoughts they would be growling at Dani: their eyes never wavered from her. Dani matched their stare with a smug smile.

This was bad.

She trusted Dani to keep things civil, but Yaz was a different kettle of fish. They'd never been anything but lovely to Ashley, but she'd heard snippets of conversation, things she didn't like: snide remarks, put-downs that weren't deserved, mean observations. Sometimes about perfect strangers.

'Been here long?' Hazel asked.

Was everyone just going to stand around and watch

them talk? Ashley wished she could click her trainers together and be transported to anywhere but here. 'Just a couple of hours.'

'Staying for the bells?'

'Of course.' Weird question: this was a Hogmanay party, after all. Then it dawned on Ashley like a punch in the gut: Hazel was nervous. Nervous to talk to her, someone she'd dated for years, been engaged to. Guilt multiplied tenfold. 'I like your outfit,' Ashley added, hoping to ease Hazel's anxiety a little.

'Thanks.' She was dressed in a shirt with blue vertical stripes, white trousers, and a white server's hat, like someone would wear in an American restaurant. Yaz was dressed the same. 'Do you get it? Yaz said no one would know who we were.'

'I think so. Kenan and Kel?'

She glared at Yaz, who was still challenging Dani to a stare-off. 'See! Good Burger, to be exact.'

'Classic.'

'Yeah.'

An uneasy silence filled the tiny space between them. Ashley wracked her brain for an excuse to leave. Her drink was still half full. She could hardly down it and proclaim she needed another.

'Ash, can you help me? I need the loo and you know what this zipper is like,' Dani said leaning close to Ashley but talking loud enough everyone could hear.

A mumbled compliance followed polite excuses from Izzy about needing another drink, and they were off.

Dani's hand laced with hers and Ashley felt the warmth travel up her arm and settle in her chest.

When they finally hit the bar area, Dani didn't turn left to the toilets. Instead she took a sharp right.

'Where we going?' Ashley shouted.

'Time to bust a move.'

Ashley grinned. She didn't need a party to see in the new year: one Dani was more than enough.

The cold air hit like a slap in the face and Ashley felt like a chain had been removed from her shoulders. She had no time to appreciate it, though, as Dani yanked her hand and broke into a run.

'Come on, before Hazel sees us.'

She only slowed down when they were safely round the corner.

Dani stood, hands on knees, wheezing like a broken toy.

'You okay? Got your inhaler?' Ashley asked.

Dani waved a hand between them. 'No.' A deep breath. 'I'm fine. Cold air.'

A few minutes later she straightened herself, her cheeks obviously rosy even in the orange glow of the street lamps above.

'Will I phone a taxi?'

'Tonight? We should be so lucky,' Dani replied, her breath not quite back to normal. 'It's not far, we can walk.'

'Just don't die on me,' Ashley joked, hoping humour would banish the stark reality of the situation. Asthma was no laughing matter.

'Would you miss me?' Dani asked, playfully grabbing at Ashley's side as they walked.

Butterflies tumbled in Ashley's stomach. 'Can't have you declaring your love then karking it.'

Dani winced like she'd just touched something hot.

'What's wrong – you embarrassed?' Ashley gibed, putting on a silly voice.

'A little. I've never said it before. It's a big deal.'

'Now that's a lie.'

'What is?' Dani retorted, grinding to a halt and putting her hands on her hips, oozing mock anger. Her monkey tail swayed in the breeze.

'You have said it before.'

'Nuh-uh.'

'Uh-huh. To me,' Ashley laughed, stabbing a finger to her chest. 'When we were seventeen.'

Dani set off walking again. 'Yeah, well, that hardly counts. Same person and all that. Double jeopardy, innit?'

'So not that much of a big deal?'

'It is, it is. A massive deal. That's what I'm saying: it feels like the first time.'

'I get ya.' Was she meant to say it back now? The words felt like marbles in her mouth. Now wasn't the right time. They'd waited this long; why rush it?

Dani laced her fingers with Ashley's again. 'I hope you don't mind us leaving. I just figured it was awkward as hell for you and Yaz was about two seconds away from tearing my throat open.'

'They're quite imposing, eh?'

'I'll say. If they stared any harder I'd have been dust.'

They walked in silence for a bit, their conversation carrying on without words. Dani's thumb gently stroked Ashley's in rhythm with their steps and Ashley felt desire swell low in her belly. Never had such a simple gesture made her so wet.

'Sorry for being weird on Christmas Day,' Dani said as they climbed the hill past the old Victoria Hospital.

'It's okay.'

'It's not. I shouldn't have snapped at you. I just—'

'It's fine.'

'It's not. No one deserves to be spoken to like that. Especially not you.'

'Well, apology accepted, then.'

'Thanks.'

The opportunity was here to push further, but Trip's warning rang in Ashley's ears. It didn't matter why Dani had pretended to have a blackout. All that mattered was now and this moment, the one where Dani's hand was perfectly slotted with Ashley's.

'Think we'll make it home in time for the bells?' Ashley asked.

Dani gave Ashley's hand a squeeze. 'Guess we'll have to keep an eye out for fireworks.'

Ashley's bag vibrated against her hip so she pulled her phone out: Hazel. She silenced it with a click of a button.

'I'd better text Kirsty, actually, let her know we've headed off,' Dani said, unzipping the front of her monkey suit and producing her phone.

'Dare I ask where that came from?' Ashley asked with a chuckle. Dani didn't have the boobs to nestle hardware between.

She opened and closed the flap of her suit quickly, flashing her sports bra and a hint of bare flesh. Ashley's skin tingled.

'I got Mum to sew me an inside pocket. Nearly lost my phone last time I wore this, so thought I'd play it safe this time.'

'Really? You weren't that drunk last time you wore that.'

Dani pulled a face as she plopped her phone back into its pocket and zipped her suit up. 'Not that you saw. Didn't exactly react well to you and Hazel getting together. I was sick on Rhona.'

'Ew. Yuck,' Ashley responded, pulling a face. 'I mean about the sick, not the Hazel thing.' She was going to ask for further explanation but Dani hurried her along with a change of topic.

'You going to call her back?'

'Nah.'

'Not going to at least text her?'

Ashley grimaced. 'Whose side are you on?'

Dani made a show of skipping as they walked down the side of Queen's Park. Thank God they were nearly at her flat; it was bitterly cold to be wearing next to nothing.

'Just playing devil's advocate. Don't start the new year on a bad note.'

It was a fair point. She fired off a quick text to Hazel saying they'd catch up soon. It was a message drafted in haste, and maybe with less alcohol in her system and her focus more on her words, not the monkey wobbling along the top of a brick wall, she would have said it differently. But it was done now, no going back.

Dani jumped onto the pavement with a thud and in one fluid movement her hand was back in Ashley's.

They'd barely seen a soul on the walk home. Everyone else was probably out partying or crowded round a TV, waiting for the clock to strike twelve. It had to be soon.

'Nearly home,' Dani said as they reached the top of Tantallon Road. 'You must be frozen. I'd offer you my suit but I don't want to be done for indecent exposure.'

Ashley giggled. 'It's fine; we can have a cup of tea when we get in. Warm up.'

'A cup of tea?' Dani bellowed. 'To see in the new year? Never! Can't start things off with a cup of tea . . .' She trailed off, still mumbling away.

'Okay, fair point. I'll need to do something to warm up, though.' X-rated ideas flashed through Ashley's head, providing their own form of central heating.

'A few jumping jacks and you'll be fine. I'll crank the heating up. Just don't tell Kirsty.'

They picked up pace once on Tantallon Road, their destination now excitingly close. Ashley could no longer feel Dani's hand in hers but a quick glance confirmed they were still linked.

It didn't take long to cut along Kilmarnock Road and soon they were at Dani's close door. She fumbled with the keys, her own hands obviously frozen.

Finally, they were inside. Dani took the stairs two at a time. 'Come on, let's get the heating on. If we're quick we might make the bells yet.'

Chet greeted them with a big stretch. 'Hey, Chetty-boy,' Ashley said, crouching down to give his chin a scratch.

Dani wandered off to the front room and by the time Ashley followed she was lolling on the sofa, searching through the channels, looking for a Hogmanay countdown. She settled on one and a large timer in the bottom corner announced there was just five minutes to go.

Ashley stopped at the edge of the sofa. 'I'm going to quickly change,' she said, throwing a thumb in the direction of Dani's room.

'Hold on,' Dani replied, extending a hand to take Ashley's. In one fluid motion she pulled her down to her knee, so Ashley was now straddling her.

Ashley's breath caught.

'You're not going anywhere,' Dani said, her voice breathy.

Their noses were nearly touching as their eyes locked. Ashley didn't dare move for fear of breaking whatever was happening. A smile flickered on Dani's lips as she closed her eyes.

Ashley mirrored her move and soon they were kissing.

Slow at first, then Dani's hands gripped Ashley's bum, pulling her closer. Fresh fervour ramped things to a frenzy. Ashley's nipples stiffened and her core pulsed as Dani's tongue found hers through parted lips.

This was nothing like their Ibiza kiss. That was sloppy and drunk, over before it really ever started.

The walk home had sobered them both. This was like kissing Dani for the first time. Purpose and passion commanded every move.

All the years of imagining this moment didn't have a patch on reality. She'd hung a hat on their teenage kisses, drawing on them for inspiration, desperately trying not to forget every feeling and nuance. But so much had happened in the intervening years. How could it not be different?

Dani's kisses were like gold back then. Now they were platinum. Best of the best.

Their heavy breathing masked the countdown being shouted from the TV.

Ashley shifted position and Dani's hand slid under her dress, coming to rest on the hem of her knickers. Soon, her other hand joined the fun.

This wasn't the time for hanging about.

They'd done twenty years of hanging about.

Tonight was about finally doing what they should have continued doing nearly two decades ago.

Sex with Dani was always fun and exciting. They took their time. Explored and learned together. Stolen chances while parents were out or private moments carved at parties.

Now they were adults, and the experience they'd garnered in the time apart was already evident in the way Dani's tongue worked in rhythm with Ashley's.

Ashley ground her hips, but there wasn't enough to get purchase on: the monkey suit was in the way.

As if reading her mind, Dani's right hand snaked downward, grazing along Ashley's inside thigh to find her knickers again. Ashley shuddered as Dani's thumb ran the length of her centre, only the thin fabric of her underwear keeping them apart.

Outside, fireworks thundered overhead.

A huge bang, worryingly near the window, made them both jump.

Dani stilled her hand. 'Happy New Year.'

'I'll say,' Ashley purred.

Another bang erupted close by.

Dani narrowed her eyes, her mood shifting. 'That sounds super close.'

'Probably kids letting them off by cars. You know what they're like.' Last fireworks night one of the sixth years had got written up by the police for letting a firework off outside Langside Hall and nearly hitting a pedestrian. The sooner shops stopped selling the bloody things to the public, the better.

Another wince-inducing bang made Dani pat Ashley's thigh. 'Sorry to be a bore,' she said, forcing Ashley to stand. 'But I'd better check Chet is okay.'

'Yeah, of course.'

She followed Dani through to her bedroom. 'He's probably under the bed. He always hides there.'

Sure enough, Dani dropped her chest to the ground to find the cat cowering in the corner.

'Do you want me to pop some music on? Ashley asked. 'Drown the sound out?'

'Good idea,' Dani agreed, still lying on the floor. 'My poor baby. It'll be over soon, promise.'

Ashley flipped Dani's laptop open and quickly hopped online. Indecision slowed the process. With a disgruntled huff she clicked on a 'daily mix' and hoped for the best.

Dani had obviously been reminiscing herself, as old-school tunes blasted out her laptop's speakers. New Found Glory serenaded them as Ashley rummaged in her bag for a jumper and joggers. Dani never even noticed her change, causing her to do a double take when she finally rose from the floor.

Ashley slumped onto Dani's bed, getting comfy between her pillows. 'He okay?'

'Yeah, the music's helping,' she replied, climbing onto the bed by Ashley. 'Nice choice, by the way. It's like being seventeen again.'

'Is that all that's bringing you back?' Ashley joked, grabbing a handful of monkey suit and pulling Dani in for a kiss.

She stopped halfway. 'Hold up, I need to get rid of this. It's ridiculous.'

She unzipped the suit and shucked it off her shoulders. Ashley raked her eyes over Dani's exposed upper half. She'd always been a sucker for a sports bra, but Danielle Hamilton in one? There was no hope: she was a goner.

Dani pivoted, shimmying the suit fully off and onto the floor. 'I hope you don't mind,' she said, her voice low once more as she climbed on top of Ashley.

'Not at all.' Ashley ran her hands up Dani's bare thighs and her palms tingled. She'd forgotten how soft Dani's skin was.

Dani leaned over her, grabbing a baseball cap off her bedpost, and popped it on backwards. 'Keep my hair out the way,' she informed, her lips already finding their way onto Ashley's neck.

She groaned in response. Usually she'd be worried

about marks, but screw that. The pulse between her legs wasn't going to let Dani stop anytime soon.

Dani parted Ashley's legs with her knee, quickly finding purchase with her thigh against Ashley's core.

A fresh groan escaped, even more needy and wanton than the first.

'Can these come off?' Dani asked, pulling at the hem of Ashley's joggers.

She didn't need to be asked twice.

25

Dani's chest ached with happiness. Ashley was a thrill like no other: pure dopamine. When Ashley sat up on her elbows and reached round to undo her bra, Dani thought she might actually burst.

This wasn't just sex.

Yes, Ashley looked phenomenal, but she'd seen her fair share of boobs. This was more than a physical connection.

Ever since they'd met, Ashley had scratched a part of Dani's brain no other human could reach. When hormones kicked in and romantic feelings were added to the mix, Dani had never doubted for a second Ashley was her one.

Everything just clicked.

A small part of her wanted to cry with happiness right now, but that would be mortifying. If Ashley knew the whole truth of her reluctance over the years and she became a blubbering mess during sex, it would be game over. Some things you can't recover from.

Ashley didn't need to see the letter. Over time she would open up, give her glimpses when the timing was right. But that letter? It was way too heavy.

Given the first opportunity, she would burn it. There was no use keeping it now: it was surplus to requirement.

Dani took Ashley in once more. She'd imagined this moment a million times, but Ashley exceeded expectation at every turn.

Her body had changed since they were teens. Maybe it was dating a personal trainer. Now her waist curved to sexy hips that hadn't been there before.

Not that it mattered. Ashley could look any goddamn way she liked and Dani would still be attracted to her.

Dani puffed her cheeks out as trailed her eyes south. 'You're beautiful.' She dipped her head and took Ashley's pert nipple into her mouth, gently sucking and biting as Ashley groaned.

Ashley had already been wet on the sofa, Dani could see that much, but she wanted to savour their time together.

She pushed her thigh harder against Ashley's core as she ran circles with her tongue round the stiff bud of her nipple. She gave Ashley's other breast attention with her free hand, the other holding Dani up.

Ashley gripped her bum, pulling her closer.

'I want you inside me,' Ashley groaned.

Dani wasn't giving in that easily.

Instead she traced a line of kisses to Ashley's navel, enjoying the way her muscles stiffened with each touch.

Goosebumps flushed over her skin.

'Do you want to go under the covers – are you cold?' Dani asked.

'No, I want to watch you.'

Dani smiled. Older Ashley was confident.

She resumed at her hip bone, paying it extra attention. She marked a trail of kisses to the waistband of her knickers.

Dani pulled at them with her finger. 'I think these can stay on a while longer,' she teased.

Ashley lifted her hips, disagreement clear.

Dani's natural instinct was to concede but this was an exercise in appreciation. Every inch of Ashley was to be explored and enjoyed. She couldn't waste a moment thinking she'd seen it before. That was the old Ashley. New Ashley deserved attention.

Dani kissed down the lace of Ashley's knickers, ending her journey where she assumed her clit would be. She was already so wet: Dani's own clit stiffened at the thought.

Ashley raised her hips again, inviting Dani to shed the final item of clothing, but it was too soon.

She leaned back on her thighs and lowered her head to just above Ashley's knee before tracing a fresh line of kisses up to Ashley's core. She moaned with every touch and Dani found herself smiling against the soft flesh of Ashley's leg.

This was new territory for Dani. She already felt so close, like she would come with just one touch, and Ashley hadn't done a single thing to her.

With that in mind, she needed a new way to prolong the foreplay.

She straightened and rid herself of her pants before doing the same for Ashley.

'What are you up to now?' Ashley asked, her voice dreamlike.

Dani didn't bother with an answer. Instead, she scooted forward, bringing a thigh over Ashley's, and tilted herself so their cores touched. Ashley cottoned on quickly, arching herself into position so they connected perfectly.

Fuck, that felt good.

They'd barely passed the basics when they were younger.

Dani watched as Ashley's breathing mellowed to long, deep lungfuls. Her eyes were closed as they ground against each other, the heat of their cores sending a swell of desire all the way to Dani's ribs.

Dani pushed down harder, intensifying the pleasure.

She ground into Ashley, rolling their hips in perfect rhythm, creating a fresh wave of want with every brush.

Any more and she might come just from this.

She stopped and leaned back, parting them. Ashley's face creased with disappointment, but Dani knew it wouldn't last long.

She dropped to her knees, bringing her face level with Ashley's slick core. She smiled as she licked her lips, excited for what was to come.

She kissed Ashley's core, the gentlest of touches, like she was kissing her on the cheek.

'Oh God,' Ashley groaned just as a firework exploded on the road outside.

They both ignored it as Dani ran her tongue up Ashley's centre. She tasted divine.

Dani kissed Ashley's clit before sweeping her tongue over it.

Outside, the fireworks took on a new life. Either their mates had turned up or someone had raided a local shop, because every second brought a new bang, still annoyingly loud despite the music.

Tuning out the chaos outside, Dani tended to Ashley with care and precision. She varied her pace and rhythm, hoping all the love and affection that had built inside her over the last two decades could be translated through kisses.

She sucked on Ashley's clit and felt her muscles stiffen.

As predicted, this wasn't going to last long.

Dani slowed her pace, flattening her tongue against

Ashley's hard clit as she swept two fingers to her core. Another loop of the tongue and she slid her fingers into Ashley, instantly feeling her tighten around her.

It only took a few thrusts of her fingers and Ashley came completely undone.

Her hips bucked twice before she put her hand on Dani's cap, urging her to stop.

'Jesus,' she huffed, her cheeks rosy.

Dani met her gaze, still nestled safely between Ashley's legs.

She didn't care what happened next. She would happily crawl into Ashley's arms and fall asleep against her chest. She didn't need to be touched. She just wanted to live in the moment.

They held each other's stare and smiled. If only there was a way to capture this feeling. Old photos, you could look at and be transported back to that moment: Dani would kill to bottle how she was feeling right now.

Happy didn't cover it. There wasn't a word for how alive she felt. She'd always known Ashley liked her, but being in a position where they could actually be together had all too often felt like a pipe dream. Somehow, through what could only be described as magic or divine intervention, Dani had got her shit together enough to be here, right now, between Ashley Davidson's legs, with the promise of a future sitting proudly on the horizon.

Good stuff like this didn't happen to people like her.

This was the stuff of fairy tales and Christmas movies.

'You okay?' Ashley asked, still catching her breath. She cupped Dani's jaw with her hand.

'Golden.' She paused, wondering if she should say what was on the tip of her tongue. Fuck it. Let's start the new year as she meant to go on. 'I love you.'

'Love you too.'

A fanfare played in Dani's head. She spun cartwheels. High-fived the motherfucking sun.

A loud bang made them both jump. 'Sorry to be a damp squib, but I'd better check on Chet,' Dani said, hanging over the edge of the bed and finding her pants. They had all the time in the world: if World War III continued to rage outside, Chet had to take priority.

DANI SHIFTED, reality hitting like sunshine on her face as she blinked awake. She pawed at her phone. Nearly noon. Not bad considering she and Ashley had stayed up until well past two.

Chet had been okay once the worst of the fireworks stopped, and was currently curled up at Ashley's feet.

She gave him a quick pat before sliding back into position. She pulled Ashley closer, her bare skin like velvet against Dani's.

'Mornin.' Ashley greeted her, her voice groggy. She scooped Dani's hand in hers and pulled it to her chest.

'Morning.' Dani kissed her shoulder.

'Sleep okay?' Ashley asked, twisting to face Dani. A new swell of happiness erupted in Dani's chest.

She ran a hand over Ashley's mussed-up hair. 'Very well, thanks. Someone tired me out.'

'Oh, really?' Ashley joked as she ran her hand the length of Dani's waist, settling it on her hip. Dani's skin tingled.

Dani planted a long, slow kiss on Ashley's lips, ignoring how badly she needed to pee until her bladder was screaming louder than her core.

'Need to pee, back in a mo,' she said, scooting down the bed.

Ashley pulled the covers closer around her, her features clouded with deep thought. 'Can we have a quick chat?'

Dani's blood ran cold as she pulled her joggers on. 'When I get back, yeah, no problem.'

'Or now?'

'Now?'

'Just, don't tell Kirsty.'

'Tell her what?' Dani asked, yanking her top on. Any longer and she'd need to dance to stop an accident.

'That we slept together.'

'Okay. Now, I really need to pee.'

She was back in minutes, desperate to know what Ashley was on about.

'That was quick,' Ashley said with a smile, putting her phone on the bedside table, screen down.

Dani perched on the edge of the bed. Did she regret last night? 'Are you – do you – you're okay, yeah?'

Ashley looked perplexed. 'Yeah, why?'

'You still like me, yeah?'

Ashley snorted, lunging forward to take Dani's face in her hands. 'Of course. Sorry. That came out weird cause you were rushing.'

'Well?'

'I just . . . the whole Hazel thing still feels very fresh. I don't want to upset anyone. Can we keep us between us for the time being?'

'Like a dirty little secret?' Dani half-joked.

Ashley moved closer, the cover fully slipping away to reveal her bare upper half. 'Okay, that makes it sound bad. No, of course not. Just, it feels respectful to Hazel to keep to ourselves for a little longer. Do you get what I mean?'

She did. Kinda. 'I think so. I'm fine with that.'
For now.

26

Kirsty was due back from work any minute, but Dani was making it hard to leave.

Her kisses were too good to simply walk away from. You'd need nerves of steel and an unwavering disposition to do that. Ashley had neither. When it came to Dani she was a quivering mess, unable to do anything but listen to the carnal impulses of her brain.

Kirsty wasn't the only thing imposing a time limit, though. She needed to swing by her flat, grab some things. Hazel would be out for another hour: now was the perfect time.

The thought of her coming home early was enough to induce a headache, though. Ashley couldn't bear how awkward that would be.

'I really need to go,' Ashley said, leaning back from Dani. She'd been and put her coat on, returned to say a quick goodbye, and somehow they'd been making out for – she checked her watch – fifteen minutes.

'Just stay,' Dani whined playfully as she traced the lapel of Ashley's coat between her fingers.

'You know I would if I could,' Ashley replied, forcing herself to her feet. It was like elastic bands were woven between them, drawing Ashley back, making it harder to leave the farther away she became.

Dani pouted. 'I know. But I'm still okay to come to yours on Tuesday, yeah?'

'Course.' Ashley rubbed at her temple. 'You got any painkillers? I've got a cracking headache.' Hazel hated taking anything that wasn't 'natural' and there was no way she could wait until she got back to her parents'.

'Top drawer of my bedside. I'll get them,' Dani replied, making to rise. Ashley stopped her with a wave of the hand.

'It's cool, I'll find them. It's on my way anyway.'

To risk another kiss or not? She'd only just broken away. Stuff it. She kissed Dani on the cheek, knowing anywhere else was asking for trouble.

Ashley looked at Dani's bed as she called in past her bedroom. The urge to climb back in and forget her responsibilities was strong. But she needed her stuff. If she didn't do it now, work hours would force her into seeing Hazel for sure.

Her head throbbed with a fresh wave of anxiety.

She opened up Dani's bedside drawer. It was a shambles. Christ on a bike, how did she find anything? Rummaging, Ashley found: money, an old watch, string, pens, receipts, a mini torch, lube, hair ties . . .

She did say bedside, yeah?

Ashley looked over her shoulder at the dresser.

No, she definitely said bedside.

She resumed her search: a gift voucher, a packet of make-up wipes, her blue emergency inhaler, and a decongestant spray. Everything but what she needed.

Further back was just as fruitless. Ashley reached

deeper and pulled the contents forward, hoping to scoop the tablets up in the process.

She tilted her head, looking at the envelope now on the top of all the junk. It had her name on it.

She picked it up.

A sealed white envelope. It was definitely Dani's handwriting. Why would Dani be writing to her?

What could be so important she needed to put it in writing?

'Find them?' Dani asked from the doorway and Ashley jumped so high her head must have nearly touched the ceiling. She stuffed the envelope in her pocket, panicking blindly as her heart rate rocketed.

'Not yet,' she replied, surprised she was a little breathless. 'How do you find anything in there?'

'It's easy,' she said, shoving her hand in and retrieving the tablets a second later. She opened the packet and gave Ashley two. 'You want some water?'

She shook her head. 'I'd better scoot. I can take them at mine.'

Ashley slipped them into her pocket, along with the offending letter, which was already burning a hole in her coat and conscience.

She smiled weakly, certain that guilt was oozing from every pore and Dani would soon cotton on.

She didn't, though. Her eyes flicked from Ashley's to her lips and back again. 'You'd better go or I might change my mind about letting you leave,' she joked.

'Don't. I'd hardly take convincing.' She kissed Dani on the cheek again and made a speedy exit.

'Shit, fuck, shit,' she said, marking every step in Dani's close with a fresh expletive. When she hit the cold air of outside and was safely on the pavement, she rammed her hands in her pockets. It was there. She hadn't imagined being an absolute idiot.

She'd have to return it before Dani noticed. If she was meant to have it, Dani would have given her it.

Her head hurt even more now.

'Ashley!' Kirsty called, suddenly level with her as she passed in the opposite direction.

'Oh, hey,' she replied, snapping back to reality.

'You were in your own wee world there,' Kirsty said with an amused smile. 'You been at ours?'

'Nah, just on my way to the flat. Picking up some stuff while Hazel is out.'

Kirsty offered a sympathetic smile. 'Ours after? We could get pizza?'

'I can't tonight. Thank you, though.' She totally could, but too many sleepovers at Dani's and her parents would get suspicious.

'Right, well, see you around. I need to get home. Totally bushed.'

Pleasant goodbyes exchanged, they went their separate ways. Could Kirsty see how uncomfortable Ashley was? Her palms were sweating.

Should she tell Dani she'd taken the envelope? No. She could easily return it without Dani knowing.

She'd calmed down slightly by the time she reached her flat in Waverley Gardens, one anxiety-inducing problem replacing another.

Hazel would definitely be out. Ashley knew her schedule like the back of her hand.

If she wasn't, though: a quick hello, grab her stuff, and leave. That's all there was to it. It was only Hazel. No reason to get so worked up.

If only someone would tell her stomach that. It did a flip as she unlocked the close door and entered the building.

She could have sworn they'd added a new level of stairs. They took an age.

Finally on their – her – landing, she took a deep breath and unlocked the front door.

'Hello?' she called. No answer. Every fibre of her being relaxed.

It was strange feeling like a trespasser in her own flat.

The air hummed with cautious energy: she was relaxed, but on edge. This wasn't the flat she knew and loved. It looked the same, but it wasn't hers. It was Hazel's domain and Ashley was just passing through.

No time to waste. She headed to the bedroom and dumped the empty tote bag she'd brought on the bed, intending to take some books back to Mum and Dad's. There was only so many reruns she could watch on TV: she needed time on her own in her room. A little space to be adult Ashley, indulge in her own interests.

She grabbed a few handfuls of pants and put them in the holdall she'd got from the top shelf of the wardrobe. She added a few tops, a pair of trousers, and a dress. No sense in emptying it just to bring all her clothes back when Hazel moved out. The idea stole her breath. She was nowhere ready for the conversation.

Without thinking, she plonked onto the edge of the bed and stared aimlessly at the wall.

What a mess to be in the middle of.

Dani was worth the turmoil, though.

Ish. She would rather be without it, and the thought of hurting Hazel was enough to rim her eyes with tears, but being with Dani was the right option. She couldn't imagine a future with anyone else.

She pulled the letter from her pocket. It would be so easy to read it and put it back.

Naughty.

She examined the seal. Glued down, with no way to pick it apart without tearing it. Maybe she could steam it?

That was bad. But it's human nature to want to know a secret, isn't it? Especially when it's about you.

The flat door clicked open and Ashley's heart leaped from her chest. *SHIT.* Why was Hazel home early?

That's assuming it was her. No one else had a key. Did they?

Oh my God. What if Hazel had moved on? Ashley had. Would certainly make Ashley feel better if that was the case, but what a kick in the teeth.

She stored that thought away, intent on unpacking it later, and what that meant for her and Dani going public. She was fast learning her middle name should have been hypocrite, not Fiona.

Ashley heard the clink of Hazel's keys as she put them in the bowl by the door. She really should say something or Hazel would shit herself, unaware she wasn't alone until Ashley appeared out of nowhere.

She was still holding the letter. This was too much to focus on, too many balls being juggled in the air.

She rammed the letter into the tote bag and shoved under the bed, as if Hazel might know it was stolen contraband if she saw it, before giving her coat a smooth down. She looked okay; presentable. Certainly not someone who'd spent the afternoon having sex with her secret girlfriend.

'Hazel, hi!' she called. 'It's Ashley,' she awkwardly tacked on, in case it wasn't obvious.

Hazel's footsteps stopped in the hall and a moment later

they doubled back. Her grin was wider than the Clyde when she appeared in the doorway.

'Ashley, oh my God, hi.' She stood, looking goofy, with her adorable dimples making Ashley's chest ache more than her head. Actually, she still had to take those tablets.

She stood, aiming for the kitchen, but Hazel took it as an invite for a hug and lunged forward, pulling her into a tight embrace. Ashley returned it, gingerly.

'Hey,' Hazel said again, her voice quieter.

This was weird.

Ashley stepped back and put on her most friendly smile. 'I've got a cracking headache, I just need to take some tablets.' She scooted past Hazel. Was it just her or were the rooms smaller than when she last visited?

Hazel was hot on her heels. 'You here for a while? Will you stay for dinner?'

Ashley was glad she was in the cupboard looking for a glass when she asked. She cringed, like she'd just stood on a plug. 'Not tonight, I'm afraid. Just here to pick up some clothes.'

Hazel's face was sullen when Ashley turned around. She nodded slowly. 'I've not heard from you since Hogmanay. You been busy?'

'So-so. School's just gone back, so . . .' She trailed off, punctuating the sentence with a shrug as she filled her glass with water.

She popped the tablets and wished it was as easy to end awkward chit-chat as it was to get rid of a headache.

'Well, not tonight, but another night?' When Ashley didn't answer straight away she added: 'I miss you.'

Pow, a punch straight to the gut, the knockout blow.

Ashley needed to leave. She emptied the remaining

water from her glass and took her time putting in the dishwasher, knowing if she lied to Hazel's face her own features would give her away. 'Yeah, sure. Work is super busy just now, you know how it is at this time of year, but yeah. I'll message you.' She stood, gasping a little, as if she'd just been diving and come up for air.

'Sounds good.' Hazel smiled.

Silence descended on the kitchen like a deadly smog, making Ashley's chest tight and uncomfortable.

'I'd best be off. Mum needs me to go to the shop,' she lied. Again.

'No worries.'

It felt like she should say something in return, but nothing was coming quick enough. They lingered, caught in an excruciatingly bizarre trap. For a second, Ashley thought Hazel was going to hug her again.

She took a deep breath, kept her eyes fixed on the hall, and walked straight past her.

'See you around,' she called from the bedroom as she grabbed her bag, zipping it up as she walked, half-hopping to use her thigh for leverage to get it closed properly.

See you around? See you around?! *Urgh.*

'Bye, Ash,' Hazel said, flat.

'Bye!' She'd wanted to sound upbeat, but what came from her mouth was far too cheery. Anyone would think she was a presenter on kids' TV.

The flat door closed behind her and she mouthed a silent *fuck*.

Awkward didn't cut it.

It was only when she was on the second floor landing that she realised what she'd left behind.

Dani's letter.

There was no way she was going back now. It would have to wait. Surely Dani wouldn't notice its absence for a day or two?

27

'Hi, Mary,' Dani said, having let herself into the Davidson household and gone straight to the kitchen. If Ashley wasn't there, someone else usually was. It was second nature to go there first when she visited.

'Oh, hi Dani,' Mary replied, cheery as ever. She was decanting leftovers from dinner into Tupperware, presumably to go in the fridge. 'You had your tea?'

'Oh aye, ages ago.' She leaned her forearms on the counter. No point moving: Ashley would be about soon.

'Plenty leftovers if you're hungry.'

'It's cool. Thank you, though.'

'We're going to watch a film anyway,' Ashley added, bang on time. She joined Dani at the counter, choosing to stand at the far side. Any further away and she might as well be in a different room.

'Oh, what film?' Mary asked, her eyes gleaming with excitement.

'Dunno. Some action film Dani picked out.'

'It's got Daniel Craig in it,' Dani said, knowing Mary was particularly fond of the former Bond actor.

Mary took a deep breath, her mouth open in anticipation. 'Oh, it's never his new one, is it? That . . . oh, what's it called?' She snapped her fingers a few times. 'Nope. It's gone.'

Ashley looked at Dani for answers. Her mind was blank. 'I can't remember the title, but yeah, it's his newest one.'

'Oh, it never is,' Mary cooed, hands now on hips as if this was the revelation of the century. 'Watch it down here, will you? Please.'

Dani watched Ashley's muscles stiffen, her right eyebrow twitching. This wasn't Dani's excuse to conjure. She held Ashley's gaze, fighting to keep the smug smile in her heart and not on her lips.

'Yeah, sure,' Ashley conceded.

Dani's inner smile faded. She'd signed up for a night of cuddling and kissing, not sitting in the living room. She wasn't going to see Ashley again for a couple of days. This was worse than dating as teenagers.

'Girls, you've made my night.'

As Mary rushed to the living room to tell Brian about their change of plans, Ashley sulked her way over to Dani's side.

'Sorry. I couldn't think of an excuse quick enough,' Ashley whispered.

'It's okay. One to keep me going for now?' Dani asked, tilting her head closer to Ashley's, their lips now nearly touching.

They were millimetres apart when Ashley jumped back at the sound of Mary's footsteps in the hall and reinstated the unnatural distance between them. She pulled a face, showing how fed up she was.

'It's fine,' Dani lied.

'When do you want to start?' Mary asked, stacking her filled Tupperware and carrying it to the fridge.

'Just as soon as,' Ashley replied.

Dani pouted as Mary busied herself in the fridge, moving stuff around to better fit her dishes.

Ashley gave her a thin-lipped smile in return.

It wasn't her fault. It didn't stop the disappointment from oozing through Dani's veins like treacle, though.

'Bring on dishy Daniel,' Mary chirped, closing the fridge door with gusto.

There had to be a way to get Ashley alone.

SHE'D CHOSEN this film because, in all honesty, Dani wasn't that fussed about actually watching it.

She stared at the screen, not taking any of it in.

Ashley was on the same two-seater but oceans lay between them. She was hunched up in the corner, cushion pulled to her stomach, eyes fixed on Daniel Craig and whatever he was doing. Something involving guns and a trip to a desert, by the look of it.

Dani craved her touch.

Even a gentle stroke of Ashley's hand would satisfy her. Anything. Having her so close and not being able to connect was worse than being apart.

Mary and Brian sat oblivious to Dani's needs.

Maybe she could yawn, stretch her arms wide and accidentally graze Ashley? Far too obvious.

There was no getting round it. Even with the lights dimmed so low it was like the shadows were crying out for Dani to use them to her advantage.

Dani's chest contained a stiffly wound spring, getting

tighter with every passing second she couldn't gain the attention she needed. Her jaw was set, her muscles locked, everything on edge. Soon it would be too much and the spring would snap, bursting her open in a horrible mess.

Ashley was as essential as air or water.

An explosion on the screen made Ashley jump. God, she was too bloody cute sometimes. She shifted position, trying to cover up her embarrassing reaction. Her hand fell to the centre of the chair.

Dani kept her head facing forward and eyed the offending limb in her side vision. So close, yet so far.

She darted her eyes to the other side of the room and Brian and Mary. They were engrossed in the film.

Given the angle and the big poofy cushion Ashley was holding, she could get away with this. Just. It had to be subtle, though. No full-blown hand-holding.

Dani pretended to be getting comfy but her movements had never felt so stiff. She let her hand fall to the middle of the sofa, centimetres from Ashley's. Guilt filled the air surrounding her, a neon light above her head screaming *romantic intentions!* with a huge flashing arrow.

She crab-crawled her hand closer, not daring to take her eyes from the TV. Her pinky finger hit Ashley's, coming to rest by its side, and a jolt of electricity went through her. It was a surprise not to see a spark in the dark room.

Now bolder than ever, she hooked Ashley's pinky with her own and lightly pressed down, pulling the digit closer. Ashley waggled hers back.

They sat, fingers twisted together, both facing ahead.

Dani sucked on her bottom lip, desperately fighting to contain the smile wanting to burst out of her. Given all the other things she and Ashley had done together, Dani had no clue that a spot of light pinky touching would stir so many emotions.

Her skin fizzed with anticipation, the point of contact on her pinky a beacon of light linked straight to her heart. It glowed hot.

She moved her hand slightly, grazing the bottom of her finger along the top of Ashley's.

So delicate; so dangerous.

She chanced a look at Ashley and watched as the flickering lights from the TV illuminated her profile. Dani's heart skipped a beat. Sometimes, she was certain she was dreaming.

Her past troubles still lingered under the surface, but Jenny-the-therapist was slowly bolstering her toolbox of coping mechanisms. If a new problem arose, they tackled it together.

Dani woke every morning hoping not to fuck things up. Self-sabotage? Just her way of pretending she was in control and able to predict the future. She didn't need a crystal ball to know she was lucky as fuck. All she had to do was keep her cool and it could go on forever.

She'd not destroyed the letter. Yet. Sometimes Dani could swear she heard it calling from the back of her bedside drawer, dying for attention.

It could strengthen their relationship or destroy it.

Jenny was yet to convince her it would do good. In fact, the lilt of surprise in her voice when Dani told her she'd kept it and was actually considering giving it to Ashley told her all she needed to know. If Jenny was hesitant, Dani would be doubly so.

Ashley moved her finger, sending a new wave of euphoria through Dani.

The film would be over soon. Then what? This wasn't enough to satisfy her.

She chewed on her cheek, thinking. She'd stayed over millions of times. It was the weekend, so Ashley was off tomorrow and Dani was on a late shift. A nocturnal stay wasn't out of the question.

She just needed an excuse.

Daniel Craig was wrapping things up: taking the bad guys out and saving the damsel in distress.

Why had she stayed over in the past? Drinking, staying out, going to parties? She wasn't up for any of that: she just wanted a night with Ashley.

The Davidson house was a place of escape in her late teens. A breather from the stifling air of home.

An idea occurred.

'Well, that was brilliant,' Mary sighed as the credits rolled on the film.

'Wasn't it just?' Dani replied, knowing it was the only correct answer. Ashley pulled her hand away and Dani tucked hers under her thigh. Nothing to see here.

Brian clicked the side light on and rolled his neck. 'Can't beat a bit of Daniel Craig. You wanting a lift home, Dani?'

Time to put her plan into action. 'Actually, Rhona and Kirsty are having a proper coupley date thing in the flat; that's why I popped round in the first place. Think I could stay a while longer?'

She avoided eye contact with Ashley, scared she'd break character and ruin the deception if she did. Ashley knew fine well Rhona was in Inverness and Kirsty was at home alone.

'Of course, just stay over if you like,' Mary beamed, exactly as Dani had hoped. Mary Davidson was never averse to entertaining.

'Is that okay, Ash?' Dani asked, still loyal to her part.

'Yeah, course. As long as you behave,' she joked.

No chance of that.

~

'I DON'T HAVE ANY PYJAMAS,' Dani said, taking her joggers off and sliding onto sofa bed beside Ashley. 'Is that going to be a problem?'

She giggled. 'Yes, go, get out, g—'

Dani silenced her by kissing just below her ear and scooping her close, Ashley's back to now pressed against her chest.

Ashley arched her hips, pushing her bum into Dani's core.

Staying over was a brilliant idea.

There was no way she could have gone home without doing this. Frustration would have killed her.

Dani snaked her hand under Ashley's T-shirt, danced her fingers up to her breast, and gently squeezed, Ashley's stiff nipple now held between her fingers.

She'd been wet through the whole film, imagining what she would do if given half a chance. The pulse now throbbing between her legs took it to another level.

But this was Ashley's time.

Dani couldn't settle until she'd given her all the attention she deserved.

She continued attending to Ashley's neck with her mouth and trailed her hand down her torso, just the lightest touch. Enough to mark her journey, but soft enough that Ashley wiggled against her again, begging for more.

She stopped at the waistband of Ashley's pyjama bottoms.

'You're going to have to be quiet,' Dani hummed into Ashley's ear. 'Do you think you can do that?'

'Yes.' Her voice was just a husky breath.

Dani nibbled her earlobe and Ashley groaned.

'I'm not sure.'

Ashley let out a quiet chuckle. 'Me neither.'

Dani smiled against the skin of Ashley's neck. It was warm; soft. Dani could set up home here. She closed her eyes and breathed in Ashley's scent. Heaven.

'The slightest sound and I'll stop.' Dani playfully threatened but her tone was firm; in control. She pressed her lips hard against Ashley neck, adding weight to her words.

Ashley nodded, not making a sound.

'Good girl.'

Dani dipped her fingers into Ashley's pyjamas, her fingers tangling with the hair that greeted her. She cupped her hand to Ashley's core, enjoying the heat. Ashley was as pent-up as her.

She lifted her leg backwards and hooked it over Dani's, creating space.

Dani sighed into Ashley's shoulder as she ran a finger up her core, her slick folds enough to send a shock wave of desire through her own centre.

Ashley shifted, pressing her bum harder into Dani.

Never mind Ashley being quiet: Dani was going to struggle herself.

Ashley's parents were just through the wall. She'd gone this many years: they could hold it together another night. Although the threads laced between them were old and fragile, it wouldn't take much for them to snap.

Dani flattened her finger against Ashley's clit, working the area above as well as the swollen nub itself.

Ashley's quiet groan pierced the otherwise silent room. Dani let her away with it. There was no way she was stopping.

She varied her tempo, responding to Ashley's hips. If they were dancing, Ashley was leading.

'Do you remember when I fucked you at Callum Russell's birthday party?' Dani purred into Ashley's ear, careful to keep her voice as low as possible.

'In the shed?'

'Yeah.'

Callum Russel's eighteenth birthday party. They'd snuck off to find somewhere private and discovered the shed was open. Dani had never been more grateful for an inside lock, as the door had jiggled just as Ashley came hard against her hand.

Shame there were no locks in this house. A little bit of security would be nice as they moved beneath the covers as one.

But knowing they might get caught was all part of the thrill.

At least, that's what Dani told herself, in a bid to balance out Ashley's need for secrecy. Dani's inner dialogue was a pendulum swinging between frustration and elation. But what Ashley wanted, Dani would do her best to provide.

She could ask for the moon and Dani would find a ladder long enough. Ashley deserved to be put on a pedestal and worshipped. Especially when her core felt so fucking good.

With slow, considered strokes Dani worked Ashley closer to the edge.

Ashley ground into Dani's centre and the sofa bed squeaked. The noise was like gunfire and they both stiffened.

Dani wasn't to be put off that easily though.

'You're so close,' Dani whispered into Ashley's ear, not expecting a response.

And she didn't get one, only a sharp intake of breath as Ashley teetered on the edge, her toes curled over the ledge, ready to free-fall at any moment.

Dani changed her pace, slowing her strokes before switching to decisive circles.

That was enough to tip Ashley over. She tilted her head to face the pillow and Dani only caught the tiniest of noises as she writhed against her hand, eventually stopping Dani's motion with a gentle grip of her wrist.

Dani held her hand in place, enjoying the quiet panting of Ashley as she returned to earth.

She swivelled to face Dani, pulling her in for another kiss. 'You're bad.'

'Me?' Dani joked. 'How?'

'In my parents' house, no less.'

The response Dani wanted to give sat stagnant on the surface of her mind: *when are you telling Hazel to fuck off?* She bit her tongue, took a different tack. 'We'll tell people soon, yeah?'

Ashley stroked the stray hair from Dani's face. 'Yeah, course. When I've spoken to Hazel.' Even in the dark Dani was sure Ashley saw her eyes mist with concern. She quickly followed up her answer. 'Which will be soon, honest. You can't rush me with this, Dani.'

'I didn't say I was rushing you.' Defensiveness prickled Dani's skin, making her tone more biting than intended.

'It's a big deal for me. I'll do it when I'm ready.' Ashley didn't rise to Dani's inflection.

'I know. It's just—'

'Frustrating? I understand.' She kissed Dani, as if compensating her with affection.

The last thing she wanted to do was rush Ashley, but there was only so long she could go on like this.

The thought that Ashley was having doubts had crossed her mind more than once.

She needed to prove she was sticking around this time.

Dani kissed Ashley on the tip of the nose.

The only way to do that was by baring the truth: every dirty, embarrassing part of it.

The letter. She would give Ashley the letter.

28

Keeping things on the down-low was harder than Ashley had anticipated. Between her living at home and Dani living with her sister and her partner, they didn't exactly have anywhere private to enjoy.

It was nearing the end of January and Ashley wondered how and when would be appropriate to ask Hazel to vacate the flat. It was Ashley's, after all. She'd bought it years before meeting Hazel. But, between giving the dust time to settle and the inconvenience of Christmas and New Year, it would seem Hazel was in no hurry to move out.

Plus, after that colossally awkward exchange the other week, Ashley was in no hurry to call by the flat again. The only issue niggling her was the letter. Dani hadn't mentioned its absence but Ashley was well aware she was on borrowed time. Even if it was an old letter, she needed to replace it. Dani had kept it for a reason.

Well, it wasn't the only issue. Not really. Dani aside, living with her parents was close to driving Ashley insane. They were so dithery and slow. Ashley wanted to tear her hair out most days. Not to mention their constant need to know what she was doing, or the stupidly uncomfortable sofa bed. Tonight, she was in Bar Orama with the gang, having suffered twenty questions for the pleasure. Thank God she was staying at Dani's tonight.

They'd had to skip last week for fear of looking suspicious. There were only so many sleepovers you could legitimately get away with as mates. Kirsty and Rhona weren't stupid.

Dani was sitting opposite her but she might as well have been on the moon. It was torture. The need to be closer made Ashley's bones ache. Izzy had taken the seat beside Dani before Ashley got the first round in. Rookie error: that's what she got for being generous.

Only Rhona was missing tonight; she was in Athens. It was good to have the whole crew in one place, even if Kim was serving behind the bar. It had been a while.

Ashley felt a foot tap hers. She chanced a look at Dani who smiled ruefully, despite being fully engaged in conversation with Izzy.

She tuned back into Trip and Kirsty, her foot now playfully exchanging touches with Dani's.

'I just want to whack him with a book, you know?' Trip said, sipping her beer. Ashley had obviously missed something.

'Definitely can't chat with his parents?' Kirsty asked.

A troublesome kid. Ashley kept quiet, needing more info before chipping in. Dani's foot skirted her ankle. She clamped her jaw tight, knowing a smile would raise questions.

'Nah,' Trip replied, dejection clear. 'He doesn't come from the best circumstances, which is why it's so heartbreaking. If he stopped titting about he could be really good.'

Kirsty nodded. 'It's tough when things aren't good at home. Learning takes a back seat.'

'No after-school clubs you could get him involved in?' Ashley asked, feeling she'd grasped the conversation enough to contribute. The way Dani was rubbing against her ankle was making her brain short-circuit, though. Completing a logical train of thought was dicey.

'None,' Trip replied.

Trip was a good teacher: she would find a way to break through. Ashley had been gutted when Dani didn't come back to school. It was understandable, though. She had lost her light. School was never an option after what had happened.

That whole time had been a mess. Sometimes Ashley wondered what she could have done differently. Maybe if she'd tried a little harder she could have got Dani back, and the last two decades would have been less convoluted. Didn't matter now: they got there in the end.

'What are you smiling about?' Kirsty asked, making Ashley jolt to attention.

'Just thinking of something funny Diane said at work,' she lied. It was about as transparent as glass, but she had never been good under pressure. 'You really had to be there,' she added, worried she'd be pressed for specifics.

'Uh-huh,' Kirsty hummed, not falling for it at all. 'I know it's a dangerous topic, but how are things with you and Hazel?'

Ashley stirred in her seat. 'So-so,' she replied with a roll of her eyes. 'She's messaged me a few times and I've replied to be polite. But—' Ashley shrugged her shoulders.

'Definitely over?' Trip asked.

'I would say so. I just want my flat back.'

'Living with your parents must be a hoot,' Kirsty said

with a smirk. 'I'd offer you our sofa but I don't think four women and a cat is the best idea.'

'Hey, I think I've seen that film,' Trip joked.

'It's cool. I need to bite the bullet and have a chat with her.'

'Tough though, eh?'

'I've never broken up with anyone.'

Kirsty's face grew sympathetic. 'You've done the hardest part. It would be worse to keep her hanging on. Plus, it's your flat.'

'I know. I just hate being the arsehole.' Ashley took a deep breath. 'I need to nip to the loo.'

She knew she'd been putting it off, as if ignoring Hazel could make the problem go away, but the time had come for her to grow up and be honest.

Plus, the sooner she did this, the sooner she and Dani could go public.

Ashley sat for a second in the shabby stall, enjoying a moment of peace to let her brain reset. The main door swung open with a clunk: peace over. Someone else wanted in.

She was surprised to find Dani by the sink when she came out.

'You okay?' she asked, not budging.

'Yeah, fine. How come?' Ashley replied, washing her hands.

'Just, you know, Hazel stuff, and then you came here. I wanted to check you were okay.'

'I'm good.'

Dani closed the gap between them. 'And also, I wanted to do this.' She pushed Ashley against the porcelain sink, her leg slotting between Ashley's legs with ease.

'Oh, really?' Ashley replied with a breathy chuckle. 'Was

that all you had to say?' She put her hands on Dani's hips, pulling her closer.

'Not quite.' Dani pressed her lips against Ashley's, wasting no time in ramping the passion up to eleven.

Ashley's core pinged with desire. Not being open about their relationship was hellish. Inside she felt like a lovesick teenager. All she wanted to do was be with Dani. Outside, she was a stoic tangle of repressed longing. It couldn't last. Even the sturdiest balloon would pop if put under continual pressure.

Dani deepened the kiss by tangling her tongue with Ashley's. How early was too early to declare they needed to go home?

Every kiss with Dani felt like the first. The build-up, the hesitation, the whack of adrenaline. Sneaking about did have its benefits.

Dani cupped Ashley's centre through her jeans and she was just about to call time when the main door creaked open, followed by Kirsty's voice: 'Just a wine, ta!'

Ashley instinctively moved back, but had nowhere to go. Instead she smashed her arm off the tap, making her funny bone throb. Dani jumped a mile, like someone had just thrown a grenade between them.

Heat filled Ashley's cheeks as she rubbed at her elbow.

'You guys alright?' Kirsty asked, searching the room for clues as to why she felt so suspicious.

Dani oozed guilt. She leaned against the toilet cubicle like she'd forgotten how to human. 'Yeah, it's just, uh . . . you don't have a tampon or something? I'm early.'

Kirsty made a show of patting the pockets of her skintight jeans. 'Not on me. I can give you a pound for the machine?'

'Nah, it's okay,' Dani said, waving a hand between them. 'I'll just leave it.'

Ashley pulled a face. How could you just leave it? Kirsty didn't seem to care.

'Okay, cool. Izzy's just getting another round in.'

'Cool,' Ashley replied, feeling she needed to contribute. Her elbow was sending odd tingles up her arm. There was a reason they called it a funny bone. She gave it a quick shake.

No one moved.

'Something I should know about?' Kirsty asked, eyes narrowing.

'Like what?' Dani asked with a quick shrug.

'Dunno. You guys are up to something.'

'Us?' Ashley blurted. 'What would we be up to?'

'Not so much you. I'm more worried about my bad influence of a sister.'

'Me?' Dani whined.

Ashley needed out of this room, stat. It wouldn't be the end of the world if Kirsty found out, but once the cat was out of the bag it would only be a matter of time before everyone knew.

She avoided looking at Dani and focused on Kirsty. They'd had plenty of close calls in their teenage years, but apparently guilt compounded over the years, because Ashley was not playing it cool. At all.

'Hmm,' Kirsty hummed. 'I'm watching you two. Something is definitely up.' She wagged a finger between them both.

'Alright, Poirot,' Dani joked, with an exaggerated eye-roll.

That was close.

29

'Everyone ready?' Fergus the instructor asked.

Dani nodded with unmatched enthusiasm, making her mask jiggle.

They'd come to the newly opened paintball experience in Pollok Park, the whole crew: birthday gal Kim, Trip, Kirsty, Rhona, Izzy, Ashley, Dani, and Travis. Dani couldn't remember the last time they'd had full attendance without Kim working behind a bar. Never mind the addition of Kim's bestie, Travis. Dani hadn't hung out with him in yonks. Today was already starting strong.

She'd never been paintballing before, only seen it in films and TV shows. It was going to be epic. They were split into two teams – Dani had Kim, Trip, and Kirsty – and the aim of the game was to take the opposing team's flag without getting shot. Seemed simple enough.

'Right, to your base camps!' Fergus announced to a few semi-excited whoops.

Safety rules covered, now it was time to play.

Kirsty walked by Dani as they crossed the forest floor. Stacks of tyres, old barrels, wooden shelters, and fences for cover were scattered throughout a cleared zone, along with a few girthy trees. This in turn was bookended by dense woodland, hiding the team's bases at the opposite sides of the fenced space. There was even an old car made to look burnt out, its windows and doors nowhere to be seen.

'This is going to be amazing,' Kirsty buzzed, showing unusual emotion for her usually stoic demeanour. They both looked the part in their supplied uniforms: a camo hoodie with matching trousers and a heavy-duty mask which covered the entire face, leaving just the eyes visible through a large goggled section. Something told Dani this was going to be a little more exciting than the time Dad bought them both potato guns.

The four women formed a circle in their base. 'Trip, I want you to cover Dani and Kirsty as they advance, but also defend the base,' Kim said, taking command. You'd think she'd served in action with such a convincing tone. 'Meanwhile, I'll skirt round the outside, go for their base, and get the flag.'

It was a good plan. Trip was a bit of a walking target and at half Trip's height, Kim could scuttle where needed basically undetected. Kirsty and Dani could distract, no problem.

She held her hand out, palm down, into the middle of the circle. The remaining trio piled theirs on top. 'Go team!' Kim shouted and they raised their hands in the air.

Adrenaline fizzed in Dani's veins.

Fergus bellowed in the centre: 'Let the game begin!' The sounding of an air horn sealed the deal.

Dani crouched low, heading for the nearest stack of tyres. A quick run and she ducked down, safely hidden.

It was a shame Ashley wasn't on her team. She'd barely seen her this week. Half term was coming up and school was crazy. Given the space to think, Dani had successfully talked herself out of giving Ashley the letter. Talk about flip-flopping. She needed to get a grip.

Reasons for Ashley's reluctance to go public danced daily through her brain. There was no need to add fuel to the fire. Yet.

She hadn't expected to still be hiding their relationship. There had to be other reasons for it. She got the initial logistics and reasoning at first, but now it was boring. Yeah, there was a thrill to start with, but now she wanted to enjoy finally being with Ashley. She wanted to take her on dates to the pub, out for dinner: heck, she'd settle for a walk round the park together. Even finding reasons for Ashley to stay over was a pain in the ass now. Maybe she should just tell her sister, swear her to secrecy. She knew something was going on. She wasn't as stupid as she looked.

She met Kirsty's gaze as she sat slumped behind a wooden barricade. Kirsty nodded, signalling for them to advance further towards the other team's camp. In her very outer vision a camo blob sped past, low to the ground. She presumed that was Kim.

Kirsty entered the danger zone first and Dani wasn't far behind. She set her sights on the wrecked car: she could either run or go low and slow.

Her sister opted for the latter and Dani jumped as the pop of an air rifle sounded through the trees. Kirsty flinched, an explosion of red paint decorating her shoulder.

Shit.

Speed was the answer. She hoofed it to the car.

She was safe. For now.

Kirsty held a hand in the air, the signal Fergus had told them to give when they were out of the game, and walked off the field.

Dani stole a look over her left shoulder, quickly peeking over the bonnet of the car. She ducked back, airgun to chest, and pondered her next move.

The closest cover was a wooden shelter about seven metres away. Or, she could cross diagonally and go for another stack of tyres. But the shot that got Kirsty came from that direction.

Shelter it was.

She checked her surroundings once more before scrabbling to her feet and running. A metre or so before the door to the shelter, she spun, facing her back to the structure and covering herself.

This was amaaaazing.

She barrelled through the door and tumbled backwards.

Safe.

Maybe.

She yelped as her back made contact with another human.

A gun jammed into her back.

'Hands up,' a familiar and gloriously sexy voice purred.

'Ashley,' she said, putting both hands in the air.

As she turned, a wicked smile took over Ashley's face. She could tell by the way her eyes creased. The sound of her gun took Dani by surprise. Green splattered her chest.

'Hey! No fair!' she growled.

'All's fair in love and war, babes,' Ashley joked.

Dani bit her bottom lip. Ashley was so strait-laced it did silly things to Dani's insides when she misbehaved.

'Oh, it is now, is it?' Dani asked, pumping her eyebrows, trying to look suitably miffed.

Without breaking eye contact with Ashley, Dani pulled the trigger on her gun, splattering her belly yellow.

'Hey!'

Dani shed her mask. Fergus the instructor would kill her: he must have said a thousand times not to take it off.

'Your word against mine now,' Dani replied, with a grin as wicked as Ashley's had been. She stepped closer. Ashley took her mask off and lobbed it to the ground.

Two seconds later they were inseparable as Dani slammed Ashley against the wooden wall.

Ashley brought a leg around Dani's waist, pulling her closer.

'I've missed you,' Dani mumbled, breaking their kiss temporarily.

Ashley's answer was lost as Dani slipped her tongue between her parted lips. Just as Ashley's hand found the waist of Dani's trousers and dipped inside, a cheer erupted in the distance, making them both freeze.

'Game!' Fergus shouted via a megaphone.

'Fuck,' Dani groaned.

Ashley stepped back, grabbing her mask off the ground. 'Better put these back on.'

Dani huffed. 'Meet me back here, next round?'

'I'll try,' Ashley replied with a wink as she pulled her mask on.

Dani snapped hers on and trudged outside to see a dancing Kim frolicking by the car, red flag in hand.

'We won!' She beamed, holding the flag up for Dani to see.

'Nice one, Kimbo!'

'Where did you disappear to?' Trip asked, appearing from behind.

'Got shot in the shelter,' Dani replied, pointing to her chest.

'Then who shot Ashley?'

Ashley's eyes widened. 'Fired at the same time.'

'Unlucky,' Trip gibed.

'Super,' Dani agreed.

Her core pulsed between her legs. These were quick games – how was she meant to carve out ten minutes with Ashley? That was all she needed. She was desperate, suffering from Ashley withdrawal.

There had to be somewhere they could be alone?

'Right, everyone reset!' Fergus shouted.

Dani traipsed back to base with her team mates. Her mind should have been on tactics and winning but all she could picture was the feeling of sliding her hand between Ashley's thighs.

This predicament was making her into a sex monster. Her mind was polluted, gagging for release.

'Okay,' Kim grunted, bringing them back into a huddle. 'We did well. This is best of three, so if we get this one, we're golden.'

Murmurs of agreement filtered through the group.

Kim continued: 'They'll be wise to our plan now, so Kirsty, you take the lead. I'll go up the side again, but we'll bluff them. You make a run for it on the opposite side. Dani, you distract in the middle. Trip, you cover again. Excellent chest shot on Travis, by the way.'

Trip's smile turned full beam. 'Thank you. Quite proud of it myself.'

Kim clapped her hands together. 'Bring it on!'

Dani nodded, but her head was computing what this meant for her rendezvous with Ashley. It would be impossible to do without being spotted.

Shit.

The air horn sounded. She had to focus, for her team.

Exiting the base, Dani went low, aiming full pelt for the car. She slid into position like a professional baseball player.

That bought a little time.

She checked the shelter in her peripheral vision. No sign of Ashley.

This was for Kim's birthday – she could hardly sabotage her winning streak for the sake of a quick snog.

The fire of air rifles sounded around her. With no sign of Kirsty or Kim, they must be aimed at them. Time to do her job.

Dani popped up from behind the car and scanned the immediate treeline past the clearing. No one.

Time to run.

Thank God she'd used her inhaler before this.

The first few metres were a blur, then Izzy appeared from behind a tree. *Bam*. Straight to Izzy's chest. Dani carried on, like a rugby player intent on scoring a try. Soon she was in the trees, covered once more.

Had Ashley gone to the shelter?

God, she wanted to kiss her so badly. This was worse than long distance. It was like having a sheet of glass between them. She could look, but not touch.

Maybe this was comeuppance for all the years of waiting Dani had put them through.

She popped her head around the chunky tree currently serving as protection. Their base lay ahead, a dot through the forest.

Twigs snapping signalled she wasn't alone.

Dani spun to find a sneaky Ashley approaching. *Pop*. Straight to the crotch.

'Again? Seriously?' Ashley laughed.

Pop. Dani's arse cheek stung. She twirled to find a dancing Travis. 'Later, losers!' he shouted, thumb and finger to his head, as he ran to the clearing. Hopefully Trip would take him out again.

Dani raised her hand, leading her and Ashley out to the active play area.

'You didn't go to the shelter,' Ashley said, stepping over a log.

'Neither did you,' Dani replied with a smirk.

'We'll just need to wait until Kirsty and Rhona go away next week.'

'But that's ages,' Dani whined. She couldn't wait. She picked the biggest, closest tree and gently pushed Ashley against it. She didn't take much persuading. She lifted her mask to rest on her forehead as Ashley did the same.

Kissing wasn't to be, though: their masks clashed together with a thump. Ashley creased in an eruption of giggles.

'Ash, this is no good,' Dani moaned as she stepped back. She kicked at a tree stump.

Ashley pulled her mask back down and enveloped Dani in a hug from behind, her hands looping around Dani's waist. They moved together like they were joined at the hip before settling in one spot.

Dani turned to face Ashley, pulling her mask back down as she remembered the stern warning from Fergus earlier.

Ashley touched her mask to Dani's as if leaning their foreheads together. 'I'll talk to Hazel soon. Promise.'

'Like really soon, yeah? I'm so over this.'

'Not over me, I hope.'

Dani shook her head. 'No, no, no. Never.'

Ashley smiled, breaking herself free from Dani's embrace. 'Good. Now, let's stop acting shady. We've got a nice meal after this, we'll have a good time. It'll be next week before you know it.'

Seven days. One hundred and sixty-eight hours. She could do this.

30

'Have a good evening, Susan,' Ashley called over her shoulder to Dani's mum as they left the freshly locked Café Odyssey. They'd told Susan they were going to the pub for a drink.

Really, they were rushing home for some alone time. And when Ashley said rushing, she meant it: Dani was practically running the length of Pollokshaws Road. She marched around a granny with a trolley bag on wheels and Ashley wondered if she'd be needing a moment with her inhaler before anything happened between them.

It had been a long week. Today felt about a week long in itself.

She'd meant what she said about speaking to Hazel, but the right time hadn't presented itself yet. Would there ever be one? She could come up with an excuse for every chance. She just had to bite the bullet and get on with it. It definitely wasn't top of the agenda for Ashley today.

They arrived at Dani's flat in record time and Dani did the steps two at once, pulling Ashley along by the hand.

They didn't bother to call out to check the flat was

empty. Rhona had a job in Alloa this weekend and had taken Kirsty with her, planning to have a minibreak once her job was finished.

A quick peek into the bedroom and they saw that Chet was sound asleep on the bed. Not for long.

'Mummy needs alone time,' Dani said, giving him a kiss on the cheek as he was put in the hall and the door closed in his face. Poor bastard.

A gentle tap on the shoulder and Ashley fell backwards onto the bed. In a blink, Dani had her work T-shirt off.

She paused, one leg over Ashley's thigh. 'Do you want me to wash? I've been at work all day.'

Ashley yanked her closer with a hand on the back of her neck. 'Bloody shut up, will you?' She silenced her with a kiss.

The release of finally having alone time was euphoric. A few times this week she'd physically ached at the thought of Dani's touch. Today she'd woken up with a pulse between her legs. It's a good job she wasn't a bloke or there'd have been no hiding how excited she was today. She was already wetter than she'd ever been, and Dani had only kissed her.

This was taking too long. She used her feet to push her trainers off as they kissed. Dani looked impressed as Ashley shimmied her jeans and knickers off. A wicked smile crossed Dani's face, the same devilish glint in her eye from when they went paintballing.

There would be no interruptions today.

Dani slotted between her legs, gasping with delight as she put her hand between Ashley's legs.

'You're so wet,' she moaned into Ashley's neck as her thumb found her clit and two fingers slid inside her centre. The thumb was barely necessary as Dani thrust inside her, building her release with every sweep of her G-spot.

'Fuck,' Ashley shouted, already teetering on the edge.

Dani moved her leg behind her hand, giving better purchase to the deep drive of her digits. The headboard hit against the wall, marking their rhythm.

Ashley desperately wanted this to last longer, but she also needed to come. It had been building for so long: if it didn't happen soon she might pop.

She gripped Dani's bum as she toppled over the edge, riding the wave of pleasure like a bucking bronco.

'Fuck,' she repeated, now fully out of breath. She gently gripped Dani's wrist, sensitivity begging her to stop for now.

Dani brought her hand to rest on Ashley's core, her own breath heavy from exertion.

Despite feeling slightly light-headed, she couldn't wait. With a gentle push she swapped places with Dani, angling herself to slot between her legs. Dani wrapped her ankles around Ashley's waist. Now would be the perfect time for a strap-on, but they'd not quite reached that stage yet. Probably best to be out and open about your relationship before buying toys together.

Ashley dipped her head inches from Dani's. 'I've thought about this all week.'

'Oh yeah?' Dani mumbled as Ashley moved south, taking Dani's stiff nipple into her mouth.

She'd made the right decision. There was no doubt.

Being with Dani was different to being with Hazel. She momentarily scolded herself for thinking of her while with Dani, but it was important. She had to acknowledge her choice.

It was like having an itch between her shoulder blades for half her life and suddenly someone had given her back scratcher. The relief was enough to make her teary. A part of her had been missing for so long she'd become numb to its absence, indifferent to its pain. Now she was complete again, she finally felt alive. She could never go back.

She ran her tongue down the centre line of Dani's stomach, all the way to her belly button.

Now there was the tough decision of what to do next.

So many choices.

She'd had her fun; the urgency was gone.

By the way Dani was arching her hips, Ashley would bet she didn't feel the same.

She took a deep breath, pawing at the waist of Dani's joggers. Ground coffee stained the lower thighs, a straight line running across them where her pinny had protected the fabric.

'We should probably take these off,' Ashley purred, pinging the elasticated edge against Dani's hip bone.

'Wholeheartedly agree,' Dani replied with a smirk, untangling herself from Ashley as she worked her clothes off.

Ashley took the opportunity to slide into position beside Dani and reposition the pillows to support her back. 'Come, sit here,' she commanded, patting the space between her legs.

The grin on Dani's face said she liked that idea. A lot.

Ashley brought her legs together, creating a seat for Dani as she straddled her. Her wet core grazed Ashley's stomach and she shivered with anticipation.

'Like this?' Dani asked, knowing fine well she was driving Ashley crazy.

'Just like that,' Ashley replied, her eyes fixed on Dani's centre.

She ran a hand up her thighs, bringing one to rest on Dani's hip, the other flitting down the line of her groin, straight to her core. Ashley used her thumb to stroke Dani's clit and the stiffening of her muscles told Ashley all she needed to know.

She teased the hard nub with a few strokes then dipped her hand lower. There was no need for lube today. Her fingers slid into Dani with ease.

Touching Dani made Ashley's whole body feel alive. Suddenly, anything was possible. With every stroke she wanted Dani to know how much she loved her. She wanted to cry out and shout about it. She could say it all day and Dani would never know how she truly felt.

Dani gripped the headboard with both hands for stability as she rode Ashley's fingers. Their last time was slow and sensual; dictated by the need to be silent. This was fast, furious; no holding back, time to be loud as possible and let go of pent-up frustration.

Thank God no one was in to hear them.

'That feels so good,' she groaned, pushing harder against Ashley's hand.

She brought her other hand round and gently massaged Dani's clit with her thumb.

Dani's features changed, her eyes creasing as her breathing deepened.

'Jesus, fuck,' she cried out, still moving with Ashley's thrusts as her internal walls tightened around her fingers.

Slowly, she stilled.

'Wow,' she huffed, bringing her head to rest on Ashley's shoulder.

'You felt good.'

'Mhmm,' was all Dani could manage.

∼

ASHLEY PADDED after Dani to the kitchen, and hugged her from behind as she got a glass of water.

They'd lain as a tangled mess in bed for a while before deciding it was too late to nap. They'd get a pizza and watch TV instead.

Ashley kissed Dani's neck before speaking. 'I'm starving.'

'Me too,' Dani replied, gulping freshly poured water. 'I think we worked up quite the appetite there.'

Ashley smiled against Dani's skin. 'I love you.'

'I lo—'

The creaking of a door made them both jump a mile.

Instinctively, Ashley took a step back to lean against the counter.

Kirsty and Rhona were away. Who the hell was here?

They exchanged looks.

Dani reached behind her, feeling for the knife rack.

A few disembodied footsteps later, a sleepy Kirsty appeared in the doorway.

'Hey, guys,' she said, stretching as she yawned.

'Kirsty, what the fuck?' Dani yelped, looking her sister up and down. She had on pyjamas. She'd definitely not just come in the front door.

Ashley gulped.

Surely not.

Kirsty rolled her neck, cracking it. 'Have you not looked at your phone? I texted you. Bride got appendicitis. Whole thing's been cancelled, so Rhona and I rescheduled. We're going to head north tomorrow.'

Dani's mouth was agape. Ashley's brain worked overtime, wondering the best way to word her questions without giving the game away: how long have you been here and what did you hear?

Rhona appeared. Was that a smirk on her face? She

leaned on the counter, rubbing at her eyes. 'Sorry if we scared you. I told Kirsty to leave a note or something.'

'No, no. It's cool,' Dani lied. 'So you were asleep?'

'Yeah,' Kirsty replied, pulling a face as if it was the strangest question in the world. To be fair, it kind of was.

'Out like a light, this one,' Rhona said, throwing a thumb towards Kirsty.

'And you?' Ashley asked, too impatient to beat about the bush any longer.

'Couldn't sleep, mind was too awake.' There was a smirk. A definite *I know* smirk.

'A shame,' Dani replied, her voice rising an octave as if it was a question.

The three of them exchanged looks. Kirsty was oblivious as she rummaged in the fridge.

'So,' Ashley started, with no clue where the sentence was going.

'So,' Rhona repeated.

'I need wine,' Kirsty said to the inside of the fridge.

Her words hung in the air as if the letters might be rearranged by Rhona to *I heard you shagging*.

'I'm going to head to the shop,' Kirsty said, closing the fridge, truly ignorant to the conversation happening in silence around her.

'I'll come with you,' Rhona said, ending their charade with a smile. Ashley could have sworn the look in her eye said she had gossip to spill.

'Me too!' Dani blurted.

'And me,' Ashley added.

'Okay,' Kirsty said, the word lasting a few beats as she picked up on the weird atmosphere. 'Flat trip to the shop.'

∽

As Kirsty perused the wine aisle, Dani sauntered up to Rhona by the beers. Ashley stood in the middle aisle of the supermarket. Have idle chit-chat with Kirsty about white wine, or get the low-down direct from Rhona?

Her nerves were shot.

She needed to know now, before she became a jittering mess.

Dani was talking nonsense about an IPA, that much was obvious. Rhona looked like she was enjoying making them squirm.

What was the worst that could happen? So Rhona and Kirsty knew? Big deal. At least it wasn't Trip. There'd be no hope then.

But still. One weak chain soon became a break.

The pressure was on to tell Hazel.

Ashley felt her shoulder muscles tighten with the weight.

Dani continued to wax lyrical about stouts.

Ashley cut her off. 'Rhona, what did you hear?' she asked, matter of fact.

Rhona bit her bottom lip. 'More than I would have liked, if I'm honest.'

'Shit,' Dani said, screwing her face up as she put the random beer back on the shelf.

'Why shit?' Rhona asked, her brow creased. 'This is amazing! I'm so happy for you guys. I mean, I could have done without the audio, but regardless, this is good, no?'

'It's complicated,' Dani replied with a huff.

Rhona's face fell. 'What's going on? Kirsty said you were being shifty lately, so I guessed I should keep my mouth shut earlier.'

Ashley checked the aisle. They were alone, but she kept

her voice low anyway. 'I haven't told Hazel things are fully over. I want to tell her about Dani before I – we – go public.'

Rhona nodded. 'I get that. But why not tell Kirsty? She's your sister.'

Dani shrugged.

'It just seemed easier to keep it to ourselves,' Ashley replied.

Another gentle nod from Rhona. 'Will you tell her now?'

Dani looked at Ashley, uncertainty clear.

'Do you want us to tell her?' Ashley asked.

'I'd prefer not to keep secrets from her.'

Fair enough. 'Okay, we'll tell Kirsty. But no one else.'

'Your secret's safe with me.'

Dani picked up another bottle of beer, examining the label. Her face was emotionless but Ashley could feel the hurt radiating. She focused on Rhona: she'd talk to Dani later. 'Thank you.'

31

Life was easier now Kirsty and Rhona knew. No more sneaking about. A week later, though, and Ashley still hadn't arranged to see Hazel. Dani wasn't going to rush her, but the farce had worn thin a long time ago.

Still, it was nice to be cuddled on the sofa with Kirsty lounging on the armchair opposite. No more hiding in her room.

'I need to pee,' Ashley announced, shuffling between Dani's legs and the coffee table as she made to leave the room.

Dani repositioned herself, getting comfy without a body to lean on.

Kirsty scooted closer, her tone conspiratorial. 'Has she told Hazel yet?'

Dani shook her head, not wanting to discuss it. She kept her eyes on the TV.

Kirsty leaned closer, not willing to give it up. 'Psst, hey, look at me. You need to move her along. You've been together ages.'

'Since when are you the relationship expert?' Dani hissed.

'I've got a better track record than you.' Dani whipped a cushion in Kirsty's direction, wiping the smug look from her face. 'Hey!'

'Everything's fine.'

'It's not.'

'You need to tell her, or I—' She shut up as Ashley reappeared.

Dani needed time to wind this up; put any notions of meddling to bed. 'Ash, can you grab me my charger, please? It's in the top drawer?'

'Sure.'

Dani checked over her shoulder, just to be sure Ashley was out of earshot. 'Honestly, I'm fine. Just let me handle this in my own way. Okay?'

Kirsty slumped back, crossing her arms. 'Fine. But I think she's taking the piss.'

'As if.'

Ashley was back. 'Want me to plug your phone in now?'

'Yeah, sure.' Dani said, passing it over the back of the couch.

She knew Ashley was dragging her heels, but she didn't need Kirsty sticking her oar in too. This was between the two of them and no one else. Yeah, she was fed up, but it was her business to be fed up of. Kirsty just needed to keep her big mouth shut.

Tension hung between Dani and her sister like a frayed thread. The slightest move in the wrong direction and it would snap, tumbling their problems into the open.

Dani put her arm out, letting Ashley get comfy again. If she didn't look at Kirsty she could ignore the death stare currently being shot her way.

Before Rhona, Kirsty hadn't dated anyone. What did she know about girlfriends?

Dani ran her tongue along the back of her top teeth. The thought near killed her, but the truth was, Kirsty was right. They needed a chat.

'You okay?' Ashley asked, lying on her side beside Dani in bed.

The lie was on the tip of her tongue: she was ready to say *yes* and turn the light out. Lies got you nowhere, though.

She'd spoken about her and Ashley with Jenny last week and they'd agreed the current set-up was doing nothing for her mental health.

She was doing this because she wanted to. Not because Kirsty had said anything.

'Actually, can we have a quick chat about something?'

Ashley's body language stiffened. 'Yeah, sure. What's up?'

Dani turned to mirror her. She swallowed. Now or never. 'You're going to talk to Hazel soon, yeah?'

Ashley's face softened. 'God, I thought you were going to say something awful.'

Dani chuckled. 'Like what?'

'I dunno,' Ashley said with a deep breath, shaking her head and thoughts free. 'Erm, yeah. Of course. Soon. Promise.'

'Like, really soon?'

Ashley cupped Dani's jaw with her hand. 'Yeah. I'm sick of hiding too.'

'Okay.' She chewed on her cheek, her mind still whirring.

'What's is it? You can tell me anything.'

'It's nothing. I just really want you to talk to her.' It wasn't. The thought still bothered Dani that Ashley might be holding off because she was having second thoughts. Otherwise, why drag her feet for so long?

Ashley caressed Dani's cheek with her thumb. 'I will. As soon as possible. Come here.' She scooted closer and kissed Dani on the lips.

Dani smiled, but the gesture felt empty. She was suddenly numb. Until Ashley actually talked to Hazel, she wouldn't believe it.

'Let's sleep,' Ashley said, turning round. 'I've got a big day tomorrow.'

Dani clicked the light off and slotted into position behind Ashley. The feeling of her skin against Dani's never got old.

'Yeah, big day,' Dani mumbled into Ashley's shoulder. It was her nephew's birthday. In years past Dani would have been there, but Ashley worried her sudden presence after years of Hazel would rouse suspicion. The whole thing was getting ridiculous.

Dani closed her eyes, trying to sleep, but her brain was too awake. She stayed still, not wanting to disturb Ashley.

Her body was tired but her mind was on a hamster wheel, running full pelt through scenarios, working itself up.

All this time and this is what she ended up with: hidden away, not to be discussed in public.

She should be shouting about them from the rooftops: *FINALLY!*

Dani took a deep breath as Ashley gently snored. Getting angry at this time of day did no one any good.

She had Ashley. Was that not enough?

TIRED AND SWEATY from working all day, Dani collapsed onto her bed. Ashley wasn't staying over tonight; she thought her parents would get suspicious if they did two nights in a row.

The sooner she got her own place back, the better.

It was bad enough sneaking around friends, never mind nosey parents.

A knock on her door signalled that Kirsty was on the prowl.

'Yeah?' she called, lifting her chin to touch her chest.

'Can I come in?'

'If you must,' she replied with a chuckle, flopping her head back on to the bed.

Kirsty took a seat on the edge. 'Sorry for being a pest last night.'

'Just last night?'

Kirsty thumped her in the thigh. 'Oi, I'm trying to be nice.'

'Hit your head today?'

'Dani,' Kirsty whined, climbing onto the bed by her sister. Chet wasn't best pleased with all the people on his bed. 'Listen, you know what's best for you and Ashley. I'll keep my trap shut.'

'Can I get that in writing?'

Kirsty whacked her again. Chet opened one, very disapproving, eye. 'This is why I never apologise to you.'

Dani was done playing. She'd run out of comebacks. Her glass wasn't just empty today: it had been on the spin cycle and blow-dried. She was drained. 'I told Ashley she had to speak to Hazel.'

'And what did she say to that?'

Dani shrugged. 'That she would.'

'You don't sound convinced.'

She ran her hands over her eyes and down her face. 'She's not exactly given me confidence in her actions so far.'

'So diplomatic.'

'Trying to be, eh?'

Kirsty sat up on her elbow. 'Look, she'll talk to her, but honesty is key. If she doesn't, you need to have another chat. You can't just let things lie.'

'I know,' Dani grunted. She pondered, her brain whirring into action again. 'Speaking of honesty: do you think I should tell her why it took so long for me to say anything in the first place?'

'Huh?'

'Like, why I left her hanging for so long?'

Kirsty's eyebrows met in the middle. 'Are you comfortable telling her? Do you think it will make a difference?'

They'd had plenty of drunken chats about it. Only Kirsty and Trip knew the circles Dani's brain ran in: the thought of letting someone else in, even Ashley, was terrifying. 'You just said honesty is the best policy.'

'There's honest and there's honest. I thought Jenny had helped with all that?'

'She has but what if things get—' she wiggled her hand through the air like a writhing snake. 'Squiggly, again?'

'You do what feels right to you. Ashley isn't going to care.'

It was a lot of baggage. It was like thinking Dani was

bringing one small carry-on with her, only to find she'd filled the whole fucking plane with cases.

'Jenny got me to draft a letter, ages ago, about how I felt. Should I give it to her?'

'A letter?'

'Yeah, you know, those things we had before phones? Sheet of paper? Ink?'

'You know I could throttle you and Mum would take my side?'

Dani smirked. 'Calm down. What do you think, though? Should I give it to her?'

Kirsty pursed her lips. 'Up to you.'

Dani turned onto her side and opened her top drawer. She peeked inside: no sign of it. Not unusual – it was usually stuffed up the back, out of sight. She put her hand in and rummaged. When that came up short she sat up, pulling herself closer to the open drawer so she could get a better look.

Her heart rate rocketed.

It had to be here. She moved her passport, inhaler, earplugs she'd stolen off Kirsty, a stack of euros left over from Ibiza. Nothing.

She felt sick. The blood drained from her face like she'd been dipped upside down into an ice bath.

'What's up?'

'I can't see it.'

'You sure you kept it there?'

She was about to clap back when her mind rattled into action. She had been meaning to destroy it for a while. Had she done it, and just forgotten?

Dani thought. No. She hadn't. Had she? No. But she couldn't remember the last time she'd physically seen it, either.

'Shit,' she snapped.

'Definitely nowhere else it could be?'

Dani collapsed face first into her duvet. 'Nope. This is bad, Kirsty. Really bad.'

'Surely not that bad?'

'There was a lot of private stuff in there.'

'Okay. Well. It didn't just walk out of here. Think Ashley took it? Doesn't seem like something she would do.'

'It had her name on it.'

'Okay.' Every time she said the word it got longer. 'So, worse case scenario is she'd read it. You just said you wanted her to read it.'

'On my terms!' Dani shouted into the duvet.

'She's not left you, though, so whatever you're freaking out about, don't.'

Dani turned, suddenly feeling on the verge of tears. 'What if she's got it, but not read it?'

'Ah.'

'Well, text her?'

'And say what?'

'*Do you have my letter?*'

'Urgh, nope.'

'How?'

'Cause! What if she says yes? I can't ask for it back. Plus,' Dani added, thrusting a finger in the air. 'She's stolen my shit. That's not on.'

'It had her name on.'

'In my drawer. You can't just help yourself.'

'Fair. What are you going to do?'

'I dunno. I can't believe she just took it. Who does that?'

'Ashley, apparently.'

'You need to text her. You can't just pretend this hasn't happened.'

'You can stop with the sage advice now,' Dani joked. Only she wasn't joking at all. She could quite happily let the ground swallow her up and not think about Ashley and that stupid letter ever again.

Anger replaced anxiety.

Ashley wouldn't take it, would she?

32

'Hey,' Ashley said as she entered the flat. The weird feeling of being a guest once again shuddered through her like an icy wind.

'Hey,' Hazel called from the kitchen, poking her head out just enough to be visible through the doorway. A heavy rock settled in Ashley's stomach. She'd felt ill all day at the thought of having this talk, but now she was here it was a thousand times worse.

The kitchen was good, though. It was better than the living room. That was still tarnished from the last conversation they'd had. With a literal barrier between them this felt more formal, controlled. She could do this.

She put her handbag on the counter but stayed standing between the bar stools.

Hazel sipped a soda water as she stood. Ashley was sure she saw a slight shake in her hand.

This was like a bizarre stand-off.

'So,' Ashley said, testing the water to see how stable her voice was. Steady. Good. 'I'm not going to drag this out. I would really, really like to move back in here.'

Hazel's eyes brightened and Ashley scolded herself for wording that sentence so thoughtlessly. She rushed to rectify her mistake.

'Like, as in, I want my flat back. For me.' This felt a mess. She wanted to walk backwards and rewind to her entrance, start again.

'Ah,' Hazel said, her face falling. 'As in, on your own?'

'Yeah.'

Her eyes dropped to the glass on the counter.

'So that's it, then?'

'I kind of thought that was obvious.' Ashley winced internally at her callous words. She wanted this over with quickly – she'd already checked out of this relationship long ago – but she needed to remember Hazel still had feelings and a bruised and battered heart.

Hazel looked wounded but soon brushed it off, returning to her usual steely demeanour. 'How long are you giving me?'

'As long as you need.'

'And Dani?'

The question took her by surprise and left a sting like a slap in the face. 'What do you mean?'

'How soon before you move Dani in?'

Ashley dropped her head, hiding the rueful smile pulling at her lips. Her body tensed with the awkwardness of Hazel's directness. 'No plans to get with Dani just yet.'

'But she bought you a ring. Is that not enough? Although, being engaged doesn't mean much to you, does it?'

Hostile Hazel was horrible. Ashley raised her head, no longer feeling sorry for the woman standing in front of her.

Since when did Dani have a ring? Had she told Hazel she was going to propose?

'What's that supposed to mean?' Ashley asked, only just keeping her voice level.

'You know exactly what I mean.'

She didn't. But, the sooner this conversation ended the better. Ashley wanted home. Pronto.

'I left my bag here. I'm going to grab that and go.' She paused, aware this was probably the last time they would speak for a while. 'Sorry for how things turned out.'

It sounded good in her head, but Hazel didn't share the sentiment.

'Sure you are,' she snapped.

Ashley walked to the bedroom, every step feeling more and more like she was walking through tar. This wasn't how she wanted things to end with Hazel. She'd fucked things up the moment she broke things off, but still, this was a women she'd loved. In an alternate world they would be getting married in six months. It was wrong to end things so bitterly.

It was like trying to mend a smashed mirror, though. Wishful thinking and good intentions were no use.

She grabbed her bag from under the bed, where it had obviously been stuffed from when she left it. She rummaged in the contents: no letter. Where the fuck had she put it?

She stuffed a few tops in the bag. No point wasting space. She was bored of the clothes she'd had on rotation recently and God knows how long Hazel would take to fully vacate.

Ashley closed the closet door to find Hazel standing behind it. She jumped out of her skin.

'Christ,' she wheezed, hand on heart.

Hazel ignored her reaction. 'One last thing,' she said, thrusting an envelope at Ashley.

Dani's envelope.

Rage bubbled through Ashley, rising with a sticky heat until it reached her cheeks. 'You read my letter?'

Hazel shrugged. 'I had to know what was so important she had to put it in writing.'

'That was private.' The words rattled in Ashley's brain, screaming ruddy murder at how much of a hypocrite she was. She'd take it back, replace it. Hopefully Dani hadn't noticed.

'I always knew she loved you. You both had me for a fool.'

'Me?'

'You knew. And still you strung me along.'

She snatched the letter from Hazel's grip. The envelope was tatty and creased from how tightly she'd held it. Ashley shoved it in her pocket, her hand trembling with rage.

'I didn't string anyone along.'

Hazel pulled a face like she was sucking on a lemon while having the stick up her arse forcibly removed. 'I guess that's your prerogative. Is that why you left me? She gave you that and you went running into her arms?'

'You really think I would cheat on you? What kind of person do you think I am?'

'I have no idea these days. You're not who I fell in love with, I know that much. I don't know who she was. A figment of my imagination, by the looks of it.'

Ashley fizzed with anger. She wasn't an entirely innocent party, she could admit to that, but Hazel was making her out to be a monster.

'Did you tell Dani you'd read it?'

Hazel scoffed. 'Really? That's what you care about?'

'Well, did you?'

'No. I wanted to speak to you first. See if—' She cut herself off.

Ashley steadied herself. Even after reading the letter, knowing what she did, Hazel had still hoped Ashley would come back to her. There was no doubt that's what Hazel was hinting at: the pain in her eyes told Ashley as much. The truth hurt like a slap in the face.

She was on the verge of saying something she couldn't take back. The voice in her head told her she'd enough regrets in life already; she didn't need to add to the list.

She chewed on her top lip, hoping the right words would come. They didn't. There was nothing left but to push past Hazel and leave the flat.

Going back to Mum and Dad's wasn't an option. Not yet, anyway. She was too old to go straight to her room and climb into bed. There were always questions, well-intentioned ones, but unwelcome nonetheless.

Spring was in the air, but the cold air that hit as she left the close was a relief. Rage simmered inside, ready to spill as she no doubt would rant to Dani and Kirsty, making her cheeks hot and ruddy.

She fingered the letter in her pocket, making sure it was still there. Part of her had hoped it was lost. She wouldn't read it now; her heart was set on it. Its contents were private. She was an idiot for taking it in the first place.

A brisk walk was just what she needed and soon she was at Dani's, her heart rate having calmed to a more normal rate.

She buzzed, hoping Dani would be in after work and not at the pub.

It wasn't long before she answered.

Just being here was calming. Soon she'd be up the stairs, lying on the sofa, having a moan. Had she left wine in their fridge? There was a strong possibility. She prayed to whoever was in the sky that there was at least a glass left.

Her mood plummeted when she rounded the corner to Dani's landing. The rage coming off Dani as she stood, arms crossed, in the doorway was palpable.

'I'm glad you're here. We need to have a chat.'

Ashley's legs wobbled as her mouth went dry. 'Okay.'

33

Kirsty had shoved off to her room to give them space.

The longer Dani had thought about it, the more the anger built. It grew and grew until it could no longer be contained. When Ashley had buzzed the flat, it was like flipping the flood gates open on a dam. It was out now, and couldn't be put back in.

She leaned her back against the kitchen counter and crossed her arms, waiting for Ashley to follow.

Her expression told Dani she had no clue what was going on.

She had to have taken it, though. Where else could it go? Rhona wouldn't be daft enough to take it. And Kirsty had no clue of its existence until today.

'What's going on?' Ashley asked, her voice timid.

'I think you have something of mine.'

'Ah,' Ashley replied with a slight nod. 'What would that be?'

Something told Dani she already knew. 'A letter.' She was trying to keep her tone level, just in case it had been a misunderstanding, but the way Ashley was standing –

shoulders slumped, rubbing at her drooped arm, shuffling from foot to foot – spoke volumes.

'Oh.' Ashley's cheeks darkened. 'Listen. It was a mistake. I took it on impulse and—'

'So you did take it?' Dani was surprised at the sudden urge to cry. She'd secretly hoped she was wrong. Disappointment welled in her chest.

'I've not read it.' Ashley's bottom lip trembled.

'But you took it?'

'Yeah.'

Dani sucked on her lips. 'It's private, Ash. Why did you just take it?'

Ashley shrugged. 'Poor impulse control.' She stuffed her hand in her pocket and produced a tatty, and very open, envelope. The top was torn open and it looked like it had been chucked about. Had she kept it on her all this time?

'It's open,' Dani said, snatching it from Ashley's grip. She wanted to tear it up, set it on fire, put it in cement and drop it in the Clyde.

Ashley swallowed hard, her eyes unable to meet Dani's. She held the edge of the kitchen counter with one hand, as if her legs might be unsteady. 'Hazel read it.'

Dani felt sick, her skin flushed ice cold. 'Hazel read my letter? What? When?'

'I don't know. She gave it to me when I went round today. I, erm, properly called things off, asked for my flat back,' she said with a nervous chuckle. Her voice was so quiet. It was hard to erupt with volcanic rage like Dani desperately wanted to.

'So, what? You two sat around having a laugh at me?' Dani asked, shaking the letter in the air between them.

'No, of course not. I promise I didn't read it.'

'I just don't get why you took it, Ash.' Dani closed the

space between them. This wasn't over, but the need to comfort Ashley was causing a tug of war between Dani's head and heart. Tears rimmed Ashley's eyes and Dani fought the urge to hold her tight and tell her it was all okay and just a stupid misunderstanding.

But the thought of Hazel reading something so private and personal made her want to simultaneously vomit and smash something.

'I don't know,' Ashley repeated, emotion making her voice break. She took a deep, wavering breath. 'Why write it if I wasn't meant to read it?'

'My therapist told me to write it.'

Ashley cocked her head as she thought. Dani couldn't remember if she'd told her she was seeing a therapist or not. So much had happened in the last few months, it was hard to keep up with the revelations.

'What's it about?'

How to phrase it? Dani tried a few sentences out in her head, doing her best to avoid Ashley's gaze. A tear traced a line of Ashley's cheek and Dani knew it was game over if their eyes met. She would be a blubbering mess too. 'What's been going on in my head for the last twenty years.'

Ashley wet her lips with her tongue. 'You think I deserve to know now?'

'No,' Dani snapped defensively. 'It's not that, it's just, this is private stuff, Ashley. It was my choice when and if it was read. And certainly not by Hazel.'

'She took it without me knowing.'

'You took it in the first place. That wouldn't have happened if you hadn't stolen from me.'

'It's hardly stealing if it has my name on it.' Ashley reached out to take Dani's hand but she snatched it back.

'Ash. Please. You should have asked me, not just taken it.'

Ashley nodded. 'I know. But you can't be mad at me for Hazel reading it.'

'Why the fuck not? There was stuff in there I'm not comfortable sharing and now someone, who's pretty much a stranger to me, knows? How do you think that makes me feel?'

'She's hardly a stranger.'

Dani ignored her. 'Did she tell you anything? About what she read?'

Ashley wiped at her face with a sniff. 'Not really. She mentioned a ring but nothing specific.'

Why did she sound so nonchalant about it? If Ashley knew what was in that letter there was no way she would be acting like this. She wanted to go round to Hazel and shake the memories from her. She had no right to know so much about Dani.

'I feel sick,' Dani said, closing her eyes.

Ashley put a hand on Dani's forearm and gently rubbed her thumb against her skin. 'It'll be fine.'

'No it fucking won't,' Dani shouted, pulling her arm free. 'That was my truth, my private business. Actually, can you just leave? I need space to think about this.'

Ashley stood her ground. 'The way you're making such a big deal of this makes me think I need to read it.'

She had a point. They'd come this far.

But the feeling of Hazel reading it sat heavy in Dani's chest. Would she feel the same if Ashley read it, and never be able to look her in the eye again?

'No. I've decided I don't want that.'

'So, you don't think I deserve to know the truth?'

'It doesn't matter now.'

'No? It doesn't matter at all? How unloved you made me feel? How unworthy I thought I was? The amount of days

I've wasted wondering what was wrong with me, what I needed to change?' Her words held venom despite the tremble in her voice.

Finally, Dani met her gaze. Tears stained Ashley's cheeks and the thought of making her feel so horrible, even for a second, was enough to make Dani crumble. Her lip vibrated as she fought to contain the emotion wanting to spill.

'I never meant to make you feel that way.'

'And yet you were out shagging someone new every week. I tried so hard to forget you, Dani. So hard. But you always found a way to reel me back in. So what was it? An ego trip? Or maybe you've finally decided to settle for me? Good old reliable Ashley, ready to be walked all over whenever you need me. No? So what? Just got bored of sleeping around? What's changed?'

Dani played Ashley's words on repeat as she tried to make head or tail of them. Is that really what she'd thought all these years?

'It's a wonder you still wanted to be with me, if that's what you think.'

Ashley swiped at her face again, ridding herself of tears. She stood taller, as if Dani had hit a nerve. 'That's it? No explanation? So I'm right, then?'

The sensible answer would be no. But Ashley had riled her. 'Do you want to be right? Would that make you feel better?'

Ashley looked at the letter still in Dani's hand. 'Is that an apology or an explanation?'

'Both.' That much was true. 'Look, if you're that fussed, just read the fucking thing.' Dani snipped, trusting the letter towards Ashley.

After a moment of hesitation, she accepted it. They way

she held it you'd think it was a ticking bomb. 'Do you want me to read it now?'

'Not particularly.' They stood in silence for a moment, the atmosphere getting heavier by the second as they both stared at the torn envelope in Ashley's hand. 'You deserve to know the truth, but if that's the opinion you have of me you should just leave.'

Ashley put the letter in her pocket. 'What else was I meant to think when you left me in the dark all these years?'

'You still shouldn't have taken it.'

'I. Didn't. Know. What. It. Was.' Ashley groaned, each word weighted with infuriation.

Dani tensed her jaw. This could go in circles. 'I think you should go. Please.'

Ashley didn't move and for a split second Dani thought she was going to have to repeat herself and force the issue. But eventually she turned on her heel as if snapping from a daze. 'Right, yeah. Okay,' she muttered. 'I think we should stay and talk this out, but whatever, you prefer to avoid stuff, I know, I know—' She was pretty much talking to herself as she left the kitchen. Dani didn't bother to follow her.

When she heard the front door click shut she was safe to leave the kitchen, but she kept her bottom lip sucked between her teeth for fear of Kirsty flying out her bedroom, wanting the goss.

After what felt an age, she was in her bedroom. She closed the door, flopped onto the bed, and sobbed.

34

Ashley tapped the side of her phone as she contemplated texting Dani. Leanne was round with the kids for Sunday dinner and there was nowhere in the house to get peace. She'd given up trying and was currently in the conservatory. Screams and boisterous play carried through the house, tightening her nerves with every fresh outburst.

They'd not spoken since their fight yesterday.

She'd half expected a text from Dani last night, asking her to come round. Instead, she got radio silence.

She shouldn't have taken the letter, but Dani's reaction was a little over the top.

Fraser came tearing through the conservatory on the way to the patio doors, a football in his hands. 'Coming to play footie, Ashley?' he asked over his shoulder.

'Nah, not today, champ. Sorry.'

Leanne stopped in her tracks, gently guiding Seb around her so as to avoid a collision. He tumbled out the door and straight into his brother, stealing the football and starting an argument.

This was ridiculous. She needed to go for a walk.

There was the small problem of her sister now towering over her, concern so heavy it pulled her eyelids down.

'What's up?' she asked.

'Nothing.'

'You're a bloody liar, and a bad one at that.'

The both looked towards the kitchen. Not a peep from Mum.

'It's fine, don't worry about it,' Ashley said, half-rising from her seat.

With a gentle finger to the shoulder, Leanne pushed her back down. 'Spill.'

Ashley groaned. 'It's just Dani stuff.'

'So unusual for you, Ashley,' Leanne joked, blatantly trying to lighten the mood. 'What's she done this time?' She took a seat in the neighbouring armchair.

'She's not done anything. Not really.'

'But you have?'

A fresh groan escaped. 'I'd rather not talk about it.'

'Jesus, you have done something bad.'

'It's all a matter of perspective.'

Leanne leaned closer. 'Ashley Fiona Davidson, tell me right now what you've done.'

She let out a sigh to rival a deflating bouncy castle. 'You tell me if it's as bad as Dani is making out,' Ashley began, before spilling the tea to her sister.

Leanne listened intently, finally letting out a breathy, and rather judgy, whistle when Ashley was finished.

'You've fucked up, big time,' she said with a grin.

'Alright, alright,' Ashley moaned. 'Don't sugar-coat it.'

'You don't think?'

'I think she overreacted.'

'Have you read it?'

Ashley shook her head. 'No. I'd feel bad.'

'Do you want me to read it? Give you the gist?'

Ashley's eyes widened. Leanne might as well have just confessed to murder. 'I hardly think that's the solution to my problems.'

'She gave you the letter. She obviously wants you to know what's in it.'

Ashley grunted with frustration. 'Look, its contents aren't the issue. The problem is getting Dani to trust me again. She was really mad.'

'And rightly so. You little klepto.'

'Enough,' Ashley grunted, tensing her jaw.

'You've done it now, you can't take that back. What you need to figure out is A: do you want to read it?' Leanne said, holding up a finger for each point. 'And B: how are you going to make things up to her?'

'What would you do?'

'I would read it and grovel at her feet. Well, depending on what the letter says. Maybe you won't even want to be with her after you read it.'

'What do you mean?'

'It must be something significant for her to freak out like that.'

'I guess.'

A fresh cry from outside pierced the room. Leanne didn't seem that fussed. 'You need to make a choice soon. The longer you leave it, the worse it will get.'

'I know.'

'Can I be honest with you about something?'

'Of course.'

Leanne leaned closer, one eye on the door. 'Dave and I have been together forever, yeah?' Ashley nodded: they were coming up for their twelfth anniversary soon. 'Well, I've never told anyone, but after we got married, just before I got pregnant, I thought about leaving him.'

'What?' Ashley gasped. This was news. She's always thought Leanne and Dave were solid, the real deal.

'You're not to tell a soul,' Leanne hissed. 'I think it's natural to worry about stuff, especially when you've been together so long. And like, I knew the next step was babies. It's one thing getting married but a whole other thing making a brand new human. There's no going back on that. So, yeah. I really started worrying I'd made a mistake, that I was making a mistake.'

'So what changed?'

Leanne shrugged. 'I realised no one was going to love me as much as Dave loved me. And the things that were niggling me, I was creating them, cause I was scared. At the end of the day, no matter what's in that letter from Dani, if you love her, you should be with her. Obstacles can be overcome. That's what love's all about.'

'You really think I should read it, then?'

Leanne pursed her lips. 'You know I've never been Dani's number one fan. She's been a real shithead to you over the years. But, if you love her, and she loves you, don't let this end over a stupid bit of paper.'

'That's the problem. I don't want it to end; I just don't know how to fix it.'

'Take tonight and decide if you want to read it or not. Then we'll figure out how to win Dani back round.'

'Okay.'

'And listen,' Leanne said, standing up.

'Yep?'

'She hurts you again, I'll fucking kill her.'

'Language!' Mum snapped, obviously back in the kitchen and in hearing range again.

They smiled, holding each other's gaze.

'I don't doubt it for a second.'

ASHLEY LAY ON HER BED, the letter in her hands.

It was like holding a grenade. The weight of it made her fingertips tingle. There was so much power in one little sheet of paper.

She turned it over, studying its outside like it might hold some answers, if not them all.

The edge was ragged where Hazel had torn it open. That must have been horrible for her. As if the rest of this godawful situation wasn't bad enough, she had to see Dani's most personal inner thoughts, too.

She wouldn't have known, though, and once she'd started it was probably hard not to finish.

That was the difference.

Ashley had a choice.

She pondered Leanne's words as she twisted the envelope between her fingers.

Was there anything that could put her off Dani?

She'd done so much in the last two decades, hurt Ashley in ways she never thought possible, and still she forgave her again and again.

What could be worse than what she'd already done?

Dani wanted her to know why she'd acted as she had, but what difference did it make to the future?

Her phone rumbled against her bedside table, indicating a text. It had to be Dani. She craned her neck to see the sender: Hazel. Disappointment seeped through her.

Ashley stuffed the letter under her pillow and rolled onto her side.

She grabbed her phone, seeing what Hazel wanted. It was short and sweet. She was moving out next week and going to stay with Yaz.

Everything was so final.

What an absolute mess of a year.

All she really wanted was Dani. The past didn't matter. She'd spent so long thinking they would never have a future together; why would she throw away what Dani had, supposedly, overcome?

So, the real question was: how was she meant to make things up to her?

35

'Is this going to be a problem for tonight?' Kirsty asked, giving Dani's feet a shove as she walked past the armchair to the sofa.

Dani was draped over the sides of the chair like she'd become a liquid. Since her fight with Ashley she felt it, too. The wind was gone from her: she didn't have the heart or the energy to hold herself up.

Work had been a slog and Kirsty had borne the brunt of her bad mood. Surprisingly, she'd not really mentioned it until now.

'What do you mean?' Dani asked, her tone as low as she felt.

'We're meant to be going to a party and you're Sad Sack McGee. Plus, Ashley is going to be there. It's going to be fucking awkward, isn't it?'

'Thanks for the support.'

'You know what I mean.'

She didn't. What was the use in arguing, though?

They watched the TV in silence for a while. Well, Kirsty

watched. Dani looked in the TV's direction, not taking anything in.

Even Chet was avoiding her tonight: her icy atmosphere was chilly enough to force a wide berth from him.

'How can I help?' Kirsty asked, breaking the quiet of the room.

Dani shrugged.

'Christ on a bike, Dan. Come on, we need to fix this.'

'It's gone too far.'

Kirsty spun to face her, one leg up on the sofa. 'Ashley made a mistake. You really want to throw it all away cause she fucked up? You've done far worse in your time.'

That forced a little energy back into her bones. Dani shuffled straighter, literally rising to her own defence. 'That's not the point.'

'Then what is?'

'What if she's already read the letter and that's why she was holding off telling Hazel they were done? What if she's realised I'm not for her?'

'You really think that?'

'It makes sense.'

'Ashley wouldn't do that.'

Reserves used, Dani slumped back into the armchair. In a perfect world, she would lean so far back she became one with it and wouldn't have to deal with any of this stupid relationship shite.

'You are coming tonight, yeah?'

'Course.'

Today was Bar Orama's official birthday bash. There was no way Dani could miss it. The bar was such a big part of their lives that sometimes it was like just another member of the gang. If it wasn't for the bar, so much wouldn't have happened. Twenty years was a big deal and she owed it to Kev to be there tonight.

'Good, cause I'm dragging you by hook or by crook.'

'Great,' Dani replied, sounding more flat than a pancake.

'And what about this?' Kirsty asked, waving a hand up and down.

'Huh?'

'You wearing that?'

Dani looked at her tatty hoodie and joggers. 'Well, obviously not.'

'So?'

'So?'

Their scintillating conversation was cut short by the buzzer.

'That'll be Izzy,' Kirsty said, jumping to her feet. It was only then Dani fully clocked that Kirsty was dressed to go out.

'Already?'

'It's seven o'clock, Dan.'

Shit. Time flies when you're in a depression pit.

Dani slammed her head into the cushion and stared at the ceiling. She'd need to wash, pick an outfit. But even existing felt like too much effort right now.

Why did Izzy have to be here? She needed longer to wallow.

Dani screwed her eyes shut as Izzy's voice filled the hall.

Time to put on a show.

'Dani!' Izzy called as she entered the kitchen. 'Ready for tonight?'

She looked glamorous as ever in a floor-length maxi dress and denim jacket. Izzy had the worst love life of them all, and yet she always showed up and made an effort. Maybe she could teach Dani a thing or two about plastering on a smile while your heart was breaking. Although, acting was Izzy's job. Dani could barely hide a snarl to rude customers, never mind putting on a whole show for the entire evening.

'Izzy,' Dani replied, trying and failing to match her energy.

Izzy cocked her head as she put her handbag on the kitchen counter.

Kirsty was already in the cupboard, getting glasses. 'Drink, Dani?'

'Yeah, why not?'

Izzy was still studying Dani with quiet suspicion. She barely blinked as she crossed the room and took a seat on the arm of the sofa, facing Dani. 'What's wrong?'

'Nothing, I'm grand,' Dani said with a shake of her head as she sat up straighter.

'No, something is definitely off,' she replied, tapping a finger to her lips.

She didn't want to have to explain the whole sorry affair to Izzy. If she and Ashley weren't going to work out, the fewer people that knew the better.

'Ashley issues,' Kirsty said, wandering through with three empty glasses and a bottle of wine.

Dani wished she could murder her with a look.

'*Pourquoi?*' Izzy asked, with such a look of concern it made Dani want to cry.

'Long story,' Dani conceded with a huff.

Izzy's features creased with confusion as she looked to Kirsty for clarity.

'I think I've said enough,' Kirsty said, lining the glasses up, Dani's death ray hot on her skin.

'Has something happened between you guys?' Izzy

asked, her face lighting up before falling flat. 'Oh no, something bad?'

'Ish.'

'Honey, I'm home!' Rhona called from the hall as the flat door closed behind her. The living room fell silent and only the sound of some stupid TV segment about goat's cheese filled the air. By the look on Rhona's face, the atmosphere had hit her like a slap in the face as she entered the kitchen. 'What's going on?' she asked with unmistakable apprehension.

Dani felt like she was on the stand. 'Nothing,' she groaned.

'Something,' Izzy amended.

Rhona pumped her eyebrows. 'I need a shower.'

'No, no, I'm first,' Dani said, jumping to her feet. Izzy stopped her with a hand to her shoulder.

'Why do I feel like I'm the only one in the dark here?'

'You're not,' Dani said, shifting her focus to Rhona. 'You go. I'll wash after.'

'So?' Izzy said, lifting a freshly filled glass from the coffee table without even looking.

'Ashley and I kind of, well, we've been seeing each other.'

The light returned to Izzy's eyes. 'That's fantastic! So, why so glum?'

'We've fallen out.'

'Ah. Why? If you don't mind me asking?'

'It's a long story. But I don't know if it can be fixed.'

'Nonsense. Everything can be fixed. Unless it involves murder. You didn't bump someone off together, did you?'

'Not that I know of.'

Izzy scooped her dress up and tucked it under her thigh as she got comfy on the sofa. 'Listen, whatever's happened, it can be fixed. If you want it to be fixed. Do you want it to be fixed?'

'I think so.' She did. Kirsty was right. Ashley had made a mistake. Dani had made plenty of them in her time. It wasn't a competition she wanted to take part in, but Dani won by a landslide. 'But what if she doesn't want to fix it?'

Izzy pondered the question with pursed lips. 'Every good love story, well, the very best ones at least, have a few bumps to them. But that's what makes those relationships so strong. When you've weathered the bad, you appreciate the good even more.' She looked at Kirsty for backup, but just got a grimace in return. Izzy loved romance books. Kirsty was still as sceptical as they came.

'I'd rather plain sailing, if I'm honest,' Dani replied.

'Now, where's the fun in that?'

'It's not fun I'm concerned about. It's the stress I could do without.'

'Fair point. Now, listen, sit up,' she said, tapping Dani's knee. 'You're going to hop in that shower, put on your favourite outfit, I'm going to make you a ridiculously strong vodka and Coke, and then you're going to go get your girl back. Sound good?'

'You make it sound so easy.'

'Sometimes, it is.'

36

Dani had barely spoken to her, but she was here. That was the main thing.

Ashley sipped her wine, wondering how best to break the ice. The atmosphere was loaded, heavy and laden like a thick fog around their table. And the others could feel it, no doubt about it. The pressure was conspiring, as if everyone had their own agenda or was at least trying to work out what the heck was going on. She'd caught not only the occasional expected look from Rhona, but from Izzy too. There was no denying the tension between herself and Dani.

She was at the other end of the table, probably by design, so striking up a quick icebreaker wasn't an option.

Ashley flicked her gaze back to Trip, aware she'd been looking at Dani for a nanosecond too long.

It was too late, though. 'You okay?' Trip asked. 'You seem distracted.'

'I'm fine. Just in my own wee world.'

Trip carried on with her story and Ashley did her best to

concentrate, but it was no use. Knowing Dani was right there and seething made Ashley's bones itch.

'You guys okay for drinks?' Kim asked, having fought her way from the bar to her friends.

The place was busy, not packed like their Halloween or Hogmanay shindigs, but the turnout was impressive enough. It was good to know the bar was at the heart of so many others and not just their group.

There were a few familiar faces from staff of years past; it was crazy how long they'd been coming here. A lot of good memories. Some sketchy ones. Some Ashley would rather forget.

Jen of Lovefest fame was even here. According to Kim, she was a proper Bar Orama alumna, having started many of the traditions they held near and dear: the pub quiz; Saturday Slams (or happy hour shots for the less informed); and Ashley's all time favourite, Mug Club. It only happened now and again, but Kev sometimes let patrons bring their own vessel from home to be filled. The most wacky got a prize. It had been a heck of a long time since there'd been a Mug Club. Maybe the changing licensing laws had put an end to it. She'd have to ask Kim later.

Kim followed Ashley's eyeline to Jen. 'Do you guys know each other?'

'Nah. Just in passing.'

Kim did a little nod. 'Just wondered, cause of the Lovefest thing. See her wife is pregnant? Weird that a dating contest can cause so many ripples.' She paused, as if debating whether to add something else, but had second thoughts as she turned on her heel. 'I'd better get back. Wave if you want me.'

'Maybe I should enter next year,' Trip mused. Lovefest was a local dating contest run every year by the neighbouring burgh's business group. As well as the chance of meeting your potential soulmate, there was cash up for grabs.

Ashley pulled an amused face. 'Don't tell me you're ready to settle down?'

'On second thoughts, yeah. Maybe not quite yet...'

Ashley smiled against the rim of her glass as she took a sip. It was impossible to imagine Trip with just one woman. It had been a long time since she'd dated.

'So,' Trip said, with a waggle of her head before dropping her voice low. 'What's the deal with you and Dani?'

'I don't know what you mean,' Ashley replied, sitting back in her seat as if to prove how laid-back she was tonight.

'Don't give me that, Ash. I've seen Dani sneaking looks your way and vice versa.'

She had been? Was that good? 'Nothing's going on.'

'Have you fallen out?'

'What makes you say that?'

'Because you've barely said a word to each other all evening.'

'She's at the other end of the table.'

'Exactly. You've both been weird for weeks.'

'Have not.'

'Something's happened. I noticed it at the paintballing, too.'

'As if.'

'And at the meal after.'

'Now you're just being delusional.'

Trip pursed her lips. 'I'm an English teacher. I can read the room no bother.'

'Aye, aye. Listen, you'll be the first to know if anything happens.'

'Izzy keeps looking at you guys, too.'

'Trip?'

'Yeah?'

'Shut up.' Ashley jested with a smirk.

She didn't want to talk about Dani. Not unless things got sorted.

Another quick look and she caught Dani's eye. It wasn't to be, though: she quickly looked away and dropped her gaze to the half-finished pint she was twisting in her hands.

She really hated her.

Ashley's insides twisted as much as the glass.

'Want another drink?' Trip asked, pushing her seat back.

'Yeah, and make it a large.'

An hour later and Dani was still doing a stellar job of avoiding Ashley. If only it was busier; if they were forced to stand she might have a chance of starting a conversation.

Ashley watched out the corner of her eye as Dani scooted between the chairs, probably on her way to the toilet.

Should she follow her? Would that be creepy?

The loos were too busy for important chats. She'd have to wait until tonight.

Trip was back at the bar, so she busied herself with her phone. Her finger hovered over Dani's name. Screw it.

Can we have a chat later? Xx

She stabbed at the send button before she could talk herself out of it.

Conversation carried on around her, but all she could do was focus on her phone. She clicked the screen on, just in case she'd blinked and missed a notification. Nothing. She checked again: you never know. Nope, no reply.

In bid to distract herself and not look like a phone-obsessed maniac, she let her eyes trace the bar, settling on Jen and Holly. They looked so happy. They hadn't won, the year they entered Lovefest. Things seemed to have worked out anyway. Was it wrong that she and Hazel had broken up now? Would the public feel cheated? God, hopefully there wouldn't be any catch-ups expected in the future.

'Kim wants to talk to you,' Trip said as she took her seat.

'Kim?'

'Yeah, you know, four foot eleven, bossy wee thing with purple hair?'

'Har har. Just now?'

'Yep.'

Ashley looked at the busy bar. *Weird.*

Without another word she weaved her way to the end of the bar, careful to stay out the way of queuing punters.

'What's up?' she asked Kim as she ducked into the fridge to retrieve a bottle of beer.

She served her customer before bounding back to Ashley. 'I need your help for a second. Follow me.' She left the bar, calling over her shoulder for Travis to hold the fort.

This was getting even more mysterious.

They walked past the entrance to the toilets and to the back door Ashley knew was only for staff. Kim punched in a code before holding it open for her.

Front of house was all dark wood and cowboy memorabilia. Back here was simple concrete flooring and white, flaky walls. Whatever Ashley had expected, it wasn't this.

'Where are we going?' she asked, confusion muddying her tone.

'Nowhere bad.' Kim chuckled.

Ashley followed in silence, knowing any more questions would just go unanswered. They took a left and traipsed down a flight of well-worn steps.

Finally, they reached a wooden door. Its peeling paint and worn edges suggested it predated even Bar Orama itself.

Ashley stopped in her tracks.

'Kim, what's going on?'

A slam from the other side of the door made her jump.

'Yo! Kim! What the fuck?' Dani shouted.

'Kim. What the hell is going on?' Ashley asked again.

Kim produced a key from the lanyard hanging from her trouser's belt loop. She kept quiet until the door was opened. She stepped in the way of a disgruntled Dani.

'Ashley, in you go.'

'Not until you tell me what's going on.'

Kim stood her ground. She huffed so loudly it echoed in the small space. 'Look, I don't know the full story, but you two—' She wagged a finger between Dani and Ashley. 'Need to sort it out. If you guys don't work out, there's no bloody hope for the rest of us.'

She yanked Ashley by the arm, and she was so taken aback by the gesture that she stumbled into the stockroom, only being stopped from falling flat on her face by Dani.

'You better not—' Dani yelped, but it was too late. Kim slammed the door shut with a click of the lock.

'Did she really just lock us in here?' Ashley asked, surveying her surroundings. It was a dingy little room with no natural light and a few dubious damp patches on the yellowing walls. Racking lined the perimeter and every available space was used for boxes, including most of the floor. The only untouched space was a couch that looked like it had lived through both world wars. Ashley presumed at some point it had been moss green, but it was hard to tell now.

She wrinkled her nose.

'At least you've got me for company. I was alone. I thought she'd left me here. She cornered me after I went to the loo.'

She was sounding like the old Dani. Ashley wanted to hug and squeeze her, never let her go.

It felt too easy, though. After what was said in their fight an unmistakable tension hung between them, like an invisible cord just waiting to be snapped.

'You okay?' Ashley asked, her tone laced with awkwardness.

Dani wandered to the grotty couch. 'Yeah. I'm good. You?'

That felt more like it. Staccato. Stiff.

'Okay, I guess.'

Dani took a seat and the sofa let out a long sigh. At least it didn't squeak with mice. 'Might as well. God knows how long Kim will leave us here.'

She was right. Knowing Kim, it could be a while. Ashley took a seat. The sofa sighed again, taking all of Ashley's words with it. It was like she'd never held a conversation before. How were you meant to start these things?

'I shredded it,' she blurted, unable to begin any other way. The sentence was choking her; she needed Dani to know the most important information first.

'Huh?'

'Your letter. I shredded it. And I put it in a wee sandwich bag thing,' she added with a nervous giggle. 'I brought it with me to show you. I didn't read it.' Ashley's gaze dropped to her hands on her lap.

'You brought me a sandwich bag of shredded paper?'

She was too scared to look at Dani, but it was obvious she was smiling.

'It seems silly now I say it out loud.'

Dani took Ashley's jaw in her hand, gently lifting it until their eyes met. 'I appreciate it; the gesture. It means a lot.'

'Yeah?'

'I guess.' She dropped her hand, letting it fall into the gap between them on the sofa. 'But you didn't read it?'

Ashley shook her head with vigour. 'Nope. Not a single word.'

It was Dani's turn to drop her eyes. 'Maybe you should have read it. You were right, what you said about me treating you badly. I've been an arsehole to you.'

There was no arguing with that. 'Well, now's your chance. What did you want to tell me?'

'Christ, I dunno.' Dani still couldn't make eye contact. Ashley didn't blame her: she felt just as uneasy.

'Hazel mentioned a ring. What was that about?'

Dani let out a little noise, somewhere between a yelp and a laugh. She ran a hand over her mouth as if wiping something away, but Ashley had seen her do it before: she was nervous.

'The ring, the bloody ring.' She played with the nail on her index finger, busying herself. Ashley watched intently, committed to giving her all the time in the world. 'You won't remember. It's really embarrassing.'

'Try me. What won't I remember?'

Dani took a deep breath. 'It was ages ago, like years; we went to Edinburgh. We passed a little antiques place, and you saw a ring in the window?'

Ashley wracked her brains as the memory floated to the surface, like a hazy image coming into focus on a rippling pond. 'Yeah, I think I remember.'

'It had sapphire stones,' Dani added, running a digit along the lower half of her ring finger as if to show where it would go.

She could remember it clearly now. She'd fallen in love with it instantly. She'd daydreamed for weeks after, imagining what it would be like for Dani to give it to her. Maybe in a parallel universe it had actually happened.

'I remember it. It was beautiful. I'm surprised you remembered it. I didn't think you were too fussed.'

'I went back and bought it.'

Ashley's jaw hung slack. 'For who?'

'You. You nugget.' Dani smiled but her eyes were clouded.

'For me?'

'Yeah. I figured I'd need it at some point.'

'Dani, that ring cost thousands. How? Why?' A million questions sat on Ashley's tongue, weighing it down, making it impossible to form an actual sentence.

'Told you it was stupid.'

'Not stupid, just – I don't understand. If you had feelings for me then, why didn't you say?' Anger nipped at her eyes and throat. 'Why did you never say? Ever?'

Dani rubbed at her eyes, keeping her palms flat against them as she leaned her elbows to her knees. 'When Dad died, I—'

Her voice cracked. Ashley edged closer, putting a hand on Dani's knee. 'You don't need to tell me: it's fine.'

'I need to,' Dani said, her voice so quiet it could be mistaken for a whisper. She cleared her throat, her hand still over her eyes. 'I thought if I didn't love you, or if I tricked the world into thinking I didn't love you, that nothing bad would happen.'

Ashley watched Dani's lip wobble as a tear fell from her

own eye. She didn't flinch as it ran down her cheek. It wouldn't be the last; no point in smudging her make-up yet.

'That makes sense.'

Dani's chest rumbled with a teary laugh. 'It bloody doesn't. I was just so scared of losing anyone else. It made sense at the time. And the longer it went on, the harder it got to go back on.'

'It's okay.'

'I'm messed up, Ash. You deserve better than me.'

That was a step too far. 'Hey, don't ever say that.' She grabbed Dani's hand. 'You hear me?'

'Therapy can only help so much. You really want to be stuck with someone like me?'

'That's kind of the whole point. I love all of you. Your past, your present, and if you'll have me, your future.'

'So it doesn't put you off?'

'Put me off?'

'Yeah. I thought that was maybe why you were holding back on telling anyone. You're not having doubts, are you?'

Ashley let Dani's words sink in. She's been so wrapped up in her own selfish motives she'd failed to see how it might be affecting Dani. 'Doubts? About us? Never.'

Dani licked her lips: another nervous habit. 'You want to give us a go, then?'

Dani Hamilton: Queen of Stupid Bloody Questions. Ashley kept her new title to herself. 'Only if you can forgive me, you know, for the whole stupidity over that letter.'

'I think we've both done a few stupid things in our time.'

Ashley leaned back into the squidgy cushion of the sofa. It was surprisingly comfy. It was like a crushing weight had suddenly been lifted: her body felt like jelly.

'If you'd told me this time last year what I'd be doing in the next twelve months, I wouldn't have believed you.'

'Tell me about it,' Dani agreed, also sinking into the sofa. 'I never in a million years thought I would be locked in the stockroom of Bar Orama, for a start.'

'I know, right.' Ashley chuckled. 'How long do you think she's going to leave us in here?'

'You know Kim and her vigilante justice. Could be hours. Never mind that she'll have to wait for a break at the bar.'

'Think they'd be mad if we cracked open a bottle of booze?'

'I've got a better idea to pass the time,' Dani said, leaning forward and pulling Ashley into a deep kiss.

Hogmanay first kisses or not, fireworks exploded in Ashley's chest. It didn't matter what inner demons Dani was battling, they would get through it. Love linked you: together they were galvanised. They could take on anything.

Ashley took a handful of Dani's T-shirt sleeves in each hand and pulled her on top as she slouched backwards to rest on the arm of the sofa.

'What's your plan, then? To pass the hours in here?' Ashley purred in Dani's ear.

'Probably easier if I show you.'

37

'Oh yeah?' Ashley replied, giving Dani's bum a squeeze as she properly straddled her.

Dani pushed down on Ashley's centre, feeling her own pulse with desire.

If she'd known this would happen she would have been less reluctant to go out.

Dani ducked down, smiling against the warm skin of Ashley's neck. She smelled amazing. Classic Ashley: flowers with a woody base. She'd worn the same perfume since they were teenagers and Dani always thought of her whenever she smelt it. Specifically, intimate moments like this, and how it felt to trail kisses down to Ashley's perfect collarbone.

'What if Kim bursts through the door?' Ashley mumbled, stilling Dani.

It was a good point. She wasn't exactly the type to knock.

Dani searched the room for inspiration before jumping to her feet and pushing a large crate of vodka along the ground.

'You think that's going to stop her?' Ashley chuckled, sitting up on her forearms.

'I'm not done yet,' Dani replied, rushing back for another box, then another. 'That should do,' she declared, jumping back on top of Ashley. She didn't protest. It would be a decent warning, anyway. Kim would have to push pretty hard to shift them.

There was no time to waste, not with the threat of Kimberly Martínez bursting through the door at any moment.

Dani popped open the button of Ashley's jeans and lowered her zipper. How far did she want to go? In an ideal world she wanted Ashley naked, stat, so she could fully appreciate her, marvel at how bloody lucky was.

This whole thing still felt like a dream. She'd spent the last few months in a daze, hoping she wouldn't suddenly wake up and discover it was just that: a fantasy.

No matter how many times she'd touched Ashley in her head, nothing beat the real thing. She dipped her hand into Ashley's jeans and smiled at how wet she was. She cupped her centre, her hand resting on Ashley's knickers.

In response, Ashley arched her hips, but the manoeuvre was tough in skinny jeans and it made Dani's hand hurt against the zipper. She weighed up her options. Persevere, or have faith in the vodka crates?

The latter would be so much more fun.

She moved her thighs to between Ashley's, so her legs were now either side of Dani, and started the job of shimmying her free. A little twisting and turning later, Dani had the best view in the whole of Glasgow.

Dani ran her thumb up the line of Ashley's core, making her shiver.

It was bizarre to think all their friends were just a few walls away. A delicious thrill coursed through Dani, adding to her own arousal.

Another pass of her thumb revealed how wet Ashley actually was. Dani's heart skipped a beat as she ran circles over Ashley's hard clit.

Ashley closed her eyes, a groan of satisfaction escaping from her barely parted lips.

Watching her fingers work their magic on Ashley was a pleasure unto itself. Once Kim freed them of their stockroom prison she was going to get Ashley home, pronto. She needed the full experience: anything less wasn't going to satisfy her tonight. She'd worried Ashley didn't want her; there was no way she was going to waste a moment now she had her.

Every sense was heightened, every feeling elevated. Dani wouldn't last long once they were back at the flat.

The way Ashley's hips were urging Dani on, pushing harder against her hand, told her Ashley shared her thoughts.

Still sweeping her clit with her thumb, Dani brought her other hand into play, using two fingers to tease Ashley's centre.

Ashley tilted her hips, inviting Dani in. She continued to tease. A little longer wouldn't kill her.

Dani couldn't hold back any longer, though. She slid her fingers into Ashley, curling them upward, hitting the spot that made Ashley screw her eyes tight.

Time thundered on but Ashley had her on the go-slow, savouring every minute, amplifying every second, searing them into Dani's heart: a memory of a perfect moment.

She worked her fingers in and out, continuing to massage Ashley's clit in perfect rhythm while keeping one eye on the stockroom door. If Kim barged in so close to Ashley's release Dani would scream.

'I'm so close,' Ashley moaned.

Dani could feel it. She changed her pace slightly, upping the ante.

It didn't take long for Ashley to tumble over the edge, pushing down on Dani's hand as she came. She could do this forever and a day. Happiness burst in her chest, warmth seeping through her like expensive alcohol. Her skin buzzed with possibility. She'd tortured herself with ideas of Ashley's future: the wedding, babies, growing old together. Now it was her future. Their future.

Ashley's eyes fluttered open, locking with Dani's. 'You're something else.'

'Likewise.' She shifted, pulling Ashley by the hips, bringing her closer.

Ashley leaned on her forearms, angling to reach Dani's jeans.

Dani gently held her wrist. 'I think we're chancing it with Kim, are we not?'

'A little. But is that not all part of the fun?' Ashley's eyes burned with wicked intentions.

Dani did the maths. Sometimes it was better to quit while you were ahead. 'How about we focus on getting out of here, then we can go straight home and do things properly?'

Ashley pouted. 'Spoilsport. But I guess you're right.'

'It happens, occasionally,' Dani replied with a smile. She shifted Ashley's legs to one side, setting her free. It wasn't long before she had her clothes back on. Dani could stop watching the door now.

'So,' Ashley said, bringing her knees up onto the sofa. 'Do we just wait it out?'

'I tried that delivery hatch when I was alone. It's locked.'

'Surely she can't leave us much longer.' Ashley closed the gap between them, bringing Dani's face closer by cupping her hand to her jaw. Before Dani had time to react, she was kissing her like there was no tomorrow, sending all sorts of signals to her already excited core.

Dani smiled against Ashley's lips, enjoying the sensation of their mouths brushing together as she spoke: 'Don't you be leading me astray,' she joked. 'We said we'd wait.'

'I know, but it's tough.'

'She'll be back soon.'

They were still nose to nose, mouth to mouth. Dani wasn't going to move an inch if she didn't have to. She could quite happily live the rest of her days in Ashley's orbit.

'Think it will be obvious when we just rush off?' Ashley asked, breaking their connection and sitting back. She took Dani's hand in hers, stroking it with her thumb.

'Does it matter? Do you care?' Dani replied, settling inside beside her.

'I guess not. They all know anyway.'

'Who did you tell?'

'No one, apart from Rhona and Kirsty. You?'

'Izzy, just before we came out.'

Ashley's attention turned to the ceiling. She traced the line of the fluorescent lights with her eyes. 'Trip totally knew, though. She's not blind.'

'I dunno. You really think Trip could keep her mouth shut?'

'Who do you think told Kim?' Ashley chuckled.

As if on command, a key clicked in the lock and the vodka boxes scraped along the floor before Kim gave up. 'You okay? What's blocking me?'

'We're having a lock-in,' Dani shouted.

'You better not be. Kev will kill me.' She shoved harder and the boxes moved another few inches, enough for a dark brown eye to appear in the gap. 'A little help, guys?'

'You going to let us out?'

'Has it really been that bad?'

'Torture,' Ashley replied, deadpan.

Dani got to her feet and shoved the boxes out the way. Kim sauntered in, her eyes narrowing as she scanned the room, as if looking for clues as to what might have occurred in her absence.

'Sorted things out?' she asked, hands on hips.

'As best we can,' Dani replied, trying to sound offhand.

'Can we go then?' Ashley added, hopping to her feet.

'I suppose,' Kim conceded, stepping aside. ' But a whiff of another falling out and I'll not be happy.'

'Never ever again,' Dani said, flashing a smile, and truly meant it.

38

'We don't have to do a speech, do we?' Dani shout-whispered in Ashley's ear.

'Not unless you're announcing something,' Ashley replied, giving Dani's hand a squeeze.

It was strange being back at her parents' summer bash. It felt like a lifetime ago she was here with Hazel, announcing their engagement. How had it only been a year?

Ashley sneakily watched Dani from the corner of her eye. The way she gave Mum and Dad her full attention, hanging on their every word despite Dad's droning speech, made Ashley's heart swell. What looked like pure love filled Dani's features, making her glow: only to be confirmed when she turned to Ashley, her smile full beam, and leaned against her shoulder as she laughed at one of Dad's terrible jokes. You couldn't fake that.

Speeches done, Ashley offered to get more drinks for the table.

Today hadn't been too bad. A few awkward questions from out-of-the-loop (and some purely vindictive) relatives, but she'd batted them away with the skill of a professional tennis player.

Having Dani by her side made the whole thing ten times easier.

She was finding that to be the general rule of thumb, in fact. Whatever life threw at her, she could tackle it head on with Dani in tow.

If only she was here now, because Mum's cousin Jessie was en route and she didn't have the best track record for being subtle. Ashley ducked behind the cupboard door, pretending to look for something at the back. Shame it was a cupboard full of plates. It didn't give her much to work with. She stared aimlessly at a serving platter, scared to peek over the cupboard door and check if the coast was clear.

She held her breath as if doing so might make her invisible.

Chatter continued around her: surely she would be gone by now?

Ashley shifted, leaning back slightly, and was met with an eyeful of garishly floral skirt. How long had she been looming over her?

'Ashley, is that you?'

'Yes, Jessie, just looking for a tray,' she lied, only just holding back a groan. She got to her feet, smoothing down her dress. 'No luck. I'll need to look elsewhere.'

The ploy didn't get her far. 'Now, now! I've not seen you all year. How's that fiancée of yours?'

The glint in Jessie's eye told Ashley she knew fine well what she was really asking.

'Hazel? She's grand. I think she's still a personal trainer in Shawlands Gym. She's not my fiancée any more, though.' She added the final sentence with a thin-lipped smile.

'Oh, really?' Jessie exclaimed, having totally just heard

this information for the first time, no doubt about it. Yeah, right.

'Yeah, we broke up a while ago.'

'Oh, I'm so sorry. Not because of anything bad, I hope?'

Did anyone ever break up because of something good? It was a snappy internal comeback but it stalled her brain for a hot second: she had, when you really thought about it. 'My choice,' she replied with another polite smile. 'Change of priorities.'

As if by magic, Ashley's number one priority strolled through the conservatory door, backwards cap lopsided and a chipolata hanging out the side of her mouth as she engaged in passing conversation with Uncle Tam. Ashley was effortless to stop the smile now plastering her face. Jessie followed her line of sight. That was enough for Ashley: the noisy woman had seen and heard all she needed to. Well, maybe not, but Ashley was done.

She bid her a friendly goodbye and crossed the kitchen to Dani, who barely had time to finish biting her sausage before Ashley planted a kiss on her cheek. She scooped her close, a hand on Ashley's waist.

'Thought you'd need a hand with the drinks,' Dani said, before demolishing the rest of her snack.

'Yeah, probably.'

'What is it?' she asked, leaning slightly back as if taking Ashley in fully.

'Huh?'

'You've got a proper goofy smile and your eyes are all big.'

'Really?'

'Yep,' Dani said, returning an equally impressive grin.

'Just happy, I guess.'

'That's what I like to hear.' She planted a fresh kiss on Ashley's cheek. 'You done the drinks yet?'

'Nope, just about to. Will you grab that prosecco for me?'

Dani waggled her head. 'Actually, can I chat to you for a minute? In private?'

Ashley's stomach swooped before being engulfed with butterflies. It wouldn't be anything bad; the question was, how good was it going to be?

'Yeah, sure. My room?' She couldn't help but call it that, despite its permanent office decor.

Being back at her own flat was a godsend. Not only were home visits more palatable, but having space to have alone time was great for her and Dani. The concept of living together had been floated, but Ashley needed time. It was a space she'd shared with Hazel: she needed to create a little distance from the memories hidden in the walls before Dani made her mark.

Dani held the bedroom-office door open for Ashley. 'Take a seat.'

'This feels very formal. What's going on?'

Dani plonked herself beside Ashley and fished her hands about behind the cushions. Was she going to propose? Knowing Dani had that ring, Ashley was always prepared for the possibility. It was far too early in their relationship, but when you've been on the bench for so long, time tends to get skewed. She would say yes, regardless.

Dani pulled a bottle of wine out. In any other circumstances it would have popped.

'Shit,' Dani yelped.

'What?'

'I forgot glasses.'

'That's okay.'

Dani pouted, looking at the bottle as if it had wronged

her. 'I just thought today might be a little heavy for you, with relatives and stuff, and maybe you'd need a breather.'

That was Dani all over. Ashley had no idea she was so romantic and thoughtful. How she hid it all these years was a mystery.

'I'm fine to drink from the bottle if you are?' Ashley said, taking the bottle from Dani and unscrewing the lid. 'Just don't tell anyone how dreadfully unclassy I am.'

'Never.'

They each took a swig, Dani watching Ashley with a smile twitching at the edge of her lips.

'What?' Ashley asked with a chuckle as she passed the bottle back to Dani.

'It's mad, isn't it? This time last year I thought it was game over. I was sitting where you are, chugging wine and wondering how I messed up so badly.'

Ashley considered her response. 'Well, everything worked out in the end. Didn't it?'

Dani dropped her gaze. 'Thank you for never giving up on me.'

'You made it kind of impossible, to be honest. You can be an annoying little pest sometimes.' She smiled, not believing a word of what she'd said.

Dani countered with a swift grab at Ashley's waist. 'Oi. But, seriously, thank you. Just a shame it took us so long.'

Ashley took a gulp of wine. 'What does the journey time matter if you get there in the end?'

She kissed Dani, long and slow, to prove a point. 'Ashley Davidson, don't you be getting me all worked up at your parents' party.'

'Why not? This sofa bed has already seen it all.'

Dani kissed her again. 'Bad.'

'Nah. Now, let's get back downstairs. Izzy wants to tell us all something.'

That piqued Dani's interest. 'Okay, but more kisses later?'

'Try and stop me.'

They had all the time in the world now. No point in rushing. It was never their style anyway.

AUTHOR'S NOTE

I hope you enjoyed Dani and Ashley's journey.

I'd originally planned something totally different, taking things right up to Ashley's wedding. She was having none of it though. Ashley isn't one to cheat or even dip a toe in those waters. She dragged her heels and made writing impossible. I had no choice but to go back, scrap what I'd written, and re-do it, Ashley's way. Here was me thinking Dani would be the issue!

I'm happy I did it though, it wouldn't have been the right story otherwise.

Don't worry about Hazel, her book is next…

Will you leave me a review?

I hope you enjoyed Long Time Coming. If you have a moment I would really appreciate an honest review on Amazon and / or Goodreads. Reviews help me grow as an author and help new readers know what to expect. The more people that take a chance on my books, the more books I can write. It doesn't need to be anything fancy, a few words will do. Thank you.

Allie McDermid is a lesbian romance author. Her debut novel, Love Charade, was published in July 2022.

Born and raised in Perth, Allie now lives in Glasgow with her ever-growing gang of cats. She is partial to a good scone.

ALSO BY ALLIE MCDERMID

Want to know what happened at the first ever Lovefest?

LOVE CHARADE

Holly Taylor didn't expect to return to Glasgow. And she certainly didn't expect her parents to enter her into a dating competition on her first day home.

Jen Berkley is happily single. Having vowed to never date again after her horror ex broke her heart, no one is more surprised when her best friend convinces her to take part in a dating contest.

Jen wants to win the money. Holly wants to regain the trust of her parents. Will they get what their hearts desire or will the charade fool no one?

Set in Glasgow and full of Scottish charm as well as lashings of delicious desire, smouldering sexual tension and even a few laughs, buy Love Charade today and find out if some things just can't be faked...

Made in the USA
Middletown, DE
10 October 2023